CHRISTMAS IN NEWBURY

A BILLIONAIRE DAD & NANNY ROMANCE

REGINA MORRIS

CONTENTS

Silkhaven Publishing, LLC
Join Regina Morris' mailing list for games, freebies,
and fun at http://newsletter.reginamorris.com
Please visit author Regina Morris on her website
http://www.reginamorris.com
Regina Morris enjoys connecting with fans on social
media. Please find her at:
Facebook:
http://www.facebook.com/ReginaAnnMorris
(@ReginaMorris)
Twitter: http://www.twitter.com/ReginaMorris
(@ReginaMorris)
Pinterest: http://www.
pinterest.com/ReginaAnnMorris

Billionaire James Nielson plans to close many of his business's installations, including the original factory started by his grandfather in the small town of Newbury, when a woman—whom he had a sexual fling with over a year ago—abandons her baby at his company's headquarters claiming he is the father.

He and his baby daughter visit Newbury during the holidays where he hires a local woman, Melanie Frank, to be his nanny. She has been furloughed from her job at his factory, and, like everyone in the town, relies on the company for her livelihood. She wants to be an artist, but is financially trapped in the town by the company.

It is obvious to Melanie that James is uneasy around his daughter, isn't finding the town charming, and doesn't feel any Christmas spirit. She's plenty attracted to James, but will this city mouse really be interested in a country mouse? As James discovers lost family members, the warmth of a small community spirit, and the compassion from his daughter's nanny, he develops a stronger sense of family and his romantic feelings for Melanie grow.

He decides he must keep the factory running, and after buying Melanie's artwork at the local Christmas auction, she has renewed interest in her studies. The two search for the perfect Christmas gift for each other while trying to save the factory, which leads to a Christmas miracle.

Silkhaven Publishing, LLC

ISBN: 978-1-948997-47-8 (EPub Ebook)

ISBN: 978-1-948997-48-5 (MOBI Ebook)

ISBN: 978-1-948997-49-2 (Paperback)

Library of Congress Control Number: 2020921758

The car slipped on a patch of ice as it drove James Nielson up the private path to the iron gate of his family's estate, but the driver quickly regained control. The vehicle hit solid ground and continued its journey to James's gilded cage.

He stared at his phone and his thumb hovered over the app that would allow them access. His world would change once he entered the home, and he wasn't in a rush to have his life ruined.

He allowed the car access and once the driver passed the stables James said, "This is fine." He waved dismissively at the driver. "I can make it from here."

Nothing mattered anymore.

One short walk up the rest of the drive and he would no longer be free.

His chest tightened and he stared at the three-story brick house. His father, who had only been curt with him on the phone when he had ordered him home, was waiting inside.

James opened the car door and stood, a slight breeze ruffling his hair and giving him a burst of renewal with the crisp winter air. His knees gave way once they held his full weight, and he held onto the car door for support. His eyesight blurred a bit as he stared into the rising sun.

The last tequila drink was one shot too many.

He closed the car door and his footsteps crunched against the crust of snow as he got out of the way of the car turning around to leave. Punching in the security code so the car could exit the property, the wind whipped around his face and he synched the scarf tighter around his neck.

The latest family scandal, when—not if—the story came out, would be the height of gossip soon enough. He needed this short, blustery walk as a reprieve. A few more minutes of calm before the storm.

He inhaled deeply during the short walk, doing his best to fight off another night of serious binge drinking to forget his problem. He reached the door sooner than he wanted and entered the mansion where he found the downstairs housekeeper quietly working. Her maid uniform was freshly pressed, and her white Keds remained silent on the polished marble floor. She replaced the flowers in the foyer with a bouquet of new ones, and the smell of them hit his nose. Another housekeeper put a leash on their family dog, likely for his morning exercise.

The sun had barely risen.

By now, James would have already worked out, eaten breakfast, and been on his third cup of coffee.

But not this week.

The last few days had weighed heavily on him. He hadn't been to the office since the incident. Drinking heavily wasn't helping the situation, especially since he needed to fly to England this evening for business.

"Good morning, Mister Nielson," the first housekeeper greeted him once she'd set the heavy vase in the center of the table. "Your father has asked to speak with you first thing this morning. I believe he is available now, sir."

A tingling of doom hit James's empty stomach. Three days had passed since his world had turned upside down, and the lab results should be in.

He nodded, unable to remember the maid's name, and then walked to his father's office. He raked his fingers through his hair, tucked in his shirt, and took determined strides. Some deep breaths helped to keep him awake and alert.

A few days ago, a woman from a two–week fling over a year ago had visited the office, claiming that James had fathered her child. It wasn't the first time a woman had made that claim, but it was the first time someone had abandoned their baby at the front desk with a note saying her lawyer would contact them.

James had learned of the news later when his father called him. Usually, a paternity suit proved the woman a liar, the press had a field day slandering him, and then life went on as usual.

But this felt different.

This felt like fate had thrown him into a brick wall.

The office door was open, and his father, Gregory Nielson, sat behind the desk in his tall, leather chair. James didn't knock, but his father saw him immediately as he stood in the threshold of the doorway. He wasn't scowling, so maybe he wanted to share some good news.

"Good morning, James," his father said, his voice way too alert for the morning hour. He then studied his son, naturally noticing the attire, unshaven face, and weary eyes. "You look like crap."

"Good. Because that's how I feel." James covered his eyes and shielded them from the bright light of the room as he crossed the office and took a seat in front of his father's huge, oak desk. The feeling was so familiar. James doing something wrong, his father calling him in to berate his indiscretion, apologies would be given, and then life would move on.

This situation was more permanent than his past mistakes.

"This week has been sheer torture," James finally said, his morning voice cracking so he cleared his throat.

In truth, the last few days had been some of the hardest ones ever. Deep down, James knew the baby belonged to him. He had come up with several escape options. Adoption, boarding schools, and even the idea of having his father raise the child. None of them seemed perfect. And no matter what happened, James would be a father.

A laptop lay open on the desk, and his father pointed at the screen. "Did you lay off twenty percent of the workers in our Colorado facility before the holiday? I thought the numbers suggested only ten percent."

His father wanted to talk about business? It'd be only a slight distraction from his real problems, but he felt a small reprieve. "The cuts were necessary," James said, his voice curt and to the point, his hands waving dismissively through the air.

"There has been bad press because of the layoffs." Gregory let out a heavy sigh, one filled with disappointment. The expression felt very familiar since James heard it often enough.

"Spinning some good news with the bad is always helpful," his father continued. "Create some charitable, tax-deductible donations that give back to the community."

James stared at the ceiling and felt anger

building within himself. Business should be business. Throwing good money after bad was only a Band–Aid for a quick marketing blitz, but donations were standard fare.

"Think of a slant different from what we normally do."

James glared at his father. Charitable creativity was not his forte, and it was definitely something he didn't enjoy doing. "There haven't been any natural disasters lately to throw money after, but I can see what I can do."

His father shook his head in a way that told James that his suggestion wasn't what the man wanted to hear. "Do something that will make an impact for those communities affected."

Of course. Let's just make the task even more difficult. James let out a slight sigh knowing that it was useless to fight with his father. "Whatever."

Gregory glanced back at the computer. "I see you laid off an average of 5% of the workers in Newbury, Dover, and San Francisco before Thanksgiving." His father pointed to the screen. "And another 15% were furloughed?"

Layoffs were happening all across the country, in all industries. Furloughs were basically the same, but at some point in the future, the employee may be called back to work.

His father had never had any trouble making the tough business decisions in the past, but his recent marriage to wife number four had softened him. "Times are tough. Business fat needs to be trimmed."

James had never been a softy when towing the bottom line, and his father knew that. Until his last marriage, the man had always taken great pride in how ruthlessly his son managed the business.

"But the workers in Newbury..." Gregory said, taking off his glasses and rubbing his eyes briefly. "That's the installation that we swore to your grandfather on his deathbed that we'd keep running."

James knew of the sentimental feelings his family had for the backwater town; he just didn't understand them. His great–great–grandfather had been a founding member of the settlement, and his grandfather a successful businessman setting up one of the largest factories the place had ever seen. The start of the Nielson fortune began there; the beginning of everything.

But James didn't wallow in sentimentality. Heck, he had never even been to the town. Didn't want to ever visit it either. "I'm sure my grandfather will be rolling over in his grave soon because I suggest we shut down the entire plant."

Gregory let out a deep breath and stared blankly at the far wall, deep in thought. "I'd hate to see the plant close. I grew up in that little town and actually worked in that facility." His father's voice held a hint of sadness, but, overall, he was a professional. True moguls didn't make their millions holding on to sentimentality. Gregory then looked back at James and reluctantly said, "Do what you think is best."

There was a brief pause and his father looked uneasy. Evidently, the man wanted to talk to him about more than just business. James's body stiffened and, even though he didn't want to know, he had to ask. "Is there any news about... the other thing?"

"You don't look like you're in any mood to discuss that matter, but, yes." Gregory stared at his son for a few seconds, as if assessing if James was truly ready to hear the answer. He then pulled a sheet of paper from a drawer. He slid the document across his desk, and it landed in front of James. "Congratulations. You're a father."

What felt like a rock lay heavy in James's gut, and his breathing became difficult. He stared at the slip of paper, his eyes unable to focus.

"No. No." He shook his head, but deep down, he had expected the result. He was just wishing for a different outcome. "This can't be right," he said, halfway hoping for a miracle.

"DNA tests don't lie." The tone of his father's voice sounded authoritative and stern, like whenever he showed disapproval. "Do you even remember being with the woman?"

Pinned to the child's outfit had been a card, signed by Vivian Saunders. Hollywood loved her, and she had slowly made her way up to a sub–A–list actress. Beautiful and brunette, their fling had lasted for two weeks off the coast of Maui, and that was nearly a year and a half ago.

"Barely."

His father frowned. "Not 'barely' enough."

"There must be a mistake," James said, leaning forward in his chair and nearly pleading. His muscles had weakened, and he was glad he was sitting. "Maybe a different lab would...?"

Gregory pulled out another sheet of paper from the desk drawer. "Here are the results from the second lab. The six–month–old girl, Arianna, is yours."

'Arianna'. James now remembered seeing the name on the note, but had forgotten it until this very moment. He snatched the second piece of proof from the table and scanned the document. The wording was too biotech for him, and the colors in the two chromosome maps were nearly the same, but the sentence across the top seemed crystal–clear. A 99.98% chance that he had fathered the child.

Crap.

"Our legal team is already working on this." He slid some additional paperwork across the desk. "If you can, our lawyers have drawn up the paperwork for relinquishing all parental rights."

A gust of hope filled his lungs, and he grabbed the paper. There was a way out. All he had to do was sign away his parental rights and the child would be placed elsewhere...anywhere else.

Scanning the document, and looking for a place to sign, he noticed his name wasn't on it. He read Vivian Saunders' name across the top and a heaviness settled into his stomach, making him want to throw up.

"This is paperwork to have *the mother* relinquish all rights to the baby."

"Naturally."

The heaviness in his chest doubled. His mouth went dry and he could hardly breath. His father wasn't onboard with sending this child away. He wanted this baby to stay. Wanted her to be part of their family. Wanted him to be a father.

His eyes locked onto his father's gaze. The man's expression was stoic, so this document wasn't a cruel joke. It was real.

Did his father really think that he wanted this child? Sure, one day, he assumed he'd settle down and have a kid or two. But that was way, way, way off in the future. James glared at his father, wishing this were just a bad dream.

"After all, the mother did abandon her baby. There's a good chance that if we act quickly, we can get her to sign." He shook his head and then added, "The mother's mental state is in question and there are some legal strings we can pull."

"We?" Today it was a 'we', but James knew his

father wasn't going to find the right prep schools and schedule time around this child. No. It was James's life that was destroyed.

"The tabloids followed Ms. Saunders during her pregnancy, but she remained tight–lipped about the father. She kept a low profile, especially since she's currently doing a television show. I'm sure the baby's arrival was announced, but the news of who the father is has never…"

James allowed his father's words to fade into the background as he stared at the two pieces of documented proof that he had a daughter and another sheet of paper that would make him the sole parent. He'd brought a new life into this world. He was responsible for her, and he hadn't even met her since he'd been in Chicago until last night on business. His father had told him the news over the phone, and James had quickly supplied a sample of his DNA to the private clinic.

A daughter.

A daughter named Arianna.

He slumped in the chair and let out a deep sigh. He didn't even know where the baby was. "Does Child Protective Services still have her?"

Could they keep her? he thought.

"It's a shame the receptionist called CPS, but I think we avoided making the incident public as much as possible." His father's face held concern, but then he shook his head as if the situation were out of his control. "My secretary will discreetly pick her up and bring her here today. We should also hire some nannies."

James needed to throw up. He didn't want this responsibility. Glaring at his father, he remembered the nannies that had raised him. He hated them all. They were uncaring women who just wanted their paychecks and not a real substitution for a caring parent. "Nannies?"

"You're her father, and you're going to need all the help you can get." Gregory's voice sounded hard and judgmental, but then his expression softened. "Our lawyers will prove the mother is unfit and can't take care of the child. We'll probably have to see what her lawyers' demands are, so we can get full custody, but..."

"Full custody." Things were moving so fast; the room spun in front of him.

Gregory leaned in, and for a moment, his father's businessman façade disappeared. In its place was the man who had taught James how to throw a baseball, consulted with him on what to study in college, and the one who had given him a place in the Nielson family business. "This baby is our flesh and blood, son. She's our family."

Looking into his father's eyes, James got a glimpse of what he always considered to be the man's softer, more compassionate side. "This little girl may be the best thing to ever happen to you,"

Gregory said. Taking a good look at his son, he added, "You didn't even know the woman was pregnant, did you?"

James pointed at himself. "Does this look like the face of someone who had months to prepare for the stork's arrival?" he asked, his voice pitching high in a desperate tone.

His father let out a heavy sigh, one that sounded full of love. "Everything will be okay. A good nanny will take care of everything."

With James's crazy schedule, he wouldn't have time to be the type of father he truly—one day—wanted to be. Even if he didn't like the idea of hiring a nanny, it was the only viable option. "Nannies would be good, then." Maybe a boarding school later, as well.

"I'd prefer if you wouldn't..." His father sat back in his chair and let out an exasperated sigh. "Your disastrous first marriage didn't last long, so my guess is you will not be marrying Vivian Saunders."

James's eyes widened. In all the scenarios that had played in his head on how he could make this situation go away, marrying Vivian was never one of them. "Heck, no." There was no way he wanted another marriage and divorce. His first attempt at marital bliss—and hopefully his last—had proven to be a nightmare with the legal fees, alimony, and crap. But being a single father, even with hired help, seemed daunting. "I can't handle this, Dad."

"Dad?" His father's voice didn't show surprise. "It's always *Dad* when you need help."

"I'm serious. I can't do this." James placed the paperwork on the desk, needing the reports out of his hands.

"You're thirty–four years old, rich, and can hire a ton of help. I think you'll do fine."

elanie rubbed the stiffness from her neck as she walked across the creaking wood floor into the kitchen. The sun had already risen and it was time to get up. Another night on her aunt's couch would kill her back, but she had nowhere else to go.

"Good morning, sunshine." Her aunt Eva glanced up from her computer, her voice filled with too much good cheer for it being only six o'clock in the morning. Eva pulled her glasses off and placed them on the table, pushing the laptop aside. "I made a pot of coffee," she said, gesturing to the old coffee maker on the counter.

The Mr. Coffee brewed satisfactory java, but not the same quality as the Keurig Melanie had at work, or the machine that belonged to her now ex–roommate. Still, the hot drink would give Melanie the caffeine jolt she desperately needed.

"Good morning." She inhaled deeply, the aroma of the dark brew filling her nostrils, and fetched a cup from the cupboard before she let out a huge yawn. Her aunt kept an eye on her and followed Melanie with her gaze, making her morning search for wakeup–juice a bit unsettling.

Showing up in the middle of the night without an explanation and seeking refuge like a criminal on the lam had been quite the display last night. Of course, no questions were asked. A pillow and a warm blanket on the couch with a "we can talk in the morning" had welcomed her.

Family was great. But here it was, daybreak, and the truth needed to come out.

Placing her full mug down on the table, Melanie pushed the heavy wooden seat—allowing the shuffling sound of the chair legs to trail against the floor —and sat. "Thanks for letting me stay here last night."

A grin, wise beyond its years, splayed across Aunt Eva's face. It reminded Melanie of how kind and beautiful her mother, the older of the two women, had been. Eva had always been the fun aunt. The family member who babysat you and fed you candy while you watched television until your parents came home. The one you could talk to.

But now...

"You showed up with a tote bag of clothes and essentials like you were going away for the weekend, but in a hurry." Eva placed her hand on Melanie's, the reassuring tug on her heart giving Melanie strength. "What's going on, honey?"

Melanie gazed into the woman's kind eyes. There was no point being embarrassed in front of family, at least, not with her aunt. "You know I was furloughed from the plant after Thanksgiving."

"Yes, dear." Eva's tone held the perfect amount of motherly love with no judgment.

Being furloughed was one step away from being laid off, but still amounted to the same thing: leave without pay. The plant would call Melanie in a few weeks to tell her if she still had a job.

It was a big *if*.

Melanie gazed into her aunt's soft brown eyes. "My roommate lost her job in September."

Eva's shoulders slumped, and a sad expression showed on her face. "I hadn't heard that." She gently rubbed Melanie's hand. "That was months ago. You should have said something."

She probably should have, but she didn't want to be a burden.

"The plant did say *you* could come back in January, right?"

Melanie took in a deep breath and let it out slowly. "If they still need me, they said I could return as early as *mid*-January."

"That's just a few weeks," Eva said, her light-hearted tone an attempt to make Melanie feel better. "That's not even enough time to get the stench of the plant floor out of your clothes." Eva's hand now caressed Melanie's in short strokes, followed by some everything–will–be–all–right taps.

Melanie didn't want to be a Debbie Downer this early in the morning, but her financial problems were consuming her thoughts. Her job wasn't a good bet. Her position seemed safer than working the plant floor manufacturing paint, but not that much better. The plant hired most of the town, and the pigments and raw materials the place used left a stinky smell in the air that permeated the town. Layoffs came from time to time, but now, they were nearly a monthly event with people having nowhere to turn.

"It will work itself out. You don't work on the factory floor, and they'll need the front–line assistant managers to come back." Her aunt's words came out weak, yet with a quiet, reassuring tone.

"How will everything work out?" Melanie shook her head and glanced at the ceiling as if divine inter-vention would somehow answer. "Mr. Ferguson allowed me back into my apartment for ten minutes before he locked the door for nonpayment. I barely had time to gather one bag of my clothes and essen-tials." She let out a sad sigh. "I had to leave all my art supplies there."

"Why did he...?"

"I haven't been able to pay rent since October." Melanie's voice sounded harsher than she wanted, and she didn't want to yell at her aunt. It felt shameful enough to admit that money had been tight, but to be evicted? At this rate, she'd never be able to financially leave this town.

Eva's face reddened, and her body tensed. "I've known Joel Ferguson since high school. I'll talk to him and get you and your roommate, Carol, back into your place."

"Carol moved back home months ago." Melanie cut Eva off, worried that she may even offer to pay some of the lost rent. Her uncle also worked at the plant. Their jobs, like everyone else's, were at stake if the place closed down. The little money Eva made owning and running the town's temporary hiring agency wasn't much, and Melanie didn't want to be a bother. One or two nights on the couch, a week at the most, was all she planned to take.

"Joel will let me into the apartment. He's sweet on me." Aunt Eva's eyebrow rose. "I'll talk with his wife down at the post office and have your mail forwarded here for the time being."

Melanie hadn't even thought about mail. She had been waiting to hear back from some schools and their scholarship programs, but acceptance letters weren't flowing in. All the colleges had either wait-listed her or flat-out said, "no."

"Thanks. I hadn't thought about the mail."

Melanie already knew the answer, but had to ask. She stared at the laptop on the table. "Have any jobs come in through your temp agency?"

Aunt Eva's face paled. "Well, not today." She sighed. "Nothing for the last few weeks really."

The news wasn't surprising.

Her aunt then beamed her a pale smile, the kind that parents give their children to have them believe everything will be all right. "The local Christmas fair is coming up in a few days. I'm sure your paintings will sell, and you'll be able to make your rent."

Aunt Eva was always hopeful, but all the paintings Melanie had planned to sell were locked in her apartment and wouldn't fetch much. She wasn't a well–known artist. She'd probably have to die before anyone cared about her work. "I doubt my paintings will bring in much money."

"Oh," Eva scoffed. "You're a wonderful artist; like your mother was. And, even if you don't make much money, you'll get exposure."

Exposure to whom? No one in this town would *discover* her and make her dreams come true. Her mother had one break in life. She had attended Vassar College and had had an internship at the White Cube Gallery in London. Of course, her mother had given all of that up when she got pregnant with Melanie. She'd left the internship and moved back to Newbury, set aside her dream of being a commercial artist, and became a housewife who worked part–time at the local grocery store designing their local ads.

Melanie didn't want to end up like her mom.

Aunt Eva waved her hand in the air. "Besides, you're welcome to stay here as long as you like."

Melanie knew she talked about the small two–bedroom home and not the tiny town of Newbury. As welcome as she was in either one, she wanted to leave.

3

James sat in his father's office, waiting for the man's secretary to return. The heater kicked on, warming the room to an uncomfortable temperature, so he removed his outer sweater. The moments ticked away slowly, but he had no other place to be.

Sitting quietly in the room, listening to the clock tick on the wall, was driving him crazy. Searching the Internet on his phone, he found the one piece of information he so desperately needed: his daughter's birth date.

A father should know when his child was born.

He should at least know that much. He had been in Greece on that day, wrapped up with his business and a personal vacation when his daughter came into this world. No worries, no concerns, no... nothing. Just him, and his needs and wants.

Everything was always about him.

That's how he liked it, and the way the world should be.

He stretched and scanned the room for any distraction that could help him take his mind off of his horrible predicament. Across from him, hung the painting *Crystal Goblet* by the artist George Brackes, a gift he had bought for his father's sixtieth birthday during that Greece vacation. James stared at the bold, red brush strokes and the contrast of colors.

He'd majored in business in college, with a minor in art history. An odd combination, but he did appreciate fine art—expensive, fine art. The more he stared and studied the painting, and as he thought about his new life as a father, the more he grew to hate the piece.

It had been a birthday gift for his father. The man didn't understand the *Crystal Goblet*, and he didn't appreciate fine art. They didn't see eye–to–eye on many things; sometimes being polar opposites to each other. James glanced back at the painting. At least his father had thought the art was a good investment and tolerated it. His dad *endured* many things even though he didn't approve of in James's life.

What if James and his daughter were contrast-ingly different people? What if they didn't get along? What if she became spoiled, demanding all his attention, time, and money? What if she became rebellious?

What if he had to tolerate her as his father tolerated him and his whims? Sure, James had a good relationship with his dad now, but he'd had to move past the nannies, the boarding school, and be in his thirties before the two of them ever saw eye–to–eye on anything—and then their business kept them civil to each other enough so they could finally be in the same room together without shouting.

What if James's daughter didn't have anything in common with him, like running the family business? What if she hated him?

He didn't know how to raise a child. Surely, he'd do everything wrong.

He felt a panic attack surfacing, so he took some deep breaths and rubbed his face. What if he focused on the fact that Arianna was only six months old and didn't despise him yet? There'd be plenty of time for her to grow into her resentment and disapproval.

The door chimes rang, and James heard the soft footsteps of who he assumed was a maid walking across the marble floor outside the office. His daughter was... *home*.

A queasiness settled in his stomach. *His* daughter was *home*. Here. In *his* home. Where she belonged.

He took a deep breath to settle his nerves, but his heart still raced, and cold sweat beaded on his forehead. He wiped his brow with the back of his hand and felt ill. This was one of those moments that defined your life. If this were his biography, a new chapter would be starting.

Shit.

His family had a dog named Izzy. James didn't walk Izzy, didn't feed her, didn't make sure she went to the vet—although he assumed she went—and now James had a human being, an innocent baby to take care of. How on Earth did that make any sense?

The office door opened, and his father's secretary carried in his daughter. James's gaze focused on the small child in the pink dress and matching head bow in the woman's arms.

She gazed at him with her big, blue eyes. Her chubby cheeks held dimples, and she smiled at him.

And then... she yawned.

The movement was a small thing, but innocent and sweet. She was too young to cover the yawn to hide it. She didn't look away. She didn't mind showing her true self.

She was so tiny. So innocent. So... beautiful.

His heart pounded, and he felt tears welling up.

Yep. Definitely the beginning of a new chapter in his life.

He had expected a baby, swaddled and small.

Even though she was little, she was sitting up in the secretary's arms, bright eyed and... gorgeous.

"Are you ready to meet your daughter?"

The woman didn't wait for an answer. She set down a small diaper bag with the logo for Child Protective Services on the side. Then she carried the baby to the couch and handed her to him.

His hands reached for her, which surprised him. He had no idea how to hold an infant, but he had chosen to sit on the big couch in case he dropped her.

'Don't drop her' he repeated in his mind. *'Please don't drop your daughter'.*

Not only was Arianna bigger than he had expected, she was heavier than a newborn. She sat on his lap and held onto the sleeve of his shirt as she stared at him with her big, blue eyes like he had all the answers in the world.

That couldn't have been further from the truth.

"Hello, Arianna. I'm your father." Quoting Darth Vader and doing a cheesy line seemed ridiculous, but he didn't know what else to say. What would a baby want to hear? Did they even care?

The girl resembled him, except for her dark, curly hair. Her skin complexion matched his. Her nose and ears were shaped like his, as well as her cheekbones. Maybe that's all he wanted to see. *Him*, somewhere in *her*.

Her hand curled around his finger, and his heart melted.

This was his baby. His daughter. His Arianna.

Tears threatened to escape. He had dreaded a day like this, and yet, here it was. And this little girl —this amazingly beautiful child—was here, and he didn't want to run from the room screaming.

Everything felt right.

She placed her free hand in her mouth and looked around, her eyes wide as she took in the room. At least, he thought she was focusing on items in the office. He wasn't sure how good a baby's eyesight was at this age.

He did know that six months old didn't talk. They couldn't sit on their own. They couldn't feed themselves. At least, that's what the quick Internet scans he'd done showed him.

Based on the stench from her diaper, they knew how to poop, though.

His face pinched and he handed the baby back to his father's secretary. "I don't... She needs..."

The woman removed a small blanket from the diaper bag and placed the cloth on the couch before laying Arianna down. The woman's lips pulled downward, and she let out a sigh of frustration, one that told James that she had no belief in him as a father.

Sure, he could help run a multi-million-dollar firm, but... change a diaper? He'd have to hire a

nanny to do that nasty chore. James wasn't a hands–
on, touchy–feely sort of guy.

Plus, he couldn't blame the woman for having
little trust in him. She had worked for his father for
several years, and he wanted to say her name was
Phyllis, but he wasn't sure. James spent most of his
time traveling for business, never really getting to
know the household's or headquarter's staff. His
reputation around the office of being a cold, heartless bastard pleased him.

God. He didn't want his daughter to have that
impression of him.

The secretary handed him the dirty diaper,
wrapped up and secure from any mess. The words
Child Protective Services were stamped on the outside,
and he could see some of the letters. "What am I
supposed to do with this?"

The woman gazed up from her duty, her piercing
eyes judging him.

"Throw it away," he said. "Understood."

He felt like an idiot. People usually didn't get a
rise out of him in the accomplishment and self–
esteem departments, but he wasn't on firm ground at
the moment. He walked to the wastebasket and
tossed the diaper in. The strong smell still permeated the air but he didn't know how to fix that. He
then rubbed his hands on his jeans to make sure
they weren't dirty.

"There she is," his father said as he entered the

room. "There's my granddaughter." He picked up the child and smiled at her. "I may not agree with how you joined our family, but you're blood." Gregory glared at his son. "Your assistant, Darin, just dropped off boarding school pamphlets." His eyes showed his displeasure about the idea, and his tone sounded stern and dismissive. "She's not going to boarding school. She's only a baby."

James had panicked when he heard the news that he was a father and had asked his assistant for some help. He now gazed into his daughter's eyes. No. She wasn't going to a boarding school. She would stay here, with him.

"Phyllis is having a nursery decorated upstairs for her and will conduct some nanny interviews."

"Nannies. Right." That would be for the best.

His father smiled at Arianna and nuzzled his face against hers. How was he such a natural around babies? Was this something new? James's childhood memories of his father were of a distant and cold man. He had always bought the most expensive gifts for birthdays, but didn't take the time to get to know James and learn what he wanted —which was just more father–and–son–bonding time.

As a child, James had wanted his father to know him, not just spend money having other people raise him. But he guessed people always went with their strengths.

He wondered what his strengths as a family man would be.

James glanced at the painting on the wall, the one he had given his father on his birthday. James was still vacationing in Greece when the gift arrived and hadn't spent his father's birthday with him. He hadn't spent many of his father's birthdays with him. Or the holidays. His father wasn't a hands–on dad. And, if James were honest, the disappointment James had felt had created a wall between the two of them.

And he didn't want to become that type of father to Arianna.

"I know you're great with the business. You make the hard decisions, you work on expanding our companies with mergers..." His father's voice trailed off. "Your tough attitude gives you an edge, but..."—he smiled once again at Arianna—"this little girl is a great way for you to show me that you're responsible when it comes to family." Gregory handed Arianna back to James, making sure that her head was balanced and that James had a good hold on her before he let go.

The baby cried once James held her. He thought about talking to her in that baby–speak way, but knew the words would sound stupid if he did. He also wanted to nuzzle his face against her as his father had done, but thought he'd scare her. He finally settled on just patting her on her back, which seemed to calm her down.

What if he did something that scarred her for life? Now thinking about what his father had said, he asked, "What do you mean about family responsibility?"

James's father nodded to dismiss Phyllis from the room. Once alone, Gregory took a seat next to James on the couch. "I'm thinking of retiring."

His father had mentioned four times over the past year about wanting to retire. The man always talked about handing over the reins, but he never did. He had been ecstatically happy lately since he had married his fourth wife, and she enjoyed traveling, so James couldn't tell if his father really meant it this time.

Taking over the company and becoming a father in the same week? James's knees grew weak, and he was once again glad that he was sitting.

"I want to travel with Joan. You've been running much of the company, especially with managing all the branches across the States and in Europe." His father shook his head, and, for the first time, James took note of the gray hairs the man had. They weren't just peppering the man's head, they covered it. "I'm thinking I can transition you in during the next six months or so, then Joan and I can travel during the summer. Maybe do a European tour or something."

"Really?" A broad grin spread across James's face, and his heart rate quickened. This is what he had wanted since graduating from Harvard business school. Heck, what he had wanted since his teenage years.

"But I want you to spend some time with your daughter first." He leaned in and coo'd at the baby and got her to smile. "It'll take a while to find a good nanny, so I want you to take the Christmas holiday to get to know each other."

The workload, especially before the holidays, always kept James busy. His schedule had him flying to London tonight. There'd be no time to take a baby in tow.

"The plant in Newbury hasn't been performing very well," his father said, his tone filled with dread.

Again with Newbury? His grandfather loved the town, and Gregory had been raised there. But why would they have such strong feelings for a place that held a population of under two thousand people? James was certain there were no good restaurants there, no good skiing, and no good vacation spots. It remained a hole–in–the–wall type of place, a town that needed to be dumped and forgotten about. "Remember, I suggested we close the plant after the holiday? It's all in my latest report."

"I want you to go to Newbury. It's the first company my father started, and that plant gave us all... this." Gregory's hands gestured around the room. "I want you to spend some time down there with your daughter and find your roots before you close the plant."

James cocked his head and his gaze locked onto his father's. "Before *I* close the plant?"

"Sure? Why not?"

Sweat beaded on James's forehead. A piss–ant town and a young baby to take care of? It would be a disaster in the making. "The plant needs to be shut down," he said, highlighting each word to get his point across. "There's no reason for me to go down there to do it."

His father pulled out three airline tickets from his suit's breast pocket. "I've already booked you on a flight. Besides, it's best to get out of town before the news of your daughter hits the tabloids."

"The tabloids?"

Gregory, who had been smiling at his grand-daughter, now looked sternly at his son. "News will travel fast, and this type of information is just fodder for those vultures."

James looked at the name and date on the three tickets, one for him, one for his assistant, and one for Arianna. The date wasn't going to work. "I'm in London tomorrow. I can't..."

James's father's face paled as if he remembered the merger James currently conducted overseas. His father took back the tickets. "The business will only take a few days. We'll send your assistant and

Arianna ahead of time. Darin can find some local, temporary help for you before he begins his Christmas vacation."

The whole ordeal sounded dreadful. He liked the idea of getting to know his daughter, but going to Newbury? "I'm skiing in Aspen for Christmas."

"Not anymore."

4

---

*D*ays had passed, and there was no job to be found. Melanie had talked to every store owner and shop clerk in Newbury. No one was hiring. If she didn't find something today, she'd have to increase her job search to the neighboring town of Wayford which held more job openings, but that was at least twenty minutes away. She'd need more money for gas, and her car would take a beating driving so much longer to work, but it was doable.

It'd be better if she moved to Wayford. The town really wasn't that far away, but moving wouldn't make sense if the plant took her back in a few weeks. Besides, if she were to leave Newbury she wanted to leave it—and all facsimilies of it and small town life —behind. A real move to New York would be better.

Right now she didn't have enough money to cover the cost of a hotel room, let alone plan for a big move. She needed a job so she could save her money and eventually escape.

She entered her Aunt's kitchen for their morning routine of coffee and disappointment. Her aunt would ask how the job search was going, and then Melanie would tell her the depressing news and promise to keep searching.

After getting herself a cup of coffee, she sat next to her aunt at the table. Before she could ask, Melanie said, "I just need a temporary job, if I can find one, until the plant takes me back." She stared down at the computer just inches away from her aunt Eva. "I'm sure I already know the answer, but has anything come in today?" She chuckled nervously. "You know, the perfect part-time job that will solve all my money issues?"

Eva put on her glasses and pulled the computer closer. Her expression looked more hopeful than yesterday. "A request came in this morning. This one is very temporary. It ends just after Christmas."

Melanie leaned in to see the screen but it was at an angle and she couldn't read the display. "Santa needs another elf?"

Eva let out a nervous chuckle. "No, but because it's under two weeks of work, I imagine the job will be hard to fill."

"A full-time position?"

The keypad clicking filled the room. "Now, don't be too hopeful. The duration is only a few days, but the pay is good. More than you would make at your position at the plant."

Finally, a ray of hope. Melanie sat straighter in the chair, her fingernails clicking nervously at the warm coffee mug in her hands as excitement tingled up her spine. "The job sounds great."

Her aunt's grim expression told Melanie it wasn't.

"I'll take the position. Whatever it is." She could shovel horse manure for all that it mattered. Better pay, a way to get back into her apartment, and then, hopefully, her job opening back up so she could continue to apply for art scholarships and get on with her life.

"You need to know CPR, first–aid…" Eva read hesitantly from the computer as though she expected bad news to follow.

Melanie shook her head. "I'm still certified in all that from this past summer when I worked as an art teacher for the Sunday school."

"And like Sunday school, this job too deals with children—well, one child." Eva's voice trailed off, and then she softly said, "A six–month–old girl."

Melanie would rather shovel horse manure, but couldn't be choosy, at least not if the job provided good money. "The job is fine."

"You *are* good with children," Eva said, encouraging Melanie with her kind words. "You could even teach Sunday school more if you were willing to put up with the little ones. I hear the teacher may retire soon."

"Children are nightmares." Melanie stiffened in the chair and felt her muscles tighten. Everyone wanted kids, everyone wanted grandkids, everyone wanted snotty–nosed, mini–versions of themselves. Why did everyone think she was a monster for not wanting them?

Because of a medical condition she couldn't even conceive a child.

She sat straighter in the chair. It was just as well. She didn't need the grief of dealing with a child.

Eva looked up from the computer. "More jobs involve children than anything else in this town." She let out a soft sigh and stared north, the direction of the Nielson Painting Manufacturing Facility, the first company of the Nielson International Corporation. "Well, other than working at the plant, which may be closing."

Melanie's chest muscles tightened even more, reminding her of how claustrophobic living in such a small town was. Living here was choking the life out of her, one stinky breath of paint pigment at a time. "One day, I'll move to the big city and escape all this." Leaving had been her plan all along, at least until her parents died in the car accident.

"I know, dear. This town is getting harder to live in with no jobs available. But I'd like to keep you here as long as I can." Eva leaned down and continued to read the request from the computer. "Full nanny care for a six–month–old girl. Twelve days. Cooking and cleaning expected. Live–in."

"Nanny and live–in maid?" Honestly? She had a mind, which no one seemed capable of appreciating. Why did every man in her life want her to be a wife and mother? Wasn't giving up her dreams of school when her parents died enough?

Eva glanced up and sheepishly said, "It'd be a place to stay."

The brick wall hit Melanie square on. She couldn't have her aunt feed and house her, not when she barely made do herself. Melanie needed to suck it up and do what needed to be done. No matter how bad the situation seemed, she was a grown woman of twenty–six and had managed to live on her own since the age of seventeen. She wouldn't allow a temporary setback due to pride get in her way.

She let out a deep sigh, allowing it to take away all her anxiety. "Where is the client staying?"

"That old mansion on Culver Road." Eva nodded and gestured west. "Down the road a bit. It's been boarded up as long as I've known the place, but I did see some lights on inside the other day, some food delivery trucks, and even a cable van."

"What?" Melanie knew the scary, old, abandoned home. "Who placed the job request?"

She glanced down and reread the name. "James Nielson."

Crap. There was no way. Melanie repeated the name in her head. "Wasn't the founder of the plant a Michael Nielson or somebody?"

Eva's eyebrow rose and hid behind her slightly graying bangs. "Mitchell Nielson, I think. He started the plant nearly seventy–five years ago." Her aunt's eyes widened. "I hadn't thought of that. I wonder if James is a grandson or something."

The Nielson family was a legend in this town, one of the founding members. Everyone had heard stories of them, including how the plant worked for the defense department during World War II, and how the family moved away nearly forty years ago. The plant had been unionized in the 1950s and had become more corporate America each decade since, showing less and less family ownership and personal touches—especially since, as far as she knew, the founding Nielson had never returned.

"If anyone will know if the plant is closing, it's this man—James Nielson." Melanie took in a deep breath and leaned back in the chair, the wood creaking with her weight.

Working with a kid would be a pain, but it'd be good money, and a way to get back on her feet. She may even find out what was going on with the plant in the meantime, and know if they really would take her back in a few weeks. "I'll take the job."

5

*J*ames parked his rental car in front of the old home and put his hands against the vents of the heater. He hadn't expected the weather to be this cold in Newbury and he paused another moment to enjoy the seat heaters. He bundled his coat around himself and buttoned it.

The howling wind whipped into the car the moment he opened the door. He stepped onto the lawn of the mansion, which would be his home for the next twelve days, and the crust of the icy sidewalk cracked under his feet. He removed his fogging sunglasses and studied the old house with its sun-beaten shutters and snow-covered lawn.

He had seen pictures of this house his entire life. The mansion looked the same, only older. But what was that stench? He had smelled it since getting off the plane, and now it smelled even stronger. Just one more reason to be here for as little time as possible.

Not that he needed another reason.

'Christmas in a hick town', he thought. Thank goodness his grandfather had had enough sense to escape this place after setting up the first of his many businesses.

James walked up the creaking steps to the front door, carrying his suitcases. His laptop swung from his shoulder, and he wondered what Internet reception the old place got, if any.

The front door flung open before he reached it.

"Welcome to Newbury, sir," Darin, James's personal assistant said in an enthusiastic voice that sounded a bit too desperate to James's ears.

In Darin's arms lay Arianna, the baby gripping the front of the man's button–down shirt tightly and sitting squarely in his arms. Her green–goo–smeared face lit up once she saw her father, and her one free hand reached for him through the blanket she was wrapped up in.

A smile spread across James's face, which surprised him. Even though only a few days had passed, he had missed his little angel and had thought about her the entire time he was in London. He reached for the child, not caring that her smudgy fingers would stain his shirt. "How's my girl?"

She lifted easily from Darin's arms, and the

assistant sprang onto the stoop to gather the bags. "Everything has been taken care of, sir."

Feeling comfortable enough, he kissed his baby's sweet cheeks.

Darin explained the condition of the home. He mentioned something about hot water and there being only one working bathroom, but James focused in on the fact that Darin had already enrolled Arianna in a Kinder Musik program—whatever that was.

Soon, there'd be many programs, school, friends… eventually, even boyfriends for Arianna. James gazed down at the baby, knowing he was getting ahead of himself.

This needed to be taken one step at a time. He wanted to enjoy the moments he had with her, not focus on the future and her growing up too quickly.

They entered the home. All the windows were open, and it left a chill in the air even once the door was closed. "The place smelled a bit musty when we first arrived," Darin explained.

James's nose wrinkled in displeasure. "And, you're letting in whatever that smell is from outside."

"That," Darin said, pointing out the window, "is the paint smell from your plant."

James's eyebrow rose. All of the Nielson paint facilities had ventilation features in place to properly contain and vent the toxic fumes of paint. Those precautions were EPA approved and strictly regulated. Of course, the plant had been here for nearly a century. He figured it would make sense that some non–toxic scent would come from it. He just wasn't used to the smell, and he didn't recognize it as paint because it wasn't that strong stench you get by walking into a freshly painted room.

The scent wasn't horrible, just unpleasant now that he knew what it was.

Arianna held tightly to her father as he carried her around the room. He shifted her from one arm to the other to hold her more securely, causing his laptop to swing and reminding him of his agenda. "Internet?"

"Surprisingly good. This town doesn't have much, but at least there's that. There's a FedEx shop down the road, the plant is only a mile away, and there are grocery stores..."

"What about a nanny?" Arianna now squirmed in James's arms and flung her head back to look at Darin.

James didn't anticipate his daughter's movement and nearly dropped the child. He needed to learn how to hold her. How to keep her safe.

"After having no luck the last few days, I discovered a local temp agency. I contacted them this morning and they have already replied. We should have a nanny today."

James shook his head. His first order of business

was to interview the nannies and pick the best one for his daughter. He could do that.

"I'm feeding her some rice cereal mixed with formula. I tried to give her some peas, but she may be too young for baby food." Darin glanced back at the living room coffee table where the jar lay. "She doesn't care for them."

Arianna reached her dirty, pea–smeared hand up to her eyes and tried to rub them, but James stopped her. "She might be tired," he said, guessing.

He had only just arrived, and he'd hoped to spend some time with her, but if she needed a nap, she needed a nap. Good fathers always put the needs of their children first. He needed to remember that.

Geez, he loved to see her smile, to hear her laugh, to feel her hugs. It had only been a couple of days, but he had truly missed her.

"The nanny candidate will be here shortly," Darin said, walking back to the living room.

"Only one candidate?"

Shrugging, Darin said, "They only mentioned one interview."

James's chest tightened, and, once again, he felt the suffocation of being in a small town. Ever since his plane had landed—no, even before that—he just knew this rinky–dink place would not be able to meet his needs. This small dive of Newbury would more than likely send a twelve–year–old babysitter to cover his daughter's needs.

"Thank you, Granddad," he muttered under his breath.

"The agency highly recommended this woman as a nanny."

James took in the disarray of the table and the fact that his daughter was now crying since Darin was cleaning up the jar of peas. She seemed old enough for baby food, but he wasn't sure. "Maybe some formula and a nap would be best," James said, dismissively, knowing that he really didn't know what she wanted or needed. He relied heavily upon the information he had gleaned from the Internet and a book he had downloaded called *What to Expect Your First Year.*

"Here is her bottle," Darin said, handing over a small container that made Arianna happy.

"She slept in late today, sir. The cold air and different room kept her up all night." Darin grabbed the child. "But a nap would be good if she goes down." He picked up a napkin from the table and cleaned her mouth between screams. "People don't know what they need until they're staring directly at it. If they're smart, they'll recognize the opportunity and take advantage of the situation."

Darin then pointed to a sheet of paper on the end table. "I wrote out what her schedule seems to be, and her likes and dislikes." He then added, "As I mentioned, we should probably note that she doesn't like peas."

A new stroller stood in the entryway, a play mat lay in the middle of the room, and a playpen sat filled with toys. James suspected that a new high chair was in the kitchen, as well as many bottles and whatever else a child might need.

James stared at the sheet of paper, which was written on only one side. "Do what you can. I'll walk around and set up an office." James would need a lot more notes on that tiny piece of paper if he planned to properly take care of his daughter.

6

Melanie steered her late model Ford Taurus down Kipling street, gripping the steering wheel through thick gloves. The sunlight glared off the snow and ice making it hard to see. She put down the sun visor to find her way, even though she had traveled down this road many times in the past. The car sputtered and hissed, reminding her that she not only needed the heater fixed, but the car also needed a full tune–up when she could afford to do so.

She drove over the old Robin Reading Railroad tracks, crossing from the industry side of town to the residential one. The old car's worn shocks jostled the car and reminded her that she needed them looked at as well.

The house sat atop a hill, nestled between thick shrubbery now white and bare from the winter.

Clouds had formed and gave the manor an ominous appearance.

Only twelve days, she thought.

If the Nielson house had heat and a bed, all would be good.

She stepped out of the car and slung her knockoff designer bag over her shoulder. Her breath collected as foggy frost in front of her as she gazed at the house. She remembered the home fondly from her early childhood years.

Some said the place was haunted, which always put the building at risk for teenagers and their Halloween misgivings, causing the cops to swing by to have a look around. But, to Melanie, the home was a magical playhouse that she and her best friend had enjoyed for several weeks the summer they were eight years old.

A broken branch had crashed through a window, and with a dare and giggles, the two girls had wandered inside. For nearly two weeks, they'd gotten to play house and enjoy the place until the repairman replaced the window and their mothers had been told about their adventures.

Her body tightened, and a flush of anger raced up her spine as she thought about her ex-friend Stephanie, whom she hadn't talked to in nearly a year.

Thanks to Melanie's ex-fiancé's wandering eye,

Stephanie now had the ring, the house, and a bun in the oven.

Melanie gripped the strap of her shoulder bag firmly, and her eyes narrowed. The two deserved each other. She would break free of this town and never look back.

She hiked her bag up farther on her squared shoulders and walked up the icy stoop.

JAMES STOOD in front of the fireplace, his stern gaze detailing the painting over the mantel, edge-to-edge and side-to-side. The family portrait held five family members—*his* family members.

The strong patriarch stood in the center back with his doting wife wearing what James assumed was typical fare for a woman in her standing. The man's suit, his pocket watch, and spectacles, along with her long, lace dress and brooch spoke volumes about their family's fortune at the time.

Three children, one a babe in his mother's arms, stood near the parents. Their white clothes—pressed and clean—were probably just a few of many such nice outfits they owned in a town when most had nothing.

James stared at the baby. The child was his grandfather, Mitchell—born into this wealthy family and, if the stories were correct, brought into this world in one of the rooms upstairs. James's father had been born decades later in a hospital, but lived in this town, in this very house, until his thirties.

James glanced around the living room, his gaze falling on the many antiquated relics from a long-ago time scattered throughout. Gas fueled lamps, dark-wood furniture, and imported throw rugs.

They were just things to him. Objects that did not fit into his world. But to his grandfather... this town and the people in it were everything, especially since his grandfather, James's great-great-grandfather, was one of the founding fathers.

James nodded at his grandfather's image in the painting. "Personal touch," he said, noting the promise he had made to his grandfather on his deathbed.

His grandfather's words rang in his head, circling James's already established sense of right and wrong. "Never forget your roots," his grandfather had told him, echoed by his father's words of, "Treat people kindly and respect this town. The place became the beginning of everything for this family."

A smirk crossed James's lips. He was filled with not pride, but duty. A duty he took seriously.

"I'll handle the shutdown of the first plant you ever created, Granddad, with a gentle hand."

The doorbell rang, its strident tone stirring James and eliciting a scream from Arianna upstairs. James suspected that Darin would be busy walking the child and putting her down for the second time, so he crossed the living room floor and went to the door.

He opened one side of the two wooden doors leading in, expecting to either see the youngest babysitter the town could afford, or the oldest grand-mother with nothing better to do.

"Hello," he said, opening the door wider. The woman stared at him, the wind having picked up her long, brown locks and blowing them across her face. She pulled the strands free and tucked them behind an ear.

This couldn't be the nanny. Could it?

James took in the woman's delicate features. Soft, green eyes; wavy, brunette hair that flowed from her winter cap; and a pert, little nose that had turned pink from the cold. Her thin build was obvious, even under the thick coat.

She was definitely not a child.

"I'm Melanie Frank. The agency sent me." She handed a folder filled with paper to him as though she held an all-access pass.

Her beautiful eyes peeked out from behind her bangs, her red lips contrasting starkly with her pale skin as she breathed warm puffs of air between them.

"Please, come in. You must be freezing."

She smiled—warm and invitingly—at him before entering, causing him to forget the dreaded town for a moment and grin back at her. "I'm James Nielson."

She removed her glove and held out her delicate hand. "Nice to meet you, sir."

Pretty and polite? "Please, call me James." He shook her hand, noting how smooth her skin felt, and how cold her hand was.

He shook his head and sucked in a deep breath. Melanie had the same soft features as James's ex-wife. The same doe-eyes, kind smile, and even the same hair color—but Melanie was so much more beautiful. She was exactly his type of woman.

But, no.

He blinked and shook his head.

Heck, no.

Whatever might happen during the next two weeks, it was not going to be a made-for-TV, stupid, romance movie. James had too many failed relation-ships and a shattered marriage under his belt already. The last thing he needed was complications from a short-term fling.

His last complication was being rocked to sleep upstairs.

He had to break his destructive patterns.

Arianna needed him.

His businesses needed him.

He didn't need anybody else.

She smiled and nodded politely, so he added,

"Let me take your coat. Can I get you some hot tea or something?"

He then remembered that he had no idea what state the kitchen was in but thought surely there'd be some food already bought. Darin had lived here for three days already, certainly the man had taken care of the basic necessities.

"I'm fine." She removed her coat and handed the thin, tattered garment to him, her eyes shifting slightly to the noise upstairs.

"My daughter Arianna is going down for a nap." He gestured to the living room for them to sit. "She's a well-mannered child, just tired right now," he said, guessing about what the child's disposition actually was. He hoped she was well-mannered, but really had no idea.

"All children can be like that," Melanie said with a smile that looked all-knowing and wise.

She crossed in front of him and moved into the room. The light scent of her skin picked up the muskiness of the heater that had been working so hard to warm the place. The fragrance she wore wasn't a floral scent, it was warmer and more sensual, as though heat radiated from her.

She placed her bag on the couch and took a seat, her legs crossed and sitting with good posture. Why James thought that to be a good sign, he wasn't sure. He would have preferred a more mature woman, one in her fifties who had raised a slew of kids herself and who would have arrived in a white nurse's uniform like the nannies he'd had as a child. But this woman was the best the town could offer.

James stared at Melanie. If his nannies had resembled her, he would have hit puberty early.

"The paperwork includes a background and driving record check. My resume is also in there."

He opened the folder and studied the documents. She wasn't a criminal. She wasn't a crazy driver. There wasn't much to the paperwork other than some handwritten notes by the agency that had sent her over.

She pointed at the resume. "You'll see that I've been a Sunday school teacher and have all the pre-qualifications you requested." Her gaze briefly wandered toward the ceiling to where the crying came from. She then counted on her fingers. "First-aid, I'm registered in CPR..." she began.

James did his best to ignore Arianna's cries, but was tempted—if he knew how—to go upstairs and soothe her. He glanced down at the one-page sheet of paper, taking it all in at just a glance. "You're local to the town?"

"Born and raised right here in Newbury. My childhood home is just a mile or so from the *Nielson* plant." Her face hinted at the name and the underlying question.

"My family was one of the founding members of this town," James said quietly, not because it was bragging, but because he felt there was nothing to boast about.

Her glowing smile told him otherwise. She'd probably gone to Nielson High School. It was a slight joke, and an inward shudder enveloped him. Was that the name of the local high school?

Gosh, he hoped it hadn't been named after his family.

"My daughter and I will only be here for a few days. She'll need twenty-four-hour care..." He grabbed Darin's notes from the end table and read them to her. He learned more about his daughter in those notes than he had in the day he had spent with her before leaving for London.

"Oh, and she hates peas," he added, noting the green food smears on it, before setting the paper down.

"And her mother is here?" Melanie's gaze wandered down the hallway and then traveled back to James.

Yes, and that little detail. It was odd to think about it, but he'd have to explain to Arianna one day where her mother was, and try to be sensitive enough not to hurt her with the truth that her mother had abandoned her. It wasn't a talk that he wanted to think about.

"I'm a single father."

She nodded slightly. "I'm sorry for your loss."

His gaze darted to her. He was sure he had heard

her correctly, but he wasn't sure how to respond. There certainly had not been any loss, but then, he figured perhaps in this small town, there weren't many divorces—and fewer 'baby daddies'. Maybe that was why his father had suggested that he come here, for strong family values.

"What makes you think I'm a widower?"

Her jaw opened slightly, as if she had been caught doing something wrong. "Your daughter is only six months old. I just assumed."

He supposed that was a fair assumption. "I was never married to her mother, and she and I are trying to work out an arrangement."

He wasn't sure why he told her the last part, but he didn't want her to believe that he had knocked up the mother and then refused to marry her. Was this the type of town he was in now? Complete with a Bible belt?

Her lips turned slightly upward and she gave a slight head nod. "Things don't always work out. I understand."

After an awkward silence, Melanie said, "I have a lot of experience with children. My parents died when I was seventeen, and I raised my brother. After high school, I worked at a restaurant, in daycare centers, and then part–time at the church. That is until I started at the local college and began working at the plant."

His face twitched, showing his shock before he

could rein it in. "I'm sorry to hear of *your* loss." Now knowing her past misfortunes, he understood the maturity in her face, the dedication in her eyes for getting a job, and why she would be available at Christmas for a short, temporary position. She hadn't had a comfortable life in a town that you'd think would be simple.

Especially simple for a young person.

But even small towns had the Internet. Then, something occurred to him.

"There are to be no pictures of Arianna posted on the Internet." He gave Melanie a stern look, telling her that he meant business. The tabloids had not tracked him down yet, and he didn't need to give them a map to where he was hiding. "No Facebook, Pinterest, Snapchat, or whatever people do these days."

He hated social media.

Her eyes widened and she genuinely looked shocked. "She's only a baby. I won't be posting pictures and inviting predators," she said in a serious tone.

She then made eye contact with him. "I have a Pinterest account, but, other than that, I don't do social media."

She couldn't be older than her mid to late twenties—at best. Who didn't do social media at that age? Even he had a Facebook account, and he was only thirty–four.

Most of the young hires he spent time with couldn't converse for more than a minute without checking something on their phones. Melanie had good people skills. That was rare these days.

The crying upstairs stopped, and he assumed that Arianna had finally gone down for a nap. A calming sensation took hold of him, and he felt happy that she was getting the rest she needed. He was also happy to conduct the interview without any further distractions.

He glanced down at the resume and saw that Melanie had graduated from Newbury High School eight years ago. He now knew her age *and* the name of the high school.

"Cooking and cleaning are involved," he said in a nearly dismissive tone, hoping that those two extra chores would not scare her away. "The place does have a full kitchen and, my assistant, I'm sure, has stocked the shelves." Not sure what the town offered regarding home delivery, he added, "You can order meals and have them brought in."

"I'm an excellent cook, and I don't mind taking care of a kitchen."

Her smile told him that she probably enjoyed preparing meals, but the food was only for him since he had read that Arianna was still on formula, rice cereal, and maybe some baby foods. She might be ready to start more solids, but the idea scared him.

"I'm not a very picky eater. Whatever you make will be great."

THE BABY HAD FINALLY STOPPED CRYING. Melanie heard footsteps upstairs, so apparently, someone was rocking the child. But, still. How long did a baby have to cry before going down? Hopefully, the child wasn't sick.

Focusing on the interview proved hard to do with all the noise. She was thankful for the peace and quiet.

"Do you have a reliable car?" James asked. "One with snow tires or chains... whatever you do in this weather?"

Reliable? What a loaded question. She needed this job so she had to choose her words carefully. "I do have a car," she said, not wanting to lie to—hopefully—her future employer, and the most handsome man she had ever laid eyes on.

This man oozed poise and charisma. His dark blond hair featured what she suspected was a New York style, which contrasted starkly with his pale skin. And his eyes? She had never seen that shade of blue before. She had seen the concern in his gaze for his daughter, but he had dismissed the worry because he had people to take care of her. He commanded power, and his influence showed.

She wasn't even sitting next to him and she could feel his confidence.

Good Lord, the man was sexy. She shifted her position on the couch and took a deep breath. He definitely wasn't a boy from around here. His hobbies were probably far from muddin' with your truck or duck hunting. He was a man of the world, who had perhaps flown here in his own jet.

"My assistant has a rental car," he said. "I can extend the lease or reimburse you for your car expenses if..."

She needed to remain focused. She had to pass this job interview with flying colors.

"The rental would be good," she said, knowing that any car would be better than hers. "I'm assuming the baby car seat is already in it anyway," she said, in a mater-of-fact tone.

He looked unsure if the car had a baby seat, but nodded with a smile and added, "You can have use of the car outside." Melanie assumed he was happy with her decision to use the rental; he didn't look put out over spending more money on a second rental car.

Reaching into his pocket, he pulled out a credit card. "You will have access to buy whatever you need, but keeping Arianna healthy and happy is your main responsibility."

He placed the card on the table. "I don't know her eating or nap schedule." His face twisted slightly.

"Being in a different house, different people... it's bound to throw her schedule off."

Melanie's heart raced. The interview had gone better than she had hoped, at least so far. She had been holding her breath for most of the discussion, and now it looked like her prayers might be answered. At least she had a place to stay for the next twelve days and wouldn't be a burden to her Aunt.

"I'm sure I can manage all the duties needed." Her gaze fell to the credit card, the gateway to accepting the job. He must have noticed since he gestured for her to take it.

She snatched the card before he could change his mind. It was a platinum card, probably with a massive line of credit.

This man was trusting. Trusting with money and, more importantly, with his daughter. He came across as someone who had people to do his bidding and to protect him if something went wrong.

She took a deep breath. Being so rich must be nice. You could live anywhere you wanted, study whatever you wanted, travel anywhere you wanted to go. She felt herself pining for that type of lifestyle. One day, she'd be a famous artist and able to afford nicer things in life.

He stared at her, and his face pinched in an odd expression. She thought for a moment that he might change his mind. "This position is for a *live–in* caregiver."

Living with this handsome man under the same roof? Keeping everything business related would prove difficult, but it was a good thing she was raised to be a good girl. She noticed a twinkle in his eyes and his kind smile, which made her switch positions on the couch once again.

Well, maybe it was a good thing she was raised in such a way. She patted her bag on the couch. "I brought a few things with me in case you needed me to start right away."

He gazed at the oversized bag and smiled. Melanie assumed that he was either impressed by her being so well prepared, or her self–confidence that she'd get the job.

"I'll have my assistant Darin show you to your room upstairs. The job is...," he paused, and then added, "no friends can be invited over."

"Oh," she said, smiling. "That's not a problem. When I'm working, I'm working. Don't worry about anything."

He slowly nodded, so she was certain she came across as professional as possible. But, then, he stared at her as if studying her.

"I'm assuming there are no *complications* with you staying here as a live–in nanny," he said, stressing the word complications.

She wasn't sure she understood. "What do you mean?"

"Husband? Boyfriend? I'd like to avoid a jealous significant other who might get the wrong idea."

It felt odd talking to someone who didn't know every detail of her life, like everyone else did in this town. James had no way of knowing how alone she was, how she had been—by choice—left at the altar, and how she could be lifted right out of pretty much any social gathering this town offered.

"Not married. No boyfriend. No worries." She gave him a wry smile, one she hoped hid her pain.

7

*A*rianna seemed small for her age, but rather tall. Her nap didn't last long, and Melanie suspected that she'd tire before it got too late.

She lay the girl down on the bed and changed her diaper. She hated changing dirty diapers, but figured she'd have to get used to the task for the duration of her job.

"There you go." She smiled at the girl as she snapped up the outfit. "Nice and clean." She looked for a Diaper Genie but didn't find one. She tossed the diaper in a pail near the crib.

Arianna had dark hair, unlike her father. His dark blond hair was straight, and the little girl's were brunette and curly. Melanie suspected that the curls and color had come from Arianna's mother.

The fair—skinned child had the palest blue irises

with streaks of violet, like James. His eyes had mesmerized Melanie during the interview. Now, she saw their amazing color again in his child.

Melanie then thought of James's strong jaw and slight beard scruff. Did men know how handsome they were with a hint of a shadow on their face? He probably had some sexy chest hair, too.

Nothing wrong with that.

Most of the boys in this town were just that—boys. The smart ones went to college and moved away, just like her brother had done. The boys that remained in town tended to be either immature or content with living here, with no real ambition in life.

"My guess," she said to Arianna, "is that you're an only child." She played with the child's hair. "I have a brother. He graduated college a while ago and moved away." She smiled at the babe. "He has curly hair like you, but not tight curls like the darling ones you have."

Her brother was bright and ambitious. Getting him through school and off to college with a full scholarship was an accomplishment that she took pride in. She had graduated with good grades too, and with high scores on the SAT and ACT tests, but she'd had her brother to raise. College had to come later for her.

She wasn't a brainiac, she wasn't the cheer-leader–type, she was a nobody in her small graduating class of two–hundred kids. She didn't want to still be living in this small town when her ten–year high school reunion occurred. She didn't even want to attend the stupid event.

A cry from Arianna brought Melanie back to her task: moving into the Nielson home and taking care of the baby.

The child sipped from her bottle and played with one of Melanie's shirts on the bed. She handed the top to Melanie as though helping her unpack.

"Thank you, sweetheart." Melanie took the shirt from the girl and folded it. "After I'm settled, we'll go to the park." She opened the dresser drawer and tossed in her few belongings, all while keeping an eye on the baby. "Hopefully, I can get back into my apartment, or you'll be seeing me in the same three outfits."

She tossed her bag aside, and a squeal came from Arianna, who now had nothing more on the bed to play with—or more to the point, nothing left on the bed to drool on.

"That assistant, Darin, left in a hurry." Melanie picked up the child, and the muscles in her back ached from sleeping on her aunt's couch last night. "Do you not get along with Darin? Is there a story behind that, other than he had holiday plans with his family and needed to leave?" she asked in a baby speak voice.

A whiff of stale formula hit her nostrils. "Oh, dear. Your drink is sour, sweetie."

She set the bottle down and grabbed the sheet of paper detailing Arianna's schedule and routine. Unfortunately, there wasn't much information written down. She hoped that meant the child was easy going.

"Let's see what we get to do today, okay?" Glancing at the schedule, she quietly read aloud in an excited voice, "Kinder Musik! Yeah! That'll be fun." She wasn't sure what that was, but she hoped Arianna would enjoy it. The class was scheduled for later in the day and she knew the part of town the class would be in. "Maybe we can go to the park first and get some fresh air. I saw a stroller downstairs in the hallway."

A knock sounded on the door and startled her. "Are you settled in?"

James stood in front of her, now dressed in a suit and tie—formidable-looking and strong. She had noticed his height and broad shoulders the minute she laid eyes on him. Now, dressed above industry-standard and handsome, she couldn't take her eyes off him.

And, good Lord, he smelled incredible.

Her heart raced, and she stared for a moment at his full, red lips. She hadn't been involved with a man since she'd broken up with her fiancé, and she had no plan of seeing anyone again until she got her life back on track.

And, even then, the guy would have to be Prince Charming.

"Are you unpacked?" James asked, obviously waiting for an answer.

She now made eye contact with him. "Yes. Thank you. I'll bring more stuff over as I need."

He smiled at her in a boyish way. How could he be this handsome?

With an assistant, there'd be at least a buffer. But, no, Darin had left the second he could, as if a reprieve were desperately needed.

Maybe Darin left because working for James was so demanding.

Melanie studied James, whose facial expression had softened as he gazed at his daughter.

Maybe he left because he hated the town? The stench was enough to drive many people away.

"Who's my precious princess?" he asked and then leaned in and kissed Arianna on her forehead. The child squealed in delight.

Thank God Melanie wasn't interested in any man right now because that little scene would have melted her heart. James was a family man, here temporarily, and definitely off—limits. "Everything is fine," she said, shifting Arianna to her other hip. "We're about to head to the park."

James's face shifted to one of worry. "You have my cell number if you need to reach me."

It wasn't a question, but not a statement either—but it dripped of fatherly concern over his daughter.

"I'm sure we'll be fine."

8

*J*ames drove around the outside of the huge factory, noticing several large delivery bays empty with only a few trucks parked within. Circling the plant, the large Nielson company logo atop the front entrance, the sign that always gave him a sense of pride, greeted him.

It was a welcomed sight in a town that seemed so distant and strange to him.

He parked in the sparsely filled lot at the plant, getting a prime spot in front of the building. The factory worked in shifts, and plenty of parking was available.

Getting out of the car, James sniffed the air. The stench smelled stronger here than a few blocks away at his family's home. He figured it was due to the fact that he stood outside the building, which was ground zero.

He entered the building through the sales and administrative wing, hearing the hum of computers and the ringing of phones.

"Hello, Mr. Nielson. It's a pleasure to meet you." Craig Cameron, the day–shift manager, came out of his office and shook James's hand. The man had obviously been waiting for him to arrive and handed him a hard hat. "We don't get too many visitors here at the plant, so your call an hour ago surprised me."

Craig gave him a nervous smile, one filled with worry as he shifted from one foot to the other in his office. Having the top brass come down for a surprise visit was never good. This stopover, in particular, would prove to be the town's worst nightmare.

"I'm inspecting the place," James lied. No need to announce the plant's closure until he saw the factory and fulfilled his father's ridiculous request. "I wanted to see how you are managing with the recent layoffs."

Craig stood straighter, and his lips curled up into a smile that showed a certain level of accomplishment and pride. "It's been tough, but we are getting by."

James knew it wasn't exactly a lie, just a hopeful exaggeration of the numbers. Fourteen failing quarters marked the books in red. James knew the real truth.

Wood paneling covered the small office walls and gave the place a seventies feel. The stains on the worn, tile floor hinted that the space hadn't been updated in some time.

And then, there was the stink in the air again. It almost smelled more stale inside the plant. Even the coffee urn in the corner couldn't mask the horrid stench of the plant.

Craig was an older man, and his embroidered name was frayed on his uniform. "How long have you worked here?"

"Twenty–five years. My two sons work here, too, as well as my niece until this past November."

A silence filled the room, and then Craig added, "You know, your father grew up here. He and I went to school together."

James studied the man's face. He looked younger than his dad. Perhaps Craig was also thinking of retiring, and then the blow of the plant closing down wouldn't be so rough on him.

"You were classmates?"

Craig's face beamed with pride. "I was good pals with both him and your mother." He paused for a moment as though suddenly remembering something. "I'm sorry about your mother's death. She was a lovely woman, and a good friend of mine."

James's mother had died giving birth to him. He

had never been given an opportunity to know her, except through his father's eyes. As a child, James would beg his father to tell him stories of how he and his mother had met, where they had their first date, when they were married,... His mother had been the light of his father's life, and until he recently married Joan, the only love James's father ever had.

Not many people knew James's mother since she had died so young. Sitting with a man whose memories held stories of her... it felt odd. He felt nearly jealous that a stranger would have memories of his mother and not him. Well, jealousy wasn't the exact feeling. No, it was also a displacement. His mother didn't exist in his world, and yet, this was proof that she had existed somewhere—and, evidently, in Craig's world.

He shook his head, trying to shake the odd feeling. He was here on business. He needed to focus on that.

"I'm still good friends with the family," he said.

James stared at the man. His father had never mentioned a friend by the name of Craig Cameran. Even with all of the stories his father had shared with him, the name Cameran was foreign to him.

"Your mother's sister took over their parents' restaurant. Many of the plant workers eat there for lunch."

A sinking feeling hit him. Craig has good

friends with his *mother's* family, not his *father's*. He had never really thought about family on his mother's side before. And, his mother had a sister? His father had never mentioned any family from his mother's side, let alone what they did and where they lived.

"Her place, Newbury Grill, is down the road." Craig's head tilted as he studied James. The man must have found it odd that James didn't know the family history.

Naturally, James knew that his parents had met in this town. He wondered if his mother's family was why his father never visited Newbury after the death of his wife.

"The plant switched from three working shifts down to two..." Craig said, switching the conversation back to work. The daily schedule of the plant was not new information to James. Many of his factories worked such hours, but keeping this plant open around the clock made no sense these days, and eliminating one shift allowed him to lay off many people.

Craig continued to talk about the factory, and how many of his relatives relied on the company for their livelihood. James could understand taking pride in a family business, but Craig's family didn't own the paint company. They merely worked for it.

He stared at the man's beaming face full of pride. He had a good work ethic and saw his job as more than just a career. Being a 'paint man' was who he was.

Geez, it was going to be harder to lay these people off than he had initially hoped.

"Let me show you the place."

Craig took James down the hallway to the big, metal doors that led onto the factory floor, bumping into three other employees along the way. Each person wore a worried look on their faces, but each one bid Craig and James a friendly greeting.

Everyone knew one another's name.

Everyone was super–friendly.

Everyone would be in for a shock once James announced the plant's closure.

James took in a deep breath and let it out slowly. Shutting down the plant simply made sense from a business perspective. He certainly didn't need to feel guilty about doing his job.

They walked along the cement floor which had painted lines delineating the walking paths until they came to a metal stairway. The stairs led them to a walkway that overlooked the mixing room.

Hanging on the wall were protective headsets. There were plenty of them, and James knew that it could only mean one thing. The people who normally wore them had been laid off already. He paused just for a moment as he reached for one, but then they each took a hat and put them on.

James inspected the plant from the mixing room,

the label maker machines, and the loading docks. As rundown as the place seemed, it had safety signs, eyewash stations, and first--aid kits posted every-where—so OSHA and government compliant. There were also pallets, hoses, shelving, and forklifts every-where. Each safely stored or staffed.

So many of the machines were no longer in use since there were no humans to run them. James could only image how loud the place was when everything was turned on. In fact, he felt certain that the factory had an entirely different feel to it when it ran at full staff.

"This is our main assembly line," Craig yelled over the din. "The cans travel down the line and are labeled." He pointed back towards the back of one area. "From there they go down that hallway and get boxed. I'll walk you down to the boxing and ship-ping area."

James could barely hear Craig's words, but understood what he wanted to do. He saw several employees on the line and knew that most of the town relied on this plant to make a living. They operated on shift work, and this was only half of the people that worked here. Overall, a sizable number, even with the massive layoffs over the year, but not enough to get this place to full operating capacity.

All the employees seemed hard–working. James didn't see a single person slacking off. Of course, the slackers could be hiding or calling in sick but he didn't get the sense that this town had people like that.

Once back in the office, James removed the hard hat and the headset. He then sat on the metal chair with the ripped, and taped, plastic which stood across from Craig's desk. He didn't need to see any disappointing plant figures, but still said, "I'd like to review the numbers in more detail."

Craig cabled up his computer so he could project onto the screen on the wall. James waited quite a while for the system to hum to life, for the correct program to come up, and for Craig to display the figures.

Craig needed a new computer.

No, he needed a new computer several years ago.

The whole place was well overdo for an overhaul, and now it was too late.

"Each month," Craig began once he got the machine working, "I collect the company report of projected earnings and send them to my front–line manager in Chicago. We can review the trend in earnings over the last six months."

"Show the numbers for the last year." James walked to the coffee urn and poured himself a cup. The factory had reported fourteen quarters of falling revenue. Maybe having Craig see at least a year's worth of failure would soften the blow.

As Craig fussed with the computer, James fussed with the out–dated coffee maker. It wasn't a Keurig machine, or any type of machine James had used over the last several years. This didn't even look like a Mr. Coffee. It was much more like a dime-store knock off.

Burnt coffee was caked onto the heating pads and he managed to get himself a cup. He then asked, "What do you think has been the biggest reason for the lack of production here?"

"We don't get as much raw material as we used to," Craig said quickly, giving James a sense that the lack of supplies was indeed the biggest issue.

"The highway construction is keeping the trucks away," Craig added. "But once that construction completes, we should be back to full capacity." He hit a button, and his laptop screen projected onto the far wall. "The recent layoffs were necessary, but we could hire those employees back."

Craig hesitated and an expression of worry crept on his face. "Unless you see a different future for this company."

James didn't want to answer that. At least, not yet.

He didn't know what construction company was working the roads, but had seen a projected end date to the madness. "The highway construction will last another four years. Honestly, by then, we'll be producing so little that I don't see a need to continue keeping this plant open." James took a sip of the coffee, the burnt liquid half scorching his throat. He instantly regretted it and set the swill down. "I'd like to start shifting some of this work to our Springfield plant."

Craig swallowed hard and fidgeted with the computer, trying to bring up the files that James suspected would only corroborate the need to shut the plant down.

"This factory is the lifeblood of this town." Craig's gaze shifted to James, his pleading eyes nearly begging him to listen. "Without the plant, there isn't much for the people in this town to survive on."

And that was not James's responsibility. He didn't want to make it his responsibility and he didn't want to care about it. "Shutting down the plant isn't personal, it's business." Hard decisions had to be made. Why couldn't people understand that?

"It is personal if everyone in this town is suddenly without work." Craig's tone took on an air of defiance that James hadn't heard since meeting the man two hours ago. He was passionate about his job and the people he worked with. James could respect that.

"What do you suggest we do?" It was an open-ended question, and all avenues had already been exhausted by the five levels of management between him and Craig. Judging by Craig's quiet stance, he knew that, as well.

"Obviously, we'll give a month of severance to every employee."

"A month?" Craig's eyes widened. "Some of us have worked here our entire careers. I thought the severance pay was a week per year worked, with an eight–month cap on the payout."

So, there had been some serious thought given to the plant closing; otherwise, Craig wouldn't have known that. "Company policy changed a few years ago," James said, his voice flat and as matter–of–fact as possible. "We can keep a skeleton crew at the plant until we transition the work to the other loca-tion. Over the next year, we can dismantle the machinery and have anything salvageable shipped to our other factories."

Craig slumped in his chair and wiped his brow. The man looked nearly defeated. "I can show you the numbers. Maybe we can figure something—"

He had only suggested looking at the charts to break the bad news. James didn't need to see them since he had already made up his mind.

"We won't announce anything for at least another month. The complete transition will be done by May, and then we can close the doors." He didn't know where Craig's loyalties lay, so he added, "Please keep this information confidential for now."

The slides appeared on the screen. "Most of our distributors are now with other companies since the road work is bad. Once the construction is done, I'm sure they'll be back. Those companies had been loyal to us for decades. They appreciate the type of service we can offer them." His voice held a hint of hope, one that James understood he was crushing.

He wasn't sure why it mattered, but James offered a lifeline to the man. "If we can get the trucks in or find another way to bring in the raw materials, I'm all ears. Otherwise, we can't wait that long."

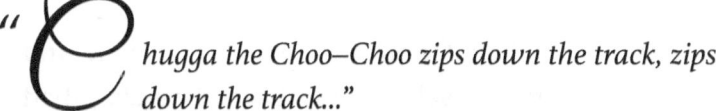 *hugga the Choo–Choo zips down the track, zips down the track..."*

Melanie knew that children's song would be stuck in her head all day, but she sang it anyway.

She playfully moved Arianna's legs in zigzag motions as the child lay on her blanket atop a mat with the other children at the Abiding Love Lutheran Church during their hour of Kinder Musik.

The mat was a bit musty, and, in truth, smelled a little like the sweat from a boys' locker room. The church played the part of one of the town's community centers with scout meetings, youth group events, and even children's athletics, so she wasn't too surprised by the smell.

Arianna was the youngest child in the group, so the class may not have been precisely age–appropriate, but she giggled and seemed to enjoy her time—which relieved Melanie. Her last time taking care of kids was at this same Sunday school. Twenty kids, their ages ranging from eight to twelve, and pure devils. Each one yelling, screaming, or crying in the church. None of them getting along with one another.

But Arianna was only one child. A happy one at that.

She gazed into the child's wondrous eyes as she stroked her hair with the back of her hand. She was a sweet baby.

Arianna giggled and then smiled at her, and Melanie caught herself smiling back. The class had lasted an hour and the time had flown by.

"Thanks for coming, everyone. Please put the triangles and other music makers back in their boxes on your way out." The instructor, Abby, picked up her instruments and said goodbye to the parents.

Melanie gathered Arianna's belongings into her big purse. She was too embarrassed to carry the bag marked with *Child Protective Services* into the classroom. She wasn't sure where that diaper bag had come from but suspected that a story lay behind it, and it was best left in the car.

Abby walked across the tiled floor, her shoes squeaking with each step. She picked up a mat, rolled it, and stacked it in the back of the long meeting room next to some folding tables and stackable chairs.

"I didn't know you had a daughter," Abby said now that everyone else had left. "I don't know if you remember me. My maiden name is Horten, and I used to go by Abigail. I graduated a few years ahead of you. I babysat you and your brother a few times."

Melanie hadn't recognized the teacher's married name of Abby Stevens. The woman had looked familiar, and now a smile spread across Melanie's face. The Horton family owned the biggest dairy farm on the north side of town. Abby sported a shorter hairstyle now and had lost some weight, but she looked about the same as Melanie remembered. Melanie hadn't seen her in years.

"Arianna's not my baby." Melanie's defensive wall came up, the one she installed years ago whenever someone mentioned her having a family. There would be no babies in her future, no snotty nosed kids to take care, no bedtime stories to read, and no tickle–times and cuddles. She gathered the musical instruments which lay around the mat, her body going rigid and stiff. "I'm watching her during the holiday."

There was no need to mention who Arianna's father was. No need to bring up the fact that the job was only temporary. All Abby needed to know was that Melanie watched the child for a friend.

Abby wrapped her long, billowy skirt around

herself and sat on the floor next to them. She tucked a strand of her long, curly hair behind her ear and studied the child.

"She sure is beautiful." Abby helped the girl to sit up and then leaned in and added, "Yes, you are. You're a pretty baby."

Arianna didn't scream or fuss. Maybe she was just a good child, but Melanie wasn't used to such sweet kids. In her experience, they always yelled when they got near her or other strangers. Either that, or, once they could talk, they tried to manipulate you.

Everyone's experience with babies seemed to come so easily. Naturally. Melanie never approached kids and talked to them, told their parents how adorable they were, or even thought to do anything of the kind.

"I heard you're married and have a son," Melanie said, somewhat happy to have an adult to talk to since the rest of the afternoon would be just her and Arianna with a side trip for some shopping.

"Married for ten years now. My husband and son, Josh, are the best things in my life." She took a deep breath, and added, "Family is so important."

A hint of frustration sounded in Abby's voice, so Melanie asked, "Is something wrong?"

Abby shook her head while she tickled Arianna's tummy and made the girl giggle. "My mother's Alzheimer's is getting worse. I've been looking into full-time memory care centers, and they're not cheap."

Frail parents were something Melanie had never had to worry about. Neither were the cost of elder care or the cost of childcare.

"I'm sorry to hear that."

Abby shook her head. "At least I have a friend watch Josh so I don't have to pay for childcare. I watch her baby on certain days, and she watches mine."

Melanie figured most single parents, or families where both parents worked, had similar situations. Day care was expensive, especially with the threat of job loss looming upon the horizon. "Sounds like a good arrangement."

"How have you been?" Abby's voice sounded soft, but her words were heavy. "You know that Trevor is my cousin, and..."

God, this town was small. She had totally forgot that Abby was her ex-fiancé's cousin. What was it? Second cousin three times removed? The relationship didn't matter. The woman would have been invited to the wedding. In any case, she knew about Melanie's past.

"I'm fine." Melanie stood and picked up Arianna, unable to look directly at Abby. Even though Melanie had been the one to call off the wedding, the break-up still wasn't easy to talk about.

Most people were angry with her for throwing

Trevor aside. He had been the high school baseball star her senior year, came from a reputable family, and was handsome. People didn't understand why she didn't want to be his baby machine—especially to a man with a proven, roaming eye.

Some were on her side, or, at the very least, took pity on her. It was either because she was now an old maid who hadn't dated anyone in quite a while, or they saw her as the poor girl who'd lost her parents, the one whose mind went when her brother moved away.

She hated having people see her like that.

Abby stood. "Trevor said he called off the wedding because you didn't want kids." Now studying Arianna and how happy she was, the woman added, "You seem good with them."

First, he didn't call off the wedding. *She* did. But that wasn't worth arguing about.

Secondly, some kids—like Arianna—were fine, but rare. She had been watching the baby for a few hours already and she was well behaved. If she ever did have a child, she'd want one as easy going as Arianna.

A familiar heaviness settled in the pit of her stomach. It was always there, but in situations like this, it grew—forcing her to suppress it. Her chances of ever conceiving a child seemed unlikely. A medical condition had seen to that, and only she and her doctor knew the truth.

Sadness crept over her, and she needed to leave.

"I do like this baby." Melanie gathered Arianna's belongings, said her goodbyes, and walked from the room. She had nothing against Abby, but she really didn't want to continue the small talk and it felt like the room was crushing in on her.

Down the hallway stood the community bulletin board with fliers. A bright, colorful sheet of paper reminded everyone about the Christmas fair in a few days. The event had always been one of Melanie's favorite holiday traditions, and she was sure to go.

Posted next to the holiday flyer was a job sheet for the church. At the bottom were pull tabs with a phone number to call. The church needed some part–time janitorial service.

A smothering sensation of being trapped took hold of Melanie. She wasn't above cleaning toilets and emptying trash, but she had wanted to work somewhere where her mind or talents were actually appreciated. She glanced around and made sure no one was looking before she pulled the tab from the flyer, knowing that she would call them after the holidays.

ames and Craig walked the short distance to the Newbury Diner for lunch, which was next to the train tracks. Although cold, the weather felt pleasant enough for the short journey, and only a few snow flurries caught on his jacket and hair.

Craig didn't seem to mind the town reeking of paint pigment, and James assumed the locals were accustomed to it and had become nose–blind, but it nearly made James lose his appetite.

Of course, he also felt nervous about meeting his aunt who owned the diner.

His father had never told him that they still had family in town. Naturally, his mother had lived here, and there was always the possibility that her side of the family remained, but he had never considered it.

The diner's parking lot was just a row of slots in front of the place that backed up onto Main Street. A few spots were in the back, but it appeared as if most people walked.

"Best apple pie in the world." Craig opened the door, the little bell atop dinging, and let James in. "Your grandmother is the baker now, and her daughter Sandra runs the place."

Grandmother?

He may have a whole slew of family in this town. Perhaps that was why his father had wanted him to visit.

Regardless, a mini–family reunion was not why he had come to town.

Only a few stools at the long lunch counter were taken. Booths were nestled against the frosted windows, which gave a view of the street and the tiny parking lot.

"This place is sort–of dead."

"Used to be pretty popular," Craig said. "The plant is within walking distance, but so many people have been let go." He shook his head and shrugged. "It's cheaper to bag a lunch or to eat at home than to pay for a hot meal these days."

James rubbed his arms and brushed the now melted snowflakes off his jacket. With how cold it was outside, a hot meal would certainly be welcome.

They found a booth in the corner. After sitting

down, Craig pulled a napkin from the packed, metal dispenser—ripping the paper towel as he did—and wiped the tabletop.

James usually dined in fine restaurants that had lace tablecloths, linen napkins, and definitely not laminated menus. He couldn't remember if he ever had eaten at such a place. At least, he knew he hadn't eaten in a place like this in a long time.

He sat and picked up the plastic, tri–folded list of food items. The sticky menu stuck to his fingers and he didn't want to think of what the mess could be.

Regardless of what the menu held, he knew by the smell alone that this diner served grilled American fare. He smelled the hamburgers, fries, and onion rings cooking. He doubted grilled salmon with a spinach salad would be available.

Hmm, grilled salmon would be perfect right now.

"Hi, Craig." The waitress approached the table, holding both a water pitcher and a carafe of coffee. "Who's your friend?" she asked as she poured water into their drinking glasses.

The gurgle of the water glasses being filled mixed with the sizzle of the food cooking, the churn and burble of the coffee machines, and the din of the few people talking. The place wasn't peaceful and relaxing. It was a strap–your–feed–bag–on type of a place that only did well because of its nearness to the plant. All that would soon change.

"Hey, Patty," Craig said, his smile and the friendly tone in his voice sounding as if he were familiar with this restaurant and its staff. "This is James N—"

"James Norman," James said, interrupting Craig. He wasn't sure why he felt the need to change his name, but it felt right. He didn't want the town to treat him differently than any other visitor; although, his suit might give him away since most everyone else in this town was dressed in jeans and a factory uniform shirt.

James also didn't need his family to know that he was the biggest employer in town and planned to take away the livelihood of many of them—especially since Patty looked nine months pregnant and ready to pop.

"I'll have the special and some coffee." Craig pointed to a sign on the table, next to the salt and pepper shakers, that had the lunch specials. Today's discount offer was for a hamburger, fries, and a soda.

James hadn't eaten many carbs in a while, but he was hungry. In a flat tone, he said, "I'll have the same."

She poured both men cups of coffee. "Two specials," she said, not bothering to write down their selection.

James's hand wrapped around the mug, and he enjoyed the warmth. He had left his gloves in New York and would consider buying another pair while in town, but he had no plans of staying that long.

He gazed across the checkered tile floor and peered through the scattered crowd, wondering who in this place was... he grimaced at the expression... *kin* to him. His eyes rested on the counter where an elderly woman worked. She wore the same pink apron as Patty did, had the same fair complexion, and a similar build, as well. She puttered around the back corner of the restaurant, wiping the counter and gathering menus.

"And two slices of pie," Craig added before Patty could walk away. "Is your mother working today?"

"Mama works every day." Patty picked up the menus and tapped them on the table. "We can't keep her away." She glanced around the restaurant but didn't seem to see her. "She left to run an errand a while ago. She should be back soon."

As Patty left, Craig leaned in and whispered. "Sorry. I assumed you were fine with people around here knowing who you are."

There was no need to apologize, and James shook his head. "I'd like to experience the town as just another person, not as the largest employer they have."

His gaze never left the woman behind the counter. Her stature was tiny, her hair gray, and her thick glasses gave her the appearance of... well, she looked like Chief Justice Ruth Bader Ginsburg. She seemed sweet and humble, but he was sure, as the matriarch of the family, she had a strong disposition.

"That's your mother's mother. She inherited the place when her father died." Craig slurped his coffee from the white ceramic coffee cup. "Do you want to meet her?"

"My maternal grandmother?" James took in the sight of the older woman. "She inherited this restaurant?"

Craig's hand gestured around the room. "The place used to be an old mill. Lorraine—well, I guess your grandmother—turned it into a restaurant with Avery Peterson back in the day." He pointed to the old woman in the back of the room. "She's worked here her whole life."

Craig gestured to a portrait which hung on a wall on the side of the space where extra utensils were placed. "That picture was taken years ago. It's the Peterson family from way back when."

James studied the portrait. The picture captured a family of four and, based on the clothes the people wore, appeared to be several decades old—especially since James suspected that the older girl in the image was his mother.

He stood and crossed the room, weaving between the empty tables, until he reached the portrait. He had never seen this picture before and was surprised by how young his mother looked.

She was the older of the two girls. Her long,

brunette hair was partially up, allowing long curls to trail down her shoulders and onto her lace dress. His grandmother and the man James supposed was his grandfather were standing, with the two girls sitting on stools in front of them—the younger child holding a doll.

A mill–turned–restaurant, with a family history spanning decades in this town—just like his father's side. A diner and a plant.

James came from two founding families of this town, not just one.

He felt relief knowing that he had used a fake name, even though his suit might give him away. He didn't want any special treatment. He didn't want to make friends. He didn't want to know anyone.

He just needed to take away the livelihood of most of the families in the town that his relatives had started.

Crap.

All this family and personal history in one place, and he had the next generation just a few blocks away, being watched over in his family's old estate. Arianna would probably be seen as a princess to most people here.

A soft voice came from behind him.

"Can I help you?"

It was his grandmother.

THE RENTAL CAR was so much nicer than Melanie's old clunker. For one thing, the heater worked. The car had just gotten toasty warm when Arianna had fallen asleep. She wanted to let the baby sleep some more, but she needed to get on with her day.

She carried Arianna inside the Nielson mansion and placed her on a play mat on the floor near the kitchen so she could keep an eye on her. Circling the child with pillows, she felt that the child would be safe for a few minutes, especially since she clipped the baby portable monitor on her belt.

The house still felt cold, but the portable heater had made that room cozy enough that the child continued to rest. She glanced at the babe's sweet face. What a blessing this little one was. It wasn't as if Melanie were an old maid, but she wasn't getting any younger either.

Tears welled up in her eyes. She never liked to admit it, but she did want a baby. Maybe one day, she thought. If her prayers were answered, she'd have a family of her own and a husband who loved her. She couldn't image it happening any time soon, but one day.

Her hand touched her abdomen and for a moment she imagined what it would be like to be pregnant and feel a life growing inside of her. To prepare a home for a baby, to make home-made baby food, and to see herself—and her parents—reflected back in the face of a child.

She took a deep breath and wiped away a tear. Stupid cyst. There'd be no way she could conceive unless a miracle were to happen, and she didn't need to be daydreaming. With Arianna sleeping, it gave Melanie time to put away some groceries and focus on the job. She needed to take advantage of nap time.

She checked the freezer and found only processed foods. Easy, convenient, but not healthy. The cabinets weren't much better. They mostly had coffee in them, but then again, for someone only staying a short while one of the most expensive coffeemakers rested on the counter.

Melanie selected a K–cup and made herself a cup of coffee. Might as well enjoy the machine while she had access to it.

She had just put away the last of the groceries when she heard Arianna stirring on the mat.

She poked her head into the living room and caught the child's attention. "Hi, honey. Are you ready for a snack?"

Arianna rubbed her eyes and stared back.

"You're not a wake–up–and–scream type of child, are you?" Melanie crossed the room and picked her up. She placed Arianna on her lap as the two sat on the couch. "I know it's difficult to be in a place that you don't recognize and to spend time with people you don't know," she said in a soft and soothing tone.

She gazed into Arianna's eyes. "But we're friends

now. You know me." She rubbed the child's back and slowly woke her.

"According to the store clerk, you're ready to start eating some new things." With a big grin, Melanie added, "Won't that be fun?"

A new high chair—one that still had the store stickers on it—was assembled and in the corner of the room. Melanie wiped the tray, cleaned Arianna's hands, and placed her in the chair before opening a jar of mashed carrots.

Scooping a bit onto a tiny spoon, she did a rendition of a choo choo going into a tunnel. The problem was that the tunnel took one taste and spit it back out.

"Now, don't be like that." Melanie wiped Arianna's face and tried again. After several more spoonfuls she realized that more carrots were on the napkin, the tray, and on Arianna's face than what actually got into the child's mouth.

She then soaked some Cheerios in some warm formula and set them on the tray to see if that helped.

To her delight, Arianna picked one up and ate it. It was funny to see the child put her fist in her mouth in an effort to eat a tiny piece of cereal, but she was getting the hang of it. The snack allowed Melanie a few minutes to fill out some more college application forms and scholarship paperwork.

She took an outdated iPad from her purse and

sat next to the child. "Do you have any idea how important college is?" She studied the child whose slobbery fist held more Cheerios bits that were more like Cheerio slush than anything else. She thought about feeding them to Arianna with a spoon, but the girl looked to be having fun.

Arianna was the daughter of a wealthy man. Doors would be open to her that were closed to Melanie. "Being born with a silver spoon in your mouth is a blessing, kiddo. I hope you take every advantage you have and enjoy your life."

She logged into her college board site and checked the status of her paperwork. A few more scholarships had opened up, but only one that was for art, so she filled it out and submitted it online.

Now to check the college portals. She sighed as she went from one university site to the next, logging into their portals. "Portals are supposed to make life easier," she said in baby speak. "Yes, they are." She put some more drenched Cheerios on the tray. "Portals just mean more passwords you have to remember."

There were no acceptance notices. But at least there weren't any rejections either. Not all of the schools had portals. She'd have to wait and get some answers the old fashioned way through snail mail.

She hated playing the waiting game.

Looking down, Melanie noticed how much of the cereal sludge made it to the floor.

"You're sneaky. Here I thought you were eating your snack." She caressed the child's face, happy that she was content to just play with her food. "I better focus on cooking a proper dinner."

She stood and wondered what type of food James was accustomed to. He probably ate at the finest restaurants and ordered delicacies that she had never even heard of. She had bought zucchini noodles and organic tomato sauce with grass–fed beef. Her cooking skills were not too shabby, so she started making her own, carb–free lasagna. The dish was one of her favorites, but not a cheap one to make. Also, cooking for one always meant she'd be eating the same food for days.

Melanie cooked the meat and kept a watchful eye on Arianna. A nice house like this, a small babe... this was what every man in her life had wanted for her. If she could combine her dream of being an artist with being a wife and a mother, life wouldn't be too bad.

Especially if the child were as pleasant as Arianna.

But Melanie wanted—no, she needed—more in her life than to play house and please a man. Especially the men in this town. Her high school boyfriend, or as she liked to call him, "Mr. Pothead," had escaped by leaving his mind. Her ex–fiancé's ambition was to sleep with half the women of the town.

If a real man were to walk into her life, a male who was confident and independent, she wouldn't know what to do with him.

11

*T*he old woman stared back at him, and James recognized the twinkle in her blue eyes.

He had never met his own mother, but he had seen pictures of her. The huge, glossy print that had hung in his bedroom as a child was an image taken of her while she'd been pregnant with him. James's father said that the photographer had caught so much of her personality and charm in that one portrait that it had always been one of Gregory's favorite images of his late wife.

Staring back at James now were those same eyes. They were older and carried more world experience than his mother's, but they were unmistakably his mom's eyes.

It was the same twinkle he saw in Arianna's eyes, too.

His maternal grandmother stood a good foot shorter than him, and her aged back bent over slightly, giving her an older appearance than her actual age. She greeted him with a smile. "This counter spot is free, son. Have a seat."

Dressed in the same outfit as the other servers, she walked around the stool, wiping the countertop as she did so, and returned to its business side where she stood next to a register and a tip jar. "Can I get you a cup of coffee while you look at the menu?"

Delicious desserts lay on the counter covered in glass casings, and she smelled like vanilla and honey. She pushed her glasses further up her nose, picked up a paper order, and read it. She then opened a case which held a pecan pie and cut a slice, placing the dessert on a plate and setting it atop the sheet of paper for a waitress to pick up.

His silence and lack of movement must have given her pause, because she asked, "You look familiar. Do I know you?"

There was no twinkle in James's blue eyes, no dark brunette hair, and nothing to tie him to the Peterson clan. James was the spitting image of his father. Everyone said so, and pictures didn't lie.

"We've never met," he said.

She took out a chilled container of whipped cream from under the counter and placed a dollop on top of the freshly cut pie before returning her gaze to James. She studied his features for a moment as if deep in thought, his suit giving her pause. "I never forget a face, but you look like you're from out of town." She then took a deep breath and motioned back to the empty stool. "Can I get you something?"

He stared at the desserts, all homemade by his grandmother. A grandmother he'd never had a chance to meet.

Until now.

"I have a booth." He pointed through the crowd to where Craig sat and chatted with Patty. "Is Patty your granddaughter?"

The woman's proud smile answered him. "One of four." Lorraine gazed at the old family portrait. "My husband, Avery, and I used to run this place once my father passed on. I took over once I became a widow. I have two daughters and four grandchildren."

An odd and pained expression crossed her face, then she shook her head. "Five grandchildren. I have five of them."

A shiver ran up his spine. He was the fifth one. The one his grandmother never thought of. She probably didn't even know what he looked like.

A few more pastry orders were placed on the counter by another waitress, who quickly left.

"That was Danielle. She's my youngest grandchild." Picking up the orders, Lorraine read them and sliced more pie.

James glanced over to Danielle who was busy with a customer. She was his cousin.

The scene felt surreal, with family coming out of the woodwork. James's father had kept all of this from him. That is, until now. Until he too became a father.

Lorraine's daughter, James's mother, had died while birthing him. The family tree became pruned after his birth. But now, he had Arianna. The tree branch was sprouting, and hopefully would continue to do so.

"Does your family all work here?" he asked, wondering if everyone but his one branch of the family tree never left this place.

"My daughters and granddaughters do. Their husbands all work with the paint company." Her voice was filled with pride and she had a big smile on her face. She then sniffed the pastries on the counter. "The air is better in here, though. Smells like cinnamon."

Everyone worked at the plant? Wasn't there a grocery store, a lumber mill, or even the post office where some people worked? Guilt swamped him, nice and slimy. He would bet that every person in this town was somehow connected to his family's company.

He glanced at the family portrait. *Unless they moved away*, he thought.

"What about, I'm guessing...," he said and pointed to the painting, "your daughter in that portrait? Do you know anything about her family?"

She adjusted her glasses and gazed at the picture. "That's my mother as a child. Her father, my grandfather, was a founder of this town." She gazed at the painting. "He died soon after that picture was taken. Think he was ninety–four."

James studied the image. His great–grandmother and great–great–grandfather? The man in the portrait was the start of the Peterson clan in this town. One of the town's founding fathers. The resemblance between his mother and grandmother was amazing.

"My family has lived here for hundreds of years." A frown appeared on Lorraine's face, one filled with sorrow. "Except for my daughter Natalie, who married a man named...he was named..." She paused and tried to remember.

James almost blurted out his father's name but bit his tongue and kept quiet.

"It wasn't George, but it started with a 'g'," Lorraine said. Her eyes narrowed and then she nodded. "Gregory. Gregory was his name. Natalie and Gregory moved away." Her face saddened even more. "My baby girl passed on a long time ago. I know Gregory made her happy the year they were married, but she missed this town."

James had heard the story before, but always from his father's perspective. It surprised him, but he found himself wanting to hear more. "Please, go on."

"You seem awfully interested in my family for a

stranger who's come to town." She put the washrag down, leaned in, and steadied the glasses on her nose. Her face creased with speculation, and her lips pursed. A moment later, she squared her shoulders and took a deep breath. Her five–foot frame held an air of strength and determination.

"Your suit and expensive haircut... You look just like the man."

James took a step back. "I look like who?"

A smile crossed her lips. "You're my grandson. Aren't you?"

A LAYER of zucchini noodles went into the pan, then sauce, meat, cheese... rinse and repeat.

The oven beeped, and Melanie placed the food in. Arianna was out of formula, but some soaked Cheerios remained. "Try another Cheerio, sweet pea."

The girl stared back as if she needed more of a selection. Melanie placed a few more Cheerios on the tray, and Arianna's sticky fingers picked one up and shoved it into her mouth.

"I guess you're more advanced than just eating rice cereal. But you're still too young for milk, choco-late, strawberries..." She stared at the tray of the high chair and tried to think of all the other foods babies weren't supposed to eat during their first two years. "You're a mess."

She let the child eat, mess and all, while she tossed a fresh garden salad.

"Your daddy should be here soon, and we can eat with him." She remembered seeing some soft books in the room and a play mat. "Let's go to the living room and play while we wait for Daddy to come home."

The scene felt all too picture–perfect. Melanie wondered if she'd even say, "How was your day, dear?" when James walked in.

An hour later, the oven dinged, signaling that the lasagna was baked. The books had all been read several times, Arianna seemed bored with the play mat, and Melanie... Melanie was done. As sweet as Arianna was, playing peek–a–boo and cooing at a child for an hour was mentally exhausting.

A car pulled up, and since there weren't many vehicles that would be driving down this street, she knew James had arrived home.

Him being home meant that Melanie's workday had ended. They'd have a meal together, then she'd give Arianna a bath and put her to bed.

But then what?

James wasn't here for her. She didn't have anything to do once Arianna was asleep, other than, perhaps, stream a movie on her Netflix account alone in her room.

That is if the Internet worked. It had been out earlier.

The door opened, and James entered, his coat covered with some snow flurries. He set his computer bag down so he could take off and hang up his jacket. "Hello."

She didn't know what it was about only having a baby to talk to for the last few hours, but Melanie felt thrilled to have an adult in the room. She didn't want to, but she said in what she hoped wasn't a Samantha Steven's sort of way, "How was your day?"

The rise of his eyebrow and the surprised expression on his face told her that he usually wasn't asked that question.

"Fine." He gazed down at his daughter who had tracked his every movement with her concentrated stare since he had entered the room. "Did she give you any trouble?"

"None. She was a delight." Even if Arianna had been a terror, she still would have said the same thing. There was no need to tattle on a baby that was doing her best to adjust to a new environment.

He sniffed the air and even let out a slight yummy sound. "Smells like Italian."

"Dinner is ready whenever—"

"I ate in town." He smiled at his baby, and his face lit up, but Melanie took note that he did not reach down to pick her up. He merely touched her cheek, briefly. "Hello, Arianna. Hello," he said in a tone that sounded like he was greeting business partners. It was cold in a way that seemed like the next step would be swapping business cards and saying 'let's do lunch soon'.

"I can eat in my room and give the two of you some time to—" she said.

Again, he cut her off. "I've got some work to do. I'll see you in the morning."

12

"I'm telling you, it's strange." The next morning, Melanie sat on the park bench next to her Aunt Eva, sipping her coffee while Arianna got some fresh air.

"Men are hard to understand, and you just met this one." Aunt Eva craned her neck so she could peek into the stroller. Arianna lay there, sound asleep, enjoying the nice weather of the outing. "She sure is a beautiful baby."

"She is, and James spent no time with her yesterday."

Aunt Eva gave her a you've–got–to–be–kidding–me look. "Many men, if you want to be stereotypical, don't know how to be around a baby. They don't play with dolls as children like girls do."

Her aunt was only one generation ahead of her.

And in that generation, and the ones that followed, men were more than just a financial supporter of the family. They took full partnership responsibilities when raising a child. At least, they should. "He holds her like a football, that is when he bothers to pick her up."

Aunt Eva pointed to the small diaper bag which sat between them. "What's the story with this?"

Melanie's eyes widened as if someone finally saw what she did. "Exactly. How does a rich man like James have a diaper bag with *Child Protective Services* stamped across it?"

"There's a story there." Aunt Eva paused as two joggers happened by. Once they were gone, she asked, "Is James married?"

It was actually none of her business. He had said that he didn't marry Arianna's mother, but that didn't mean he hadn't married someone else. Still, she had snooped. "No ring."

Aunt Eva leaned back and narrowed her eyes. "Did you Google him?"

Melanie hated how much information was on the Internet, especially false data, which is why she used computers sparingly. "You know I don't..."—she paused and took a deep breath—"I'd hate to intrude upon the man's privacy, but I do remember reading some information about him while I worked at the plant."

Aunt Eva's eyes widened and she leaned in with a grin. It was one of the many reasons Melanie loved her. It was like sitting and talking with one of her girlfriends.

"Spill," her aunt said.

Melanie glanced around, but no one was near them. She hated when people talked, but at least she knew the gossip she was going to share was factual. "He's about ten years older than I am," she said just above a whisper. Her lips turned up into a smile. "And he's single."

"Is he good–looking?"

Melanie's cheeks flushed. "He's my boss."

"And?"

"He's incredibly handsome." She barely got out the sentence because she smiled from ear–to–ear. "But he's here for just the holiday, and I'm his employee."

"Romances have started on much less."

Melanie couldn't argue with that. Many times relationships started with less and typically they ended quickly. She didn't want some sort of holiday fling. That would only complicate her life, not help it. "Trust me. He only sees me as an employee." She shook her head. "He has a personal assistant, and, from what I can tell, probably grew up with nannies himself." She then thought about it and added, "More than likely, he has a houseful of servants to do his bidding."

Aunt Eva shrugged. "There's nothing wrong with being rich."

"There is if you don't spend time with people you love." She glanced at Arianna, who still slept in the stroller. "He spent all of five minutes with her last night. This morning was no better."

"He may have had a lot of work to do."

Everyone had work to do. Work was always there, never totally completed and constantly calling you back. "I made a nice meal last night, and he didn't even try it."

Eva let out a half snort. "Is that what's nagging at you? That he didn't try your food? Or is the real problem that he left you alone with his baby until this morning?"

That was a good question. James didn't owe Melanie anything, except payment for her nanny services. But something still nagged at her. Last night's evening had been set up so June Cleaver–ish, and she'd barely gotten a nod hello.

Why did she even care?

"The lasagna, by the way, was magnificent," she said, deflecting the question.

"I'm sure it was."

"Have you heard from my landlord yet?" Melanie asked, changing the subject. "I only have one more outfit to my name."

"I left him a message. I'm sure he'll call." Aunt Eva glanced at her large handbag and let out a sigh.

"I almost forgot. Your mail came, and there's a letter you'll want to open right away." She handed a stack of envelopes to Melanie, the top one from Vassar College.

Melanie hadn't told her aunt about applying to Vassar, which was her mother's alma mater. The top–level dream school was just that, a dream. She wouldn't attend unless she were accepted with a scholarship. Now, seeing the half–worried look in her aunt's eyes over Melanie possibly leaving, she almost didn't want to open the letter.

In an attempt to delay, Melanie scanned through the other pieces of mail. It was mostly junk mail, but her electricity, phone, and credit card bills were in the pile. Some of her bills would be up to a third notice by now, others, well, they'd have to wait. There was nothing she could do until she received her nanny paycheck.

"Let's see if you're moving to New York." Aunt Eva shot a pained smile toward her and pointed to the envelope that was now at the bottom of the stack. "I know I can't keep you here forever."

Melanie opened the envelope with a trembling hand. Getting into Vassar was a long shot, but her test scores were good.

She could barely make out the words and scanned down the page. "*Congratulations*" jumped out at her, same with "*Spring semester.*"

Her heart raced as she now read the bottom

section of the letter. "*You have received the Academic Excellence Award.*" Reading the details, she nearly dropped the letter. She got a full-ride for tuition. The letter then said, "*We regret to inform you the Winchester scholarship has not been awarded to you.*" The message then went on to say that student loans would be available to help her with housing and miscellaneous college costs.

Those words deflated her, and she felt stuck once again in this town.

Living on campus, the food, the books... it was more expensive than the tuition money. She could probably easily qualify for student loans, but she didn't like the idea of being in debt. The current statistics said that college grads had an average of thirty–six thousand dollars in debt when they graduated—and Vassar was more expensive than the average school.

She wouldn't be up to her eyeballs in debt.

A heaviness settled in her chest, weighty and solid. Her dream would never come true and she'd be stuck in this town forever.

"Well? Are you going to be packing your bags?"

"Not this semester." Not ever.

A genuine display of disappointment and sorrow showed on her aunt's face. "I'm sorry, sweetie." She patted Melanie on the arm. "You're a good artist, so... the heck with them if they don't see it."

Hearing those words meant a lot to Melanie. Her

aunt had always been one of her biggest—and very few—cheerleaders. "Maybe next year," Melanie said, doing her best to hide the disappointment in her voice.

"You weren't dealt the best of cards, Melanie," her aunt said in a serious tone that was laced with just a bit of teary sentiment. "But you've done well for yourself. And, I have no doubt, the good Lord will provide for you. He is always there watching us."

Aunt Eva never missed a Sunday service, but she usually didn't go around mentioning the Lord's name either. However, coming from her, and knowing that she truly did believe that a divine power was watching over them, it did make Melanie feel better.

"So, what else should I buy at Wal–Mart today?" Aunt Eva said in a cheery voice with a smile to match.

Shopping was the reason Melanie had met with her, so she put the letters in the bottom of the stroller. "We need some baby supplies, and I have James's charge card to get what we need."

Aunt Eva picked up the tiny diaper bag and inspected it. "First thing, we need a decent diaper bag. Next, do you know if she's eating rice cereal or real food yet?"

That was a good question. Without a mother around she certainly wasn't strictly breastfeeding.

"She's doing well with the Similac formula and Cheerios I found at the house."

"So, you'll need some baby food." Aunt Eva gave her an all–knowing smile. "In my experience, it's always best to start with the strained vegetables."

"Why?"

A slight chuckle escaped. "Well, other than watching their precious little faces try something new, you get them used to veggies before you give them the strained peaches, pears and apples. Definitely don't start with the vanilla custard."

Vanilla custard. Melanie hadn't thought of that baby food in a long time, not that she remembered having eaten it as a child. "My mother always told me that one was my favorite."

"True. You wouldn't eat anything else after you had tasted that sweet treat."

It made so much sense. "You are a wise woman. We'll stock up on peas, green beans..."

"Peas, carrots... are good. But, no spinach." Aunt Eva shook her head as if there were a story behind that one.

"Why no spinach?" Melanie knew not to give eggs, chocolate, or nuts to a child. But spinach?

"Well, we can let her eat it. But, you're the one that will be changing her diaper."

That didn't sound too pleasant. Thinking back to last night's messy payload, she said, "That reminds me, I definitely need a baby bath." Melanie rubbed Arianna's lower back. "I had to hold her in the tub to wash her last night."

"Sounds like we have quite the morning." Aunt Eva finished her coffee. "We should get going."

13

*T*here was nothing to do.

James sat in his bedroom, which he set up as his quasi-office, and stared at the lack of Internet connection. Darin had set up the home as a hotspot, and now, it didn't work.

Something needed to be reset, but James had never had to worry about such things before. He had an entire IT department to fix this stuff.

Good grief. He'd have to sit at a coffee shop just to log in. An unsecure, open-to-the-public, seated-at-a-table-being-interrupted, damn coffeehouse. He wasn't going to get anything done.

He cradled his head in his hands. The merger's paperwork was complete, and his lawyers were off doing their magic. Most of his frontline managers were now on vacation, and things at the office were slow.

He *could* take the day off.

But what would he do?

More importantly, what could he do in this rinky-dink town?

A nagging voice inside his head, one that sounded a lot like his father, told him that he should spend some time with his daughter and bond with her.

He should do that, but he had heard Melanie leave with Arianna a few hours ago. Was he such a bad father that he'd actually been happy to hear them go? Knowing that he didn't have to deal with a baby for the day had made him *happy*.

And yet, a part of him wanted to be a father and get to know his daughter. Arianna was here. She wasn't going anywhere... but he didn't know what to do with her.

A total stranger was taking care of his child. Arianna would probably prefer to spend time with Melanie than with him anyway. He didn't know how to connect with a six-month-old. What did they even do? Watch Sesame Street?

An inner warmth filled him as he thought back to that show. He always did like Ernie and Bert. Big Bird was his favorite. Exposing Arianna to the educational program would be good. It was at least one activity he could do with her. He wondered when the show aired in the tiny town, because, clearly, he wouldn't be able to reliably steam anything with this Internet.

Stupid town.

Yesterday, his family at the diner had seemed happy to be in this little town. He didn't understand it, but they were content nonetheless.

James stood and decided to explore the place, maybe see more of it than the six city blocks he'd found yesterday. There was something here that made people happy. He hoped he could find it.

But first, he needed to dress down. He needed to blend in.

THERE WAS NOTHING. Nothing exciting about this town. Nothing that made it stand out as being a great place to live. Nothing that would get James excited about living here.

Nothing.

He had explored the town for a couple of hours and he was freezing. Wrapping his scarf around his neck, he noticed that the snow had picked up—not that the streets needed anymore of the fluffy white stuff. The entire town lay under a white, freezing cold blanket. A blanket that had ice under it.

A chill ran up his spine and white puffs of air came from his mouth. New York certainly had cold days like this, but he wasn't usually walking around in them. His car service, the one that he always complained about, now seemed like such a blessing.

The snow on the road had already turned to a gray slush thanks to the few cars. And the shoveled walks were now covered with another inch of snow to be removed.

He had walked pretty much the entire town, from one side of the railroad tracks to the other— avoiding the one area that looked a bit too sketchy for him to travel through. His feet felt numb and he was ready to find a warm place to sit.

Walking past what he figured was the town square, he noted the time on the clock tower. The clock had stopped at four o'clock. He stared for a minute to make sure, but he knew it wasn't the correct time.

The town couldn't even fix their clock tower.

Couldn't, or wouldn't? How expensive was it to fix something like that? Glancing across to some shops that ran down Main street, he wondered what else in this town wasn't fixed or running.

Main Street looked like a 'Come visit the historic district' for a town's brochure. The old apothecary shop, now permanently closed, was made of white brick. An ad for Coca Cola ran the length of the side of the building—painted in an old graffiti style ad. The weather-worn image was faded, but he could make out the price of a bottle being only a nickel.

The next three shops were also closed, so he

crossed the street to what looked like an old movie theater. Surprisingly, it was open. The ticket counter was unmanned and he probably would have to go inside to pay, but he wasn't interested in a movie. Walking past the movie posters prominently displayed he saw that the featured films were a good six to twelve months old, and not the latest releases from the box offices. Surely this town could get new movies.

But then again, this town didn't have much to offer—so probably not.

A sign caught his attention. This was a dollar movie place. He had heard of such places. Cheap and older movies played here. Since this was the first theater he had run into, he figured an old-style Blockbuster store would be next.

Why couldn't there be a Starbucks on every corner here?

The next store was marked as "General Store." There had been a sign at one point, but the letters had now been removed. The sign was "Woolworth's." He paused as he read it. Woolworth's stores had gone out of business years ago. If he remembered correctly, the company had been founded in the 1890s. The company was the forerunner of stores such as Kmart, Target, and even Wal-Mart.

He let out a chuckle. He may have fallen asleep in his history of businesses class in college, but he did at least remember a few things.

There were no more Woolworth stores left, at least, not in the United States. This store had certainly taken its marquee down but you could still make it out. The old Woolworth company had been renamed. He was pretty certain it was now Foot Locker.

A big change, but the company had survived. The owners knew they needed to grow with the times, learn new ways, and adapt to stay afloat.

James had never believed he was all that sentimental. You had to adjust to changes and move on, but staring at the faded markings where the old marquee was, he felt a giddiness overcome him, and he smiled.

This was the old five-and-dime store his father used to visit as a kid. He was sure of it.

He now looked back to the theater. His father had told him of taking his mother to the five-and-dime for a cream soda and then to the movies for their first date. This was the place. This was the start of it all.

A warmth spread throughout him and he felt tears in his eyes.

He knew this place.

There was a fabric and notions store on the corner where his grandmother had bought fabric to make his mother's wedding gown. Other than the drug store on one end, he saw a closed shoe store. On the other end of the street was an antique store.

The fabric store had to have been where either the shoe store now stood, or maybe the antique store.

His parents had walked these streets, had dated each other here, and somewhere uptown there was a small chapel where they had been married. The chapel was off of Willow Street and... he had to think. Willow Street and something like Gillis Street.

He then remembered that his father had told him the chapel had burned down. James had walked past that intersection already, and there was nothing there but a garage mechanic place. He hadn't even realized where he had been at the time, but now an eeriness settled upon him.

He had never been to this town before, but in his mind with all the stories he'd begged his father to tell him of his mother and their time together, he had a mental map to this entire area. Sure, his map was outdated, but there were remnants still left.

He *knew* this town. If he looked, he was sure he'd find the high school his parents went to, the park bench where they carved their initials into, and even the library where his father got down on one knee and proposed.

Everything from his childhood stories was here. Maybe not the buildings anymore, but this was the place. Another time sure, but love happened here for his parents. True love that he had always romanticized in his head. Where people met, fell in love, got married, and had a life together.

This town wasn't just the start of 'it all'—meaning the business. It was the start of *him*. His family. His *life*.

Heck, he was probably even conceived in this town.

A tiny bell sounded behind him and he turned to see someone leaving the General Store. It was open, so he went in—the little bell announcing his arrival into the place.

The warm air embraced him immediately. The worn wooden floor and wooden display stands were the first things he noticed, as well as the smell of vanilla and some flowery scents coming from a table filled with candles.

There weren't too many people in the place, but he figured enough to keep the place open during these lean times. In the past, a General Store was where people could get pretty much anything they needed for the house. He had seen such places in old movies. But this store, it was different.

It was more nostalgic in a forced but nice way. A country-charm feel covered the place in a very slight touristy way, but not distasteful at all.

He wandered down the aisle with the candles and the merchandise quickly turned into clothing, and then toys. The clothes were on cloth hangers with bows, and the toys in wooden display barrels with the smaller items—like old-style jacks—in mason jars on the counter. Arianna was too young to play with most of what he saw or he'd be tempted to buy the springy slinky, the silly putty, or even the spinning tops. These were toys from yesteryear.

Moving to the next few rows, he found some household items such as soaps, cleansers and bubble bath. He picked up the old-style box of Mr. Bubble. God, he remembered this box. He was certain that it now came in a plastic bottle like everything else, but the old box with the pink bubble on it brought back a flood of memories.

He had given Mr. Bubble a first name as a kid. Ben. Ben Bubble.

It was almost like running into an old friend.

He needed to buy a box and introduce Arianna to him.

Walking down the candy aisle he found what would have been called Penny Candy back in the day. Jars of brightly colored candies lined the wooden shelves. He wasn't much for sweets, but he had to sit at the old soda jerk counter. No one manned the fountains any more, and more merchandise stacked the bar, but he wanted to sit on the old stool.

The plastic seat squeaked when he sat down and turned in it. There were six stools. Two of them his parents would sit on, order an ice cream sundae at, and then sit and talk. Fall in love.

This stool was still here. How many couples had

sat at this counter and fallen in love? The thought became overwhelming to him.

He got up and rummaged through the store finding more items from long ago days until his arms were full and he stood in line to pay for them.

Somewhere in this town was the public library where his parents got engaged. His mother was an avid reader and his father knew the place was special to her. Back then there were no eBook readers and she spent hours in the library reading. She even had a job there one summer as a page where she returned books to the shelves.

"Next, please." The cashier said.

He purchased his load and asked, "Where is the public library?"

14

*J*ames stood on the second story of the public library in the middle of the last aisle, near the window, and in the midst of a ton of history books.

He stood in the spot he had always envisioned as a child. The spot where his father asked his mother to marry him.

No one was nearby, so he knelt down for a second and got a view from where his father would have been looking up at his mother. She had smiled and yelled a full-hearted 'yes' in reply. Their excitement even caused the librarian to walk over and shush them.

Standing, he studied the room. In his mind the book racks were made of wood and not metal. They were probably wood back then, or maybe his father had told them they were. Either way, the image wasn't exactly as he had imagined but so darn close that he felt he was a time traveler exploring the past.

Of course, there were current-day distractions. In his mother's time there wouldn't have been a movie section or a computer where you could rent eBooks from, but she had been here. She had walked the book stacks, had greeted readers, and probably did the librarian 'shhhh' to people who talked too loudly.

The place was warm and they had Internet. Reliable and fast Internet, so he took advantage of it. He studied one website after another about being a decent parent, learning what children needed, and what they wanted.

Surfing the web became exhausting. James did his best to avoid the personal blogs and remain focused on the medical journals instead, but that proved difficult to do. The blogs had the best advice on toys, foods, and programs. Surprisingly, that Kinder Musik class that Darin had signed Arianna up for kept popping up as one of the better classes to take your babies to.

After a few hours, James left and walked down the road to his family's house. The building was the one of the few oddities that stood out in this town, and he wasn't sure why he liked the home so much.

Staring at the place, he noted its size and warm exterior. The home looked happy, if a building could appear as such. The snow–covered yard didn't hinder his imagination. He could envision the place with a lush green lawn, a tire swing swaying from the big tree, and some rocking chairs on the porch.

Most of the homes didn't seem nearly as inviting. The Nielson family manor felt like an oasis. It'd be perfect if hot water and the Internet were consistently available.

James figured that people lived in this town for only a few reasons. Fear of the unknown trapped them here, their expectations of city life and making a real living were low, family or duty held them back, or the town served as a peaceful retirement place.

At least, that's what his exploration of the town had told him. From the waitresses he had met, to the people he passed on the street, down to the old librarian who had greeted him.

Everyone was so friendly.

His family's house stared back at him. The shutters over the windows looked like the half–closed eyes of a friendly face. The door was the home's nose, and the tiles on the roof were the head.

He was willing to admit that he liked the house; he liked the location, he liked how easy the town was to navigate on foot, and...he liked the people. Newbury had charm.

It was the perfect place to raise a child. He could understand his father's attraction and nostalgia for the place. He bet his father had a happy childhood here.

Walking up the front porch, James took a deep breath and reminded himself of all the information he had read today from the parenting websites. According to one blogger, his daughter needed to know that he was happy to see her. She needed to be greeted hello with a hug. She needed to feel *wanted* in his life.

Unless she was asleep. Then, he could see her in the morning since a good father would never wake their sleeping child just to spend time with them. That would be ridiculous.

He opened the door and walked in to see Melanie on the couch holding Arianna. His wide-awake daughter stared back at him and wore a huge smile on her face.

It was show time.

JAMES WAS BUNDLED up in his coat and didn't bother to remove it before placing his bags down and then whisking his daughter into his arms. His smile and care-free demeaner told Melanie one thing: he was making an effort tonight.

"I bought you some bubble bath today," he told Arianna. "It's Mr. Bubble." He reached into the plastic bag and took out the pink box. "See? He's a friendly bubble that is going to make bathtime fun."

He placed the box on the table and gave her a

hug. But the embrace, although loving, didn't last long. James cuddled with his daughter, asked her a few questions in a silly, baby–speak voice, and then handed her back as though he were done.

There was no poopy smell, nor was Arianna crying. She seemed happy in her father's arms. Perhaps James just needed to get his coat off.

A few snowflakes were melting on his sleeve and he brushed them off. "Wait, is it snowing outside?"

Unbuttoning his coat, James answered, "For at least the last hour."

Fresh snow. Melanie loved how it covered everything white and made it look so pretty when it was new on the ground. Arianna was too young to really understand, but she might enjoy it. "Let's go outside."

"What? Why?"

"To see Snow Falls."

He pointed to the door. "Like I said, it's been falling down for an hour."

"No, silly," she said, wrapping Arianna up in a warm jacket she had bought earlier that day. "You stand under a tree and enjoy the Snow Falls."

When he looked like he had no idea what she was talking about, she added, "It'll be Arianna's first time seeing it." She now studied James. "I'm guessing your first time too."

She led him out the door, huddling close to Arianna, and took them under the tree in the front yard. The tree's leaves had mostly fallen, with just a few stragglers hanging on.

"This is perfect. Are you ready?" she asked.

Melanie reached up and tapped on a low hanging branch. Snow fell gently all around in a spiral of white magic. Arianna's eyes widened and she giggled.

"Now you try Arianna." Melanie took the baby's hand and tapped another branch, causing more soft snow to flutter down around them.

Arianna let out a squeal so Melanie picked up some snow and showed it to her. "This cold stuff is snow and it comes each year to let us know that Christmas is on its way." Arianna grabbed at the small pile of snow and instantly put her hand in her mouth."

"Is it yummy?"

"Don't let her eat it."

"James, it's snow. Fresh snow that is falling. It's not acid rain."

An expression crossed his face, one not of worry, but of near embarrassment. "You're right. It's not going to hurt her." He laid his hand on the top of her head. "I used to eat it as a kid, but I don't remember it tasting all that great though."

"One day, when you're a big girl," Melanie said to the child, "you can make snowmen out of this snow." Melanie wasn't sure if that was the correct verbiage to use these days so she added, "snow women too."

"I think their just called snow people now." James smiled and, just like that, the businessman was gone. His softened facial features, his playful grin... they showed a softer side of him that Melanie enjoyed being around.

Taking his own turn, he reached up higher and knocked the last bit of fresh snow from the tree, causing Arianna to kick her legs and giggle.

"I think that's enough fresh air for now, little one." Melanie held her tighter and the three returned into the home.

He removed his coat, shook it out, and then sniffed the air. "Smells like dinner is ready. Italian again?"

Melanie undressed Arianna. "I made so much food last night that I thought leftovers would be fine. It's in the oven staying warm. I'll set it on the table."

James paused a moment but didn't say that he had already eaten. He didn't say he had to go upstairs and work. Did he plan to spend the evening with her and Arianna? Maybe playing out in the snow and having some downtime from work was exactly what he needed.

Melanie hadn't expected that he'd have time to sit down with them for dinner but had preset the dining room table just in case.

Tablecloth, glasses, placemats, and real dishes, not just paper plates.

This really did feel like playing house. She stared

into James's beautiful eyes and, for the first time, understood why so many of her high school friends had wanted to be wives and mothers.

A lovely home, beautiful children, and a husband that all the other women would be jealous of. Handsome, well–built, and...there was a certain sexiness to a man who, at least today, seemed to love being a father. The quality was hard to pinpoint, but James had that extra something.

Even though Melanie wanted a career and the ability to explore her talents as an artist and a feminist, that didn't mean she didn't want to have it all: family and a job she could be passionate about. Even if she could never have it all, she could always dream.

James stroked the back of Arianna's hair. "Please fix me a plate and bring it to the office upstairs." He pulled a sheet of paper from his pocket. "I need to reset the router." He shook his head and looked intensely at the note. "Doesn't seem too hard."

He *seemed* different from most men. But Melanie suspected one flaw. He didn't call during the day to check in, he didn't ask how their day went, and he only spent about five minutes at a time with his daughter.

James was a workaholic. It was probably how he kept his millions, but since he was a single father, Arianna would need more than a drive–by father in her life.

The bubble was burst. This wasn't playing house anymore. Melanie was a paid employee. One who had spent the entire day with a baby and was going to spend the night alone with her, as well.

"I'll bring your dinner right up."

15

James walked up the creaky, wooden steps to the large room at the corner of his family's house. The warmth of the second story hit him once he reached the top floor.

Had he really only spent five minutes with Arianna before retreating upstairs? Tonight he told himself that he was really going to try. He would be the man he wanted to be, the man his daughter needed him to be.

He wasn't even sure he could fix a router, but it was his only excuse for not...for not being a daddy.

He was a father, but not a daddy. When would he feel like a dad?

Everyone else seemed to catch onto family bonds so easily. He had an entire restaurant filled with family members to prove it. Nepotism or not, they all lived and worked together. They all had smiles on their faces and seemed to enjoy each other's company.

When was the last time he and his father had actually gone out to dinner without the outing being a business meeting?

James wasn't sure he could remember that long ago. He thought back to birthdays, holidays, and even the eve of him going to boarding school each year. His father was always either missing in action or had a phone glued to his ear.

James didn't want to be that kind of parent.

He felt a gut-wrenching pain. He couldn't even talk to his daughter with the same ease as Melanie. Snow people? There would be snow people in Arianna's future, but would he be there to help her build one? To show her how to build a snow fort and throw snowballs?

Would he have the type of relationship with his daughter where she'd rush to see him when he was done with work just so she could tell him about her day?

Right now, he hoped she would, but deep down he wondered if he would take the time to really listen.

He needed to make more of an effort, but tonight was the best he could give and he fell far short of his ambitions.

He reached the top of the stairs and thought about this house, his father's childhood home. It was large and impressive but devoid of internal warmth, just like he was. The place had a museum–quality feel, especially with the antiques inside. James wanted a *home* for his daughter, one where her artwork could be proudly displayed on the refrigerator, where her toys cluttered the living room, and where she would cuddle on the couch with him and watch Disney movies.

He didn't even know if he could name five recent Disney films. Could he even name the seven dwarfs?

Or, were there eight of them?

Taking a deep breath, he figured a real daddy would probably know the answer to that.

He had to change. His New York mansion may not be a museum, but it felt sterile and too cold to raise a child in.

He felt as frigid as this house, which belonged to the wealthy Nielsons, not the family–friendly Petersons.

That waitress, Patty—and her mother, whom he had not yet met—were not part of his world. This boarded–up and abandoned house was probably the last remnant of what his family was in this town.

Well, other than running the company that employed half of them.

And the plant was a mess. James's family hadn't kept the place up, even though they had promised his grandfather they would.

James entered his bedroom but could still smell

the dinner downstairs. It smelled terrific, but it was already seven o'clock in Chicago, and he had some business calls to make. The calls had already been scheduled, and he couldn't postpone them.

He'd have to focus on Arianna and being a daddy later.

Checking his cell phone, he only had three bars and was down to twenty–seven percent battery.

Naturally.

Frustration bubbled up in his chest: the annoyance of being stuck in a cold, dank town with little access to the modern world.

James found the router and followed the instructions he'd gathered earlier. Pull one plug, then the other. Wait two minutes, then replug the cords. Repeat if needed.

Surprisingly, it worked the first time, and his laptop now had an Internet connection.

If only everything in his life could be so easily rebooted.

A knock sounded on the door, startling him. Melanie had arrived with his dinner. "Come in."

She opened the door and placed the tray of food on the dresser but didn't say a word. She didn't carry Arianna in with her. "Where is Arianna?" he asked.

"In the playpen downstairs." She glanced away sheepishly. "I hope you don't mind, but other than the essentials, Arianna needed more baby items so I bought a few things today."

James shook his head dismissively. If his daughter needed something, it was fine. Whatever it was.

And money was no object.

His thoughts went back to his cousin, Patty. Her baby would feel the pain of the factory closure. Her husband probably worked at the plant. Even if he didn't, the diner would feel the pinch of fewer workers coming by for lunch. Fewer customers meant fewer tips.

Those in his world had money. And he controlled the wealth of other people. The town of Newbury had made that perfectly clear.

"Arianna already ate and is tired. Do you want some time with her before her bath and I put her to bed?"

James didn't know Arianna's schedule, but, for some reason, he'd assumed he would have more time with her today.

More time to be the dad he wanted to be.

The day had gotten away from him...and he still had that call to Chicago to make.

"I'm swamped, and I have things to take care of. So, if you wouldn't mind..." he said, gesturing to the door.

"But you've worked all day." Melanie glanced at the dark window. "It's late, and most people are winding down their day, spending time with their family and taking it easy." She stared into his eyes and he saw a hint of judgement in them. "Your daughter hasn't seen you today."

That hit a raw nerve. Employees didn't talk back to him. They never questioned his motives, and never pushed on his most exposed button. He didn't know how he would juggle being a successful executive and raising a daughter. He needed more than a few days to find all the answers.

He stared into Melanie's green eyes. She had seen through him and his fear of spending time with his daughter. Was it that obvious? "Most people do not broker multimillion–dollar mergers and run a Fortune 500 company," he said, knowing it wasn't much of an excuse for ignoring his own flesh and blood.

Her face pinched in disgust. "Most people don't have the blessing of a beautiful baby in their lives, either."

Anger grew, and James felt his jaw tighten and his body stiffen. Melanie only told him what he already knew, but he didn't want to hear it. She may have spent the day with Arianna, but she had no idea who he was or what he did to make a living. She lived in a small town where nobody matched his business knowledge. "Who are you to criticize me and how I raise my daughter?"

"I'm just saying...it's the holiday season, you haven't seen your daughter all day, you're here to inspect the plant—which you already did—and..."

"I'm here to *close* the plant." He regretted letting the words slip out. He didn't want to start a panic, and she hadn't signed a non–disclosure agreement.

Melanie's face paled, and he saw a look of shock on her face, followed closely by one of anger and disappointment. She had worked at the plant and had been furloughed. She would lose her job, like all the others in this town.

"Okay," she said, her frosty tone curt and dismissive. She took a step toward the door. "I'm going to finish my dinner and then bathe Arianna. We'll be up in a few minutes."

She left, leaving the door open, and he watched as she made her way to the staircase.

Of course, he wanted to see his daughter. He had only just met her this week. But he honestly had no idea what to do with her.

But he did know what to do about the plant. It, unfortunately, needed to be closed.

*a*fter his conference call, James stared at the computer screen. Instead of focusing on the merger paperwork, he searched parenting websites once again.

There was so much to learn, and he didn't have the time.

Good parents took the time to spend with their families, and he didn't want to short–change his child.

A link on one of the websites caught his attention. A news article featuring Vivian Saunders appeared with the words:*You won't believe who the father is*. He clicked for more information and was taken to a site that gave background information about Vivian. He clicked the "next" button. Now information displayed about her movies with another "next" button.

He went through five more similar pages and saw Vivian pregnant. He never thought to look her up again after their fling, but the pregnancy pictures he now saw would have had him call the woman up and ask some very important questions.

Finally, on the sixth page he saw that his name was now associated with Arianna. He hit the "next" button one more time and his stress level escalated. The next article had his latest press–release picture, his bio, and information about his companies.

He'd known it was just a matter of time before the news of him being the father would be leaked. But he had hoped for at least a few weeks' head start with his lawyers to get behind the mess. It seemed he wasn't that lucky.

James read the article. It held information about him being Arianna's father and how he had their child for the holidays... but no information about where he or the child was, and nothing was said about how Arianna was abandoned.

The article went so far as to say that the two lovers hadn't been seen together and a question was asked if wedding bells would be in the future.

Wedding bells?

He rolled his eyes. One fun fling without the cover of every cameraman and newscaster present and the secret baby scandal was on. He was the unknown father that everyone wanted to know more about.

He doubted Vivian would use such scandalous means to promote herself, but he wouldn't put it past Hollywood.

Something else caught his attention. A major Hollywood movie producer had just signed Vivian for their next release.

She'd be away on location for what he guessed would be at least a year. The movie sets may even be overseas.

Vivian would be too busy to be a mother.

Which meant he needed to step up and be the full-time parent. A tingle of excitement mixed with fear ran up his spine.

Was he up for the challenge?

He heard footsteps in the hallway leading to the bathroom. He owed Melanie an apology; he just wasn't used to giving them.

He stood and crossed the room, opening the bedroom door wider as she approached. She made slight eye contact with him as she turned to walk down the hallway, but she didn't smile at him. "Did you grab the bubble bath from downstairs?" he asked, not knowing how to begin the apology.

She turned and looked at him, the box of Mr. Bubble under her arm. "Yes. I also picked up some baby body wash and shampoo today, as well as a tiny baby bath."

His daughter seemed content to lie in Melanie's arms.

Melanie made everything look so easy.

James stepped into the hallway. "I'm sorry for my harsh behavior earlier," he said softly, his voice filled with regret. "Being a parent is new to me." He figured the news of Vivian's secret baby daddy would soon trickle to this town. It wouldn't take long for Melanie to know the truth.

Melanie swayed from side–to–side, and Arianna nestled back into her arms and rested her head on Melanie's shoulder again. "I understand. An unedu-cated girl from a hick–town wouldn't know what she's talking about. My parents died. What would I know about family values?"

He deserved that. It was precisely what he had thought when he stormed up the stairs, but Melanie wasn't some backward girl from a rural town. He could learn a lot from her. Looking into his daugh-ter's peaceful face, he could learn a lot from Arianna, too. "I'm sorry. I shouldn't have treated you that way."

"No, you shouldn't have." She stared at him for a moment, then asked, "There's no way to save the plant?"

Having already hurt her once, he didn't want to add any additional pain. "If you can find a way, I'll keep the place open. But, likely, no. I'll have the factory closed within the next six months."

She stared past him for a moment, apparently

deep in concentration. "I'll let you know if I think of anything." She then gave him a slight smile before walking down the hallway. "She'll be ready for bed in about twenty minutes."

Even though Melanie closed the bathroom door after entering the room, James heard the water pipes squeal as she turned on the hot water. This old house, museum–esque but somewhat charming, needed updating if he were to sell it. After walking past the small homes in the neighborhood, he figured the place might not be easy to offload.

The familiar scent of Mr. Bubble caught his attention and he knew his old friend 'Ben Bubble' was hard at work since he heard shrieks of delight from his daughter. She enjoyed spending time in this town—and, more importantly, with Melanie.

He pulled up the files for the merger and glanced at them again. The private company was in good standing financially, and their technology would be a welcome addition to his other businesses.

Stuff like this usually made him happy, but all he could concentrate on was his daughter's laughter down the hall. It was music to his ears. He would have joined them in the bathroom, but the room was small, and he did have work to do.

After a few more minutes, he heard Melanie walking down the hall to her bedroom, not Arianna's. Darin had said that Arianna was having problems adjusting to sleeping in the house, and James had left early this morning without getting a status report. Perhaps the two of them had switched rooms.

James left his bedroom to say goodnight to his daughter, only to find that Melanie had put the crib in her room. A small heater was on, and the place felt warm and cozy. The room also smelled of some flowery scent.

His daughter was in her pajamas and nearly asleep in Melanie's arms. The woman's back faced him as she sang a lullaby and rocked, alternating her hips.

Melanie, her hair pulled up in a sloppy bun, swayed back and forth as she patted Arianna gently on her back.

The rhythmic movement was soothing, her voice soft and sweet.

His daughter was peaceful and quiet.

The side rail of the crib was down, and the bed rested low to the floor, so placing Arianna into it for the night would be easy.

Melanie shifted her weight and put the baby on the lowered mattress, kissing her cheek as she did so. "Good night, Arianna. I'll make sure your daddy knows you're asleep."

He watched as Melanie stared at the baby. He assumed that it was the kind of gaze that mothers had when they looked into the angelic faces of their children as they slept. He couldn't see Melanie's face, but he just knew she had that look. The expression he was sure none of his nannies ever gave him.

Melanie turned and caught him staring at her.

"I'm sorry," she whispered. "Arianna fell asleep the second I put on her pajamas."

He crept to the crib, the floorboards creaking under his weight, and saw the peaceful face of his daughter. "Will she be warm enough in there?"

"I was worried about that, too." She softly nodded as though thinking what else she could do. "I can put her to bed with me." She looked nervously at him as though she had said something wrong. "If that's all right. Or, I could…"

His child, snuggled up next to a stranger? He couldn't make eye contact with Melanie. Not because of her generous offer but because it would have never occurred to him to put Arianna in *his* bed. Her comfort hadn't become one of his concerns. Not yet. He hoped it would one day be at the forefront of his thoughts.

Since he had remembered cuddling with a few of his nannies, he said, "You can put her in your bed. As long as she gets a good night's rest and is safe." He then remembered the information he had read about babies and their sleep. "Please make sure she's safe. There's this thing where babies can stop breathing…"

"SIDS. I know," she whispered. "She'll sleep on her back and I'll keep her in the crib as much as possible."

She seemed to know as much as he did, even more. He sniffed the delightful scent that lingered in the air. He still hadn't gotten used to the horrid plant smell that permeated every nook and cranny of this town. He suspected his daughter didn't like the stench either.

"What is that smell?"

Melanie pointed toward the nightstand. A device puffing out what he assumed was water vapor was plugged into the wall. "It's a diffuser with lavender oil. I also put some oil in the tub with her. The scent helps relax you so you can sleep deeper."

Diffuser? Oils? That was all new-agey stuff that James was unfamiliar with, but...looking at his daughter and how peacefully she now slept, he was grateful that Melanie was.

"If the diffuser helps her sleep and keeps her bedroom from smelling like the rest of this town, then keep it." He smiled at his daughter, who was passed out. "She looks like an angel when she's sleeping."

Arianna had been bathed and now slept in her bed—all before eight at night. Whatever Melanie was doing, it was magic. He knew, deep in his heart, that he couldn't have done so well. He now understood the panic-stricken face of Darin before he left. He had watched Arianna for three days with no help.

Darin needed a larger Christmas bonus.

"I hope you don't mind that I put her in this room. The air vents down the hall aren't working, which keeps her bedroom too cold."

"It's fine." James then gazed at his daughter. "Good night, sweetheart." James softly kissed Arianna's cheek, careful not to disturb her. He grabbed the teddy bear from a nearby dresser and placed the plush toy next to her, but Melanie snatched it from him.

"Your assistant shouldn't have bought this bear. It's not safe."

He looked at the seemingly normal little teddy bear. It was a stuffed animal not a machine gun ready to go off. "Why is it not safe?"

Her fingernail tapped on the glass beads the animal had for eyes. "Choking hazard."

Melanie moved a soft toy from the corner of the crib and placed it closer to Arianna. "This one is safe for babies."

This toy had stitched eyes and was soft all over. He had no idea he was putting a dangerous toy into his daughter's crib. He had so much to learn.

Small–town girl or not, Melanie definitely knew her stuff. "I'm sorry I doubted you earlier. I..."

"It's fine," she said, interrupting him. Even in the dim light, he saw that a slight blush rose to her cheeks. "I'm going to take a bath and turn in." She grabbed the baby monitor and left the room.

He'd never cared before what his hired help thought of him, but Melanie was different. He didn't like that he had hurt her feelings earlier. He followed her out to the hallway, but she had already entered the bathroom and closed the door.

He hadn't even completed his full apology, but it didn't look like he would get the chance. He had to put Melanie and Arianna out of his head and finish his work.

He returned to his room and saw the steaming hot lasagna waiting for him. He couldn't remember the last time someone, other than a paid servant or a restaurant, had made him a meal. And to keep it warm in the oven? Who did that?

His stomach growled, so he sat and took a bite. The melted cheese spread from his lips when he pulled the fork away. The tangy tomatoes and savory meat made a good combination with the veggie noodles.

It was probably the best lasagna he had ever tasted.

Had she found a recipe to make the lasagna? Or was she just that good of a cook?

She was excellent with his daughter, she was a wonderful cook, and she was a good nanny. Overall, a capable woman. And smart. Not to mention caring and damn good–looking, too.

The water pipes squealed to life, and he knew that she was naked and about to get into the bathtub. He now wondered what else she was good at.

he overhead water pipes squealed to life and woke Melanie. The sun shone through the window, and she knew James had already risen.

Arianna lay on her back, safely between Melanie and the wall, bundled up in warm pajamas but with no blankets. She'd woken up several times in the middle of the night, and had had one messy diaper, but overall, she had been a sweet baby.

Just the same, the night had been restless. Melanie wasn't used to sleeping with a child in her bed. She had worried about rolling over onto her, smothering her, and possibly even killing her. But the room felt too cold for the child to lay in a crib alone.

But it wasn't only sleeping with a baby that had contributed to the restless night.

James had been man enough to apologize when he was wrong. How rare was that? Most men never admitted their mistakes, and some even blamed others—sometimes, randomly.

He hadn't spent much time with Arianna yesterday, but he had only just arrived in town and was busy. Melanie didn't know much about running a huge company, but she suspected that the job was more than a nine–to–five type of position.

Plus, there was something about James that puzzled her. He seemed loving toward his daughter, but not comfortable with her. Hiring a nanny to watch her was probably normal for his world, though, and all the details of his child's life would be filtered through an employee.

He even held Arianna the way you would a sack of dirty clothes.

Melanie glanced down at the sleeping baby. She looked like an angel. Her pale skin and crooked smile were adorable. She looked so much like her daddy—a pang of excitement shot through Melanie as she studied the child's beautiful features.

James sure could make one heck of a baby.

Arianna's mother, whoever she was, was probably a sophisticated woman of the world—a jet–setting model, another corporate executive, or perhaps an exotic, wealthy foreigner who James had met while cruising the Caribbean.

An educated heiress that Melanie could never hold a candle to.

Why did the one man to turn her head in over a year have to be a visiting father who planned to be in town for only two weeks? An intelligent, city–smart, family man who would leave after the holiday and never think again of the silly country girl who had been in his employ. A country girl whose job would be eliminated if he closed the plant. She'd end up scrambling for another job, in a town that had no other employment options. James wielded much power, but did he have any compassion?

She knew James to be several years her senior. She had never thought of herself as being interested in older men, but the butterflies in her stomach whenever he was nearby, told her otherwise.

And she needed those feelings to go away.

Everything about this job felt too domestic. It had also felt too... familiar in this room with James last night. But, then again, this was her bedroom. She needed to keep all discussions between them in the more common areas of the house.

A family man like James wouldn't be satisfied dating someone like her. He probably wanted more kids, and it would be good if Arianna had siblings. But because Melanie had had a cyst and needed one of her fallopian tubes removed, she had a reduced chance of ever conceiving a child. No man would want her.

An emptiness inside bubbled up.

There'd probably be no sweet children like Arianna in Melanie's life. She may have convinced the town that she hated children, but her heart knew better. Even as a child, she wanted children. She loved playing house and loving on her baby dolls.

Years had passed, but Melanie could still remember the names she had picked out for her future children. Ten names. Five girls, five boys. And all pure fantasy.

She stroked Arianna's curly hair. James had claimed to be a single father, but not a widow. What kind of mother abandoned her child?

Or, perhaps, James was powerful enough that he'd hired the best of lawyers to win any battle he fought in the courtroom.

Just thinking about the influence the man had made her flush, and she reminded herself that she was just an employee. He was older and probably saw her as just a kid herself.

Looking at Arianna blissfully asleep, Melanie was tempted to sleep in with her, but she had to use the bathroom.

The sounds of the shower ended, and she had to force herself not to think of James naked. She waited a few minutes until she heard the bathroom door open, and then she carefully unwrapped herself from the sleeping child and made a barricade of blankets and pillows around the bed. She then tiptoed to the baby monitor so she could take it with her. She slowly opened the door, which creaked. The sound echoed down the hallway.

Looking back at Arianna, she saw the baby was still sound asleep.

Melanie entered the hallway and closed the door. She needed two minutes in the bathroom, and she was sure she could race back to Arianna if she woke up. The child could turn around, but not yet crawl. She seemed secure enough on the bed for a quick bathroom break.

Turning from the door, she saw the bathroom door open and could smell the clean scent of bath wash wafting out. She took a few steps and bumped into James as he was leaving. Startled, she tripped over her feet and bumped into him, but caught herself and managed to not fall on her face.

She felt grateful not to have fallen, but she was fully aware that she had touched him. First his chest, his arm as he tried to catch her, and... she touched—no nearly pulled off—the towel that covered him.

The dark green towel that had snuggly hugged his hips was now loose. His hand had quickly reached for it before it fell, but the terrycloth managed to slip down his body a few inches and nearly revealed way more of her boss to her than she needed to see.

Her cheeks grew hot, and she averted her eyes. "I'm sorry. I thought you were out of the bathroom."

He tightened the knot around his hips and asked her a question, but she wasn't focusing on his words right now.

Steam. He was airing out the only working bathroom after his shower and letting the steam out of the space. She should have noticed that the light in the room remained on, even though the door was open.

His cologne and aftershave smelled divine.

Still not looking at him, she said, "Arianna's still asleep. I needed to use... I mean, I thought you were done."

His hand touched her arm, which caused her to look deep into his eyes. His freshly shaven face revealed his chiseled jaw.

Of course, he had likely shaved after his shower. Just like most men. Gosh, she acted like such an idiot. She should have waited until she was sure he had returned to his room.

He glanced down the hall to where his daughter slept. "I'm glad she's still asleep, but I asked if *you* were okay."

A tingling sensation traveled up Melanie's arm and continued through her body until it captured her breath. "I'm fine," she managed to say, her voice shaky.

James stood nearly naked in front of her, and all she could manage to do was stutter? Well, that and almost fall on her butt. It had been a long time since she had been with a man, and thanks to what she saw in front of her now, she was focused on some very impure thoughts.

Why did he have to be so handsome? A great father, a successful businessman... Last night, she had imagined his body covered with a rash just to stop thinking about him as a man.

His fingers moved up her arm to her top's shoulder. The thin strap had slipped down, and he put it back into place, his hand lingering for just a moment on her skin as she steadied herself.

"I'm sorry I startled you."

"I should have been paying attention." She felt her cheeks flush.

Crap. Melanie had forgotten that she had slept in her bralette and jeans because she had no other clothes to wear. She must look half naked to him as well. She knew her hair was a mess, and her mascara was probably not just running down her face but hurdling down her cheeks.

His hot gaze wandered down her body to her legs. "Are you sure you didn't twist your ankle?"

Her jaw fell open, and then she swallowed the lump in her throat. "I'm fine." She motioned with her hand toward her feet, but the back of her fingers brushed against his towel.

She pulled away. She needed to stop touching him. Her heart racing, she said, "I need to use the bathroom for a minute."

His gaze studied her, then his lips pulled up into a smile. "I'm done in there if you need to get in."

He stepped past her and walked down the hallway. She knew better, but she tilted her head to get a better view of his back.

Strong shoulders, tan as all get-out, sexy legs, and from what she could see, a firm backside. She bit her lower lip and studied his muscular build.

"Oh," he said, turning back to her.

Her eyes widened, and she stood taller. "Yes?"

"My lawyer called this morning." His lips twisted in a way that told her he now carefully chose his words. "If the press finds out where I am, there may be some reporters around today. You'll want to avoid them."

Finds out? This man had a mystery about him. Why did that make him so much more sexy to her? "There isn't anything wrong, is there?"

His facial expression gave away no secrets. "It's about Arianna's mother," he said in a matter-of-fact tone.

Melanie had assumed legal matters kept the mother out of the picture. Was she somehow still involved?

"Arianna's mother?" she repeated, nervously.

"Yes, Vivian," he said, his voice decisive and firm. "We probably should talk about a few things."

That's when it hit her.

James may be a single father, but he still maintained some sort of a relationship with Arianna's mother. Melanie felt so stupid. Here she was, practically lusting after this man who was already spoken for.

Spoken for by the mother of his six–month–old child.

She was so dumb.

A successful, gorgeous man like James...a new baby...and Melanie had thought there could be something between them?

"Vivian is leaving for Europe to film a movie, but that doesn't mean the press won't hound us before she goes." His eyes narrowed and a sad expression crossed his face. "Or even afterward for that matter." His gaze wandered to the closed bedroom door and the soft cry from Arianna. "She's up. I'll check on her while you use the restroom, and then we'll talk."

hank goodness he had brought along casual clothes. He had stuck out like a sore thumb the other day in his suit. Today—especially today—if the reporters knew he was here, he needed to blend in.

Arianna was fussy, but James managed to take her into his bedroom and place her squarely in the middle of the bed.

He pulled off the towel but quickly put it back on. Arianna was awake. Awake and staring at him. She didn't need to see him naked in front of her.

James felt awkward, but he turned Arianna around so that her focus would be on the bed's headboard. He then walked to the foot of the bed and got dressed.

"Daddy is almost done." He put his underwear

and pants on first, just in case he had to grab her quickly. He then put on his shirt.

She rolled halfway over, but seemed content to just lay there and cry.

Cry loudly.

What was he supposed to do?

Tears formed and dribbled down her little cheeks, and her face grew red.

"You're a good baby, Arianna." He picked her up and was feeling less nervous about supporting her neck and holding her in his arms, but not better at it.

Everyone else in the world could carry a baby and not look like they were some alien conducting an abduction. Why couldn't he hold his child and comfort her?

James held Arianna tightly against his chest and bounced up and down, the same way he had seen Melanie do it. The child still cried.

Did he know any lullabies? He racked his brain to think of any and only came up with three beer commercial jingles and an ad for Ben Gay.

"Shh. You're fine, Arianna."

Her diaper smelled ripe, and he suspected that she wanted her breakfast.

He took her back to Melanie's room where the bag of diapers was, only to bump into Melanie now rushing up the stairs with some formula.

"I got her breakfast," she said, holding up the bottle and showing it to Arianna.

She walked into the room and placed the bottle in a warmer, then took Arianna from his arms so she could change her.

Melanie placed a clean towel on the bed and then put Arianna on it. His daughter lay there so helpless. So tiny. Her big, blue eyes stared up at Melanie with a sense of peace that had been missing as she'd gazed into his a few minutes ago.

Babies knew when you weren't comfortable with them. And Arianna was no fool.

"You're so good at that."

"What? Diapering?" Melanie smiled at Arianna. "She just needed a little attention. That's all." She leaned in closer to the baby, the poopy-diaper smell not seeming to upset her. "Isn't that right?" she asked in baby talk and calmed Arianna down. Melanie then expertly undid the diaper, and with just a few efficient wipes, was done and a clean diaper put on.

"She seems fine now."

Melanie picked the child up and set her on her hip so she could look around the room. "So, what is it you need to talk to me about?"

Right. He needed to tell her about the reporters. "Arianna's mother is Vivian Saunders," James said, knowing the truth had to come out.

"Why does that name sound familiar? You said she's filming a movie..." Melanie's eyes widened a moment later. "She's that woman from that movie."

Her brow furrowed deep in thought. "The one where the soldier returns home and meets his pen pal."

Why was it that most the women he knew never remembered the names of people—especially actors —and could never recall movie titles?

"*Lovers Entwined*," he said. The film had been an instant box office sensation, catapulting Vivian into a position as one of the most sought–after actors of the last few years. They had met, however briefly, during a hiatus between the two movies she had been filming in Europe. Her pregnancy, and the birth of their daughter had taken her out of the limelight, but only momentarily.

He felt like a fool. He hadn't followed Vivian's career—just didn't care to—and she had had a baby. If he hadn't been so preoccupied with his own life, he could have guessed that he was the father.

All the research he had done online told him that Vivian had never revealed who the father was. He wondered if that was due to her being a private person, or if she was somehow embarrassed by him being the dad.

Not that there should be anything to be embar-rassed about.

And now, according to his lawyers, Vivian was planning to fly back to Europe to film another movie. One of several that were sure to come, which meant she would be too busy to be a mother.

And that left only him to care for their child.

"Vivian has been in several movies, but that soldier love story one launched her career," he said, adding what was obvious to anyone who had seen the movie and followed her progress.

Melanie straightened the sheets and propped some pillows up so she could comfortably sit and feed Arianna now that the food was warmed. "I don't follow the tabloids or anything in Hollywood for that matter." She glanced down at Arianna, and in a soft voice asked, "How long have you been dating her?"

"I'm not in a relationship with her. Never was. Not really." James sat on the bed and caressed Arianna's cheek as she drank her breakfast. "Let's just say the relationship was barely long enough to conceive Arianna."

The expression on Melanie's face wasn't as judgmental as he'd thought it would be. Maybe because he was Arianna's caregiver and not just a baby daddy who tossed out money as a solution.

Melanie shook her head and a slight smile appeared on her lips. "When you said you never married the mother and were a single father, I had assumed she had run out on the two of you. I didn't realize you were just watching her while Vivian films on location. Why is the press excited about that?"

If she didn't follow the Hollywood gossip, then Melanie wouldn't know that Arianna's father had never been revealed to the press. Vivian, with whatever she had going on in her life, had not approached him during the pregnancy, nor immediately after Arianna's birth. Until she walked into his company's headquarters and publicly dropped Arianna off like last week's dry–cleaning.

"I have no formal agreement with Vivian over custody, not yet at least." He needed to tell Melanie the truth, so he relayed the story as it had been told to him by his father. How Vivian had callously dropped Arianna off and then left her at the receptionist desk with just the clothes on her back and no extra diapers.

Melanie's jaw literally dropped. "That's cold." She slowly nodded as though analyzing the situation. "But it does explain a lot."

"What do you mean?"

"You just became a father a few days ago. You don't know Arianna's routine, you don't know her favorite toy, you don't know her likes and dislikes. You don't even know how to hold a baby without her crying."

Was his inexperience that obvious? He had hoped to look—maybe not a natural—but at least capable. "I'm trying my best to adjust, but..."

"No," she said, her hand reaching out to touch his. "I'm not trying to be critical of you. I'm just saying that it's obvious that this"—her gaze moved down to Arianna—"is all new to you. And not in a six–month–old newness kind–of–way. I think you're doing a great job."

It was sweet of her to say so, and James hoped that he would be comfortable holding Arianna soon —maybe even enough to change a diaper.

"It's an awkward situation." He glanced at Arianna, knowing that she deserved someone with more experience to watch over her than a father like him.

"You're seizing this opportunity," Melanie said.

"What do you mean?"

"You have a daughter. She smiled at the baby who was enjoying her breakfast. "You can either be a crappy parent like Vivian, or you can be Arianna's biggest hero." She now looked him square in the eyes. "You're choosing to be a daddy here. Not just a father who's there every other weekend or less; you get to be a daddy full time. Many fathers don't get that opportunity. Enjoy having Arianna and spending time with her. So many people go their whole lives without such a blessing."

Her words hit home with him. Just a week ago, he had wished all of this away, then he thought he could somehow manage with just a partial—and very limited—custody. Now, just a week in, he wanted to be a daddy for Arianna. He wanted to be the one she came to when she was scared at night, when she was excited about something in her life, and the one that got to see her perform the part of a flower in a school play—even if it were the role of flower number three that didn't have a speaking part and just sat at the back of the stage.

"Thank you."

"For what," she asked.

"For putting everything in the proper perspective." The bottle slipped from Arianna's mouth and she let out a contented cooing sound. He enjoyed sitting on the bed and sharing the moment with them, but then a knock sounded on the front door.

"Are you expecting anyone?" he asked.

Melanie glanced up, but managed to place the bottle once again in Arianna's mouth. She readjusted the child and helped her hold the food up so no bubbles got into her tummy. "I'm not expecting anybody."

James stood and went to the window. His heart sank. "KKRP Television," he read. "Their van is parked out front." He glanced about the room, a surge of panic hitting him. He needed his daughter to be safe. Needed her not to have her picture displayed on all the tabloids and on the newscasts.

"KKRP?" Melanie stood with Arianna still in her arms. "That's the local news station."

James craned his neck and could see more of the yard. There was just the one van. Local or not, a news segment could be sold to a national chain. A motion from the side of the house caught his attention. "A cameraman is on the lawn."

Another knock, followed by the doorbell sounding.

"They'll hound us all day. We can't stay here." They needed to escape. James found Melanie's car keys on the dresser and picked them up. "I'll drive. Once we lose them, I'll take you to where you need to be today, and then I'll walk or Uber to the plant. I can get a ride from there back here for my car."

"This town doesn't have Uber."

Shit. Well, that was the least of his worries right now. He'd just have to find a way to...

"I'm meeting my aunt today. I can use her car." She shrugged and looked at him. "They already know what our cars look like, so maybe they'll leave me alone if I'm driving my aunt's old Chevy."

It was a plan. Probably the best one they could come up with. But first, they had to get out of this house. He gently touched Melanie's arm and escorted her and his daughter from the room.

Once downstairs, they saw a face peeking into the window by the front door. Melanie turned away and covered Arianna's face as they walked toward the kitchen.

"We'd like to talk to you, Mr. Nielson, about your relationship with Vivian Saunders."

"The stroller is already in the car." Melanie placed her purse on her shoulder. The bag shifted on her hip as she quickly went from room to room, gathering up extra blankets and clothing for Arianna.

"Here. Put these in the diaper bag," Melanie said as she handed James a few items.

A newer diaper bag, one that didn't say *Child Protective Services*, lay on the kitchen counter, stuffed nearly full of baby stuff. James placed the items next to some extra pacifiers and toys.

"Is that you, Melanie?" the reporter shouted from outside.

James ignored the question and put on his coat, he then gathered Melanie's coat and placed it over her shoulders since she was still carrying Arianna. He then went to the side door of the house, the exit closest to the car. "Ready?"

When Melanie nodded, the three of them left the house. The cold wind whipped around and sliced into his exposed skin. He hit the key fob to open the car before he locked the house door, his fingers already freezing cold.

Before he could reach the vehicle, Melanie had put Arianna in the car seat and had gotten in the back with her.

"Is that Vivian Saunders' baby?" The reporter now stood near the rental, the camera man close by and zooming in, doing his best to get a picture of Arianna. "Mr. Nielson, are you involved with Vivian Saunders?"

James jumped in, the cold leather seat depleting

his body heat. He started the car, but the cameraman blocked his exit. James rolled down the window just enough to say, "No comment."

"That's Vivian Saunders' baby." The reporter glared at Melanie. "Melanie, are you a nanny? You hate kids."

"Feel free to run him over." Melanie used a burp cloth and covered Arianna's face so the cameraman —who had moved to her side of the sedan—couldn't get a good picture of her.

James pulled out of the driveway, avoiding the reporter, who now dashed to the van with the cameraman. He wondered if he'd be able to lose the press in this small town.

MELANIE HAD NEVER HAD to make a break for it before. There was some excitement to it, but because a young baby was involved, she understood this was no game.

She never read the tabloids, but figured if an heir of the town's founding fathers were involved in something as scandalous as a secret baby, she would have heard something about it. News traveled fast in small towns, and Arianna was big news indeed.

The secret was out—and in a very public way.

Melanie felt sorry for James. An unplanned pregnancy was certainly a surprise, but he'd only found out days ago that he had fathered a child, and in a very unexpected way. Typically, you had a few months to let the news settle in, to get used to the idea, and to prepare. James had had less than a week, wasn't in familiar surroundings, and was now being chased by reporters who wanted to share the news with the world.

To make it worse, the reporter, the one who stared through the window at them, was none other than Melanie's ex–fiancé.

It sounded like a bad movie, with a villain from her past.

Crap.

The car sped down the road and nearly slid on the ice. The news van was still far behind, but not as far as she would have liked.

This was more drama than this little town had seen in a long time. And, Vivian Saunders? This scandal had a Hollywood link, so she suspected it'd be the talk of the town for quite some time.

She glanced at James, who focused on the road. He had fathered a child with Vivian Saunders? Naturally, Hollywood stars dated the elite, the wealthy, and the most handsome people in the world. You had to look good while walking on the red carpet. You needed some eye–candy to escort you to all of your Oscar appearances.

Vivian Saunders was a rare beauty with dark brunette curls and a size–two body to match.

Melanie glanced at Arianna's hair and facial features. It was now obvious that Vivian was her mother. Arianna looked like the perfect blend of both of her gorgeous parents.

"Where should we go?" James asked. His eyes darted from one side of the street to the other as they passed intersections.

"Drive to Lexington and Palmer. I'm meeting my aunt there."

James pointed at the intersection up ahead. "Left?"

Of course, he wouldn't know. She needed to be more specific. "Left. Four blocks, and then left again. You're taking me to the Shamrock Apartments."

He made the turn. "That's where your aunt lives?"

"No, it's my apartment. I'm picking up a few things, and then I'll have my aunt drop me off at Kinder Musik with Arianna. You can have the car."

James drove down the road, and Melanie was happy that they weren't hitting any red lights. She didn't see the news van through the back window anymore, and she could detect a slight smile in James's reflection in the rearview mirror.

But then James stared directly at her in the mirror, his expression filled with concern. "The reporter knows you. Will he know where to find you?"

Not likely. Melanie had moved out once their

engagement ended and she'd never told him where she now lived. "Trevor doesn't know where my new apartment is. Arianna and I should be fine."

James caught Melanie's gaze. "He said you hate kids." James turned left down the next road. "I'm not one to believe what a reporter says, and this time the guy seems way off base. You like kids just fine. At the very least, you're good with them." He gave a sideways glance at her through the mirror. "Why would he have said that?"

Her jaw tightened. That lie was hers. She had spread it, and she had owned it. To have Trevor throw it back at her—especially in front of someone paying her to care for their child—made her sick to her stomach.

"Trevor is my ex–fiancé. It's a long story," her voice trailed off and she hoped he wouldn't ask further.

An awkward silence filled the car, then he finally said, "I know how hurtful exes can be."

She leaned in and touched one of Arianna's dark, Vivian–like curls. "I'll make sure to keep her safe."

"Call me if you're in any trouble. I'll be at the plant." James shook his head. "I'll be there as soon as I can, first I'll make sure to lose the reporters." She detected a hint of anger in his strong, tight jaw. "You'd think those idiots would be more interested in the factory closing than in my daughter."

Gosh. She had tried not to think about the plant closure. She wasn't going to get her job back in January, and there were no jobs in this town. She'd have to find something before all the other plant workers started job hunting.

She couldn't breathe. Her lungs tightened, and she fought to say, "You'll kill this town if that place shuts down."

"I'd rather not close it at all, especially since I just discovered a lot of family members who rely on the place for their livelihoods." He made eye contact with her again and with a face full of sorrow he said, "But I'm not sure I can save it."

Dread gripped her. The tragic news of the plant closing would shake up her little town. She wanted to warn everyone, but a mass panic wasn't the answer.

As strong and as powerful as Melanie believed James to be, he wasn't a magician.

The train tracks were coming up, and James looked both ways, pausing only briefly. "I've been here for several days and have never heard a train go through."

He'd probably only made the comment to change the subject, so Melanie let the topic of the plant closure slide.

"These are dead tracks," she said, her voice flat and raw. "They've been out of commission since I was a kid."

Arianna began to cry, so Melanie gave her a pacifier and it calmed her down. "A terrible storm
revealed a sink hole that destroyed a huge section of
the tracks on the north side of town. They're still
under water."

Melanie gazed north up Concord street when
they passed the intersection. She hadn't thought
about these train tracks in a long time.

And that's when the stupid train song came back
to her mind, the one she'd sung to Arianna the other
day, the tune slowly gnawing at her sanity.

19

*A*unt Eva handed a cup of coffee to Melanie, its Starbucks logo and *almond milk* written on the side a welcome sight to her.

"Coffee. Yes!" She hadn't been able to make herself a cup this morning and, since she hadn't slept well last night, she needed a jolt of caffeine. She sniffed the sweet aroma, which cut through the stench of the town, and then took a sip.

"The baby seat is in the car," James said as he shut the back, passenger door. "It was nice meeting you, Eva, and I appreciate you allowing Melanie to use your car today." He looked as if he wanted to pick up Arianna and hug her goodbye, but then he leaned over and kissed her on the cheek instead. "You stay safe today." Now, looking at Melanie, he placed his hand on her shoulder and added, "Call me if you need anything."

"We'll be fine." Melanie shifted Arianna in her arms, and the two of them watched as James walked to his car and drove away.

"So that was James Nielson," Aunt Eva said as James pulled out of the apartment complex's parking lot. "That was odd."

"What was?"

Aunt Eva shrugged. "It's nothing."

Her aunt had a slight grin on her face. Melanie knew it wasn't 'nothing'. "What?"

"Well," she said, her voice trailing off and the slight smile spreading across her lips, "that incredibly gorgeous man looked like he was about to kiss you and tell *you* to have a good day." She let out a slight giggle. "Like the two of you were an old married couple."

Melanie had felt a closeness to James, especially since he had admitted to her the entire story of Arianna... but there was nothing between them. He was the man who would destroy this town by closing the plant. He was who would take away her uncle's position, and her job too, eventually. "That's ridiculous. There's nothing between Mr. Nielson and me," Melanie finally said, finding it odd to call him Mr. Nielson instead of James.

She hated breaking any trust she may have with James, but she needed to warn her aunt but not give away any details. She chose her words carefully. "The plant is probably going to close."

Eva's face paled. "Your uncle came home moody last night. I think he heard something, too. I wanted to warn you that your job might not be safe."

Melanie wanted to help her aunt and uncle out, but her position wasn't any better. Sad news definitely had a way of killing the conversation, and the two of them gazed into each other's eyes with concern.

Perhaps picking up on the slight pause and wanting to change the subject, Aunt Eva said, "James is as handsome as his father was back in the day." Her eyebrow arched. "Handsome and rich."

"You remember his father?"

"Oh," Aunt Eva said, "I think everyone knew Gregory when he lived here. It's been so long though, that I think most people have just forgotten him."

"James resembles his father?"

"Spitting image." Aunt Eva took a sip of her coffee and Melanie could see her eyes dancing their reminiscing little dance. "Handsome man. He fell in love and they moved away." One eyebrow arched and she gazed over to Melanie. "James lives in New York, right?"

A Cinderella story happening once in a small town bucked the odds. The chance of it happening twice? Never. "There's nothing..."

"All I'm saying," her aunt said, as though trying to interject some motherly wisdom, "is that it's just as easy to fall in love with a rich man as it is with a poor one."

"Enough." Melanie could feel her cheeks flushing. "He's going to drive back to the plant and see if he can distract the press." She held tightly to Arianna, not wanting to think about the plant closing. "Do you want to hold this little angel?"

Arianna squealed with delight and easily went to Aunt Eva's open arms.

"She sure is a beautiful child. It's been so long since I've had a little one to hold." Her expression soured and Melanie could mentally hear what her aunt didn't ask, which was 'when are you going to settle down and have one of your own'. Her aunt knew better than to ask.

Aunt Eva took a deep breath and shifted the child from one hip to the other. "What did you mean by James distracting the press?"

Since Joel Ferguson hadn't arrived yet to let them into her apartment, Melanie filled her aunt in on the events of the last few days, being careful not to divulge too much information about James's personal life. Since Aunt Eva was helping them elude the press, she did deserve some information, especially if the press found out where Arianna was.

Melanie told her about Vivian being Arianna's mother, the woman's abandonment of her baby, and Melanie's run–in with Trevor. She decided not to share James's life adjustment issues to suddenly being a father. That seemed too personal, and she didn't want to invade on his privacy.

"What mother would leave her child?" Aunt Eva shook her head judgmentally. "You take care of your family, no matter what."

Arianna began to fuss so Melanie took the baby from her aunt's arms and sang, *"Chugga Choo–Choo. Zipping down the tracks. So much stuff to haul, like bricks on his back."*

It was a stupid song, but one she hadn't been able to get out of her head for the last two days. She'd be back at Kinder Musik soon. Hopefully, a different song would get stuck.

"Great. Now, I'll be singing that song all day," Aunt Eva said. "This baby has lived a hectic life for only being six months old."

"She's a sweet baby, too." Melanie glanced down the street and saw the old Ford pickup Joel Ferguson drove. He parked and got out of the truck.

"Eva," he said, smiling. "You look lovely."

A slight blush crossed Eva's face. "Joel, thanks for letting my niece back into her apartment."

"Technically, I'm not supposed to... so it's only for a few minutes." He smiled at Aunt Eva, and Melanie suspected that there was a secret behind that grin. A mystery that may be decades old since the two of them used to be high school sweethearts.

The way her aunt smiled back, Melanie knew

they still had a soft spot for each other, even though both were happily married.

Melanie didn't understand being friends with past lovers. Some people could do it, but not her. Once a romance was over, it needed to be over.

Trevor didn't seem to understand that.

"I need to grab a few things," she said, knowing that a duffle bag lay in her bedroom closet and she could stuff most things into it.

Joel's eyebrow rose and hid behind his gray hairline. "I didn't know you had a baby, Melanie."

For the briefest of moments, having someone think that she did have a baby was nice. That she might be married and living a family life. Joel didn't know her—other than collecting her monthly rent—and was a generation older. Most people her own age judged her for not being content to settle down and live in this town. Of course, they were the ones she had convinced that she hated children.

"Arianna belongs to a friend. I'm watching her today." If the local news station already knew about Arianna, then the whole town would soon enough. No need to jump the gun and start advertising who Arianna was.

They walked up the creaking stairs. "This railing has been busted for months," Melanie said, taking advantage of her landlord's presence. "I reported it a while ago." She then glanced at one of the lights at the top of the stairs. "Same with the broken light."

Joel looked sheepishly at her and then moved his gaze to Eva. "I'll get those fixed right away."

He unlocked the secure box attached to the doorknob, and the three entered the apartment. The living room was small, there were water stains on the ceiling, and peeling linoleum on the floor. The mismatched furniture rested on a threadbare rug.

"This place could use some updating," Eva said, casting a stern gaze to Joel. "It's freezing in here."

"I turn the radiator off when I leave to save money," Melanie said. "It's been off for several days."

"Well, it's colder in here than outside standing in the sunshine." Eva zipped up her jacket and looked around. "Is that a dripping faucet I hear?"

Joel kept the door open, probably to let some sunlight in. "Once the rent is paid, I'll take care of the place." His eyes widened, and his face softened as he stared at Eva. "I promise," he said, his voice soft and full of assurance.

Melanie knew that bringing her aunt would be a good idea. She always had a way of getting people to do things for her, especially if she was dealing with someone from her past. "I can have the rent money for you right after the holidays." Since he looked skeptical, she added, "I have a part time job right now and I get paid right after Christmas."

Joel nodded. "I won't get rid of any of your belongings." He waved his hands around the space. "Your things will be here when you get back."

It was a relief to know that he wouldn't ship all her stuff to Goodwill. Since she still carried Arianna in her arms, Melanie said, "If you and Eva can load the paintings into her car, I'll grab my personal belongings."

Joel pointed to the stack of paintings resting against the wall. "These?"

Aunt Eva flipped through the stack of six paintings, looking at each one briefly before moving onto the next. "These are beautiful, dear."

Joel took a critical eye to them. "Abstract art. I don't get it..." he said, his voice trailing off until he finally added, "I'm sure some people like this boxy type of stuff."

The form was called cubism, but Melanie didn't want to get into that.

She knew not everyone liked her art, but at least Vassar thought highly enough of it and her that they wanted her for the spring semester. Of course, she wouldn't be attending that college. She'd probably have to be dead for her artwork to matter to anyone. Being a starving artist wasn't getting her anywhere.

"What are all these paintings for?" Joel asked.

"The Christmas Eve fair. I'm placing them in the 50/50–split art aisle." She had been selected with five other artists to display her artwork at the event. Two of the artists were sculptors and the other three were painters. She didn't know if her paintings would sell or not, but there was hope for some recognition and money.

"I'm familiar with our fair, but what's a 50/50 table?" Joel asked.

"It's new this year. Times are tough, so the fair is allowing homemade crafts to be sold with either a twenty–five, fifty, or seventy–five percent split going to the charity, and the rest going to the artist to help pay for supplies and time," Aunt Eva said.

"So, people are going to buy these paintings?" Joel's voice, once again, didn't sound judgmental, but he needed to stop talking. Melanie's feelings were getting hurt, and her hope of making some money and recognition fading.

"These are beautiful," Aunt Eva said again, high-lighting the word *beautiful* and making her expression stern as she glared at Joel. "Melanie has her mother's talent."

Melanie liked hearing that, but it wasn't true. Her mother had been a fantastic artist who had scholarships to study in Europe. If she hadn't been pregnant with Melanie, her mother could have been one of the greatest artists of all time.

Melanie had trapped her mother in this town.

Her mom could have had a different life.

Not that she thought her mother hated the life she had.

Now, staring at the paintings, Melanie wondered

if she had what it took to be a real artist. Most people didn't like cubism.

"Let's load this up." Melanie didn't want to focus on her mother's decision and sacrifice, or the fact that she may not have the same quality of talent as her mother.

Loading the paintings and her personal items into Aunt Eva's car only took a few minutes. The ordeal would have gone faster, but Melanie had had to hold onto Arianna the entire time.

Melanie placed Arianna back into her car seat as her aunt said goodbye to Joel. She noticed that they both smiled politely to each other and even ended their conversation with a friendly goodbye hug.

"You can drop me off at home and then go to... what do you have planned for today?" her aunt asked as she got into the car and buckled up.

There wasn't a whole lot on the agenda, and she wondered how much of it she could actually do with the reporters in town. "Arianna has her Kinder Musik class, and then we'll do some grocery shopping."

"What's Kinder Musik?"

Okay, so nobody knew about this class? Abby had made the program sound like the entire country knew about Kinder Musik as being the best first music introduction that kids got.

Maybe their small town was only now hearing about the program.

She began the drive back to her aunt's house and explained what she knew of Kinder Musik. Parking in front of Eva's modest home, Melanie said, "You'll never guess who the instructor is."

Aunt Eva took the last sip of her now-cold coffee. "Who?"

"Abigail Horten. Well, she's married now, and it's Abby Stevens. Her son is four years old."

Aunt Eva's brow furrowed. "Do I know Abigail?"

"She was one of my babysitters." Melanie filled her aunt in on how Abby's family was doing, especially her ailing mother.

Her aunt nodded, her face filling with recognition that she remembered the girl. "That family owns all that land up north, on the good side that doesn't have all that water." Her eyebrow rose. "They have that big house on top of that hill. Her mother shouldn't be alone in that home. She could get lost."

Arianna fussed in the back seat, so Aunt Eva turned and did her best to face the child, whose car seat faced backwards. *"Chugga Choo-Choo,"* she sang. She darted her gaze at Melanie. "Dang, now you have me singing that blasted song."

20

James didn't know where to go. It was early morning and he was dressed and ready to head to the plant, but Craig wouldn't be there for at least another hour. He thought about going to his family's diner to get some breakfast, but that would be the first place reporters would search for him.

He didn't need to bring this type of drama to his grandmother's restaurant. His family had just met him and he didn't want them to get any wrong ideas about him and the life he led.

The pit of his stomach weighted heavily in him. Did he really care when the people in this town felt about him? He took a cleansing breath. He cared what his family thought of him, and that was an odd sensation seeing how he had just met them.

Driving aimlessly, he searched for a breakfast spot. As he figured, this tiny town didn't offer much. The snow sloshed under his tires as he turned down a side street, and for a moment his car hydroplaned on the ice. Slowing down, he turned down a more traveled road with more slush than ice, which is where he found a small coffee house. A sign hung in front indicating that a bakery was inside.

He bundled up before leaving his car. Few vehicles were parked in the lot and he figured this business, like many others, was suffering due to the economy. It was at the end of a shoppette that held five stores. Only one other was still open, a small ice cream shop which was closed.

The sidewalk was freshly shoveled and he walked under the awnings, avoiding the one with the row of melting icicles dripping, until he came up to the small store's door.

The bell above him dinged, announcing his arrival as he walked in. The place was warm and cozy in a New England cafe sort of way. More importantly, the smell of freshly brewed coffee hit his nostrils and he desperately needed a cup.

The place may not be Starbucks, but the coffee would certainly be better than the one down at the plant in the out–dated, barely functioning, urn.

"Welcome to Kiefer's Cafe," an older, blonde woman said from behind the counter.

The place only held half a dozen small tables, all of which were empty. It also had huge picture windows which would allow him to see any reporter coming up the walk. Two customers stood in line so he got behind them so he could place a breakfast order.

A pastry display ran along the side of the cash register and he took a look at the offering. There wasn't much of a selection, but he found a spinach quiche that was to his liking. Unbuttoning his coat, he thought about his grandmother's assortment of pastries. She didn't offer any quiches, but he thought her selection was grander and looked tastier.

Her pie from the other day was amazing.

How was it that he already had pride in his grandmother's work when he had just met the woman? Maybe the women in this town, as thoughtful and considerate as they were, just demanded your loyalty.

Not demanded. That was too edgy of a word. They *earned* a man's loyalty just by being themselves. He actually felt a little guilty by bringing his business to this cafe instead of his grandmother's restaurant, but there wasn't much he could do about that.

The two men took their coffees and began doctoring them up with cream and, from what James could tell, a ton of sugar. "What will it be, hon?" The blonde behind the counter said, and he wondered if any stranger had ever called him 'hon'.

"Cup of coffee and a spinach quiche," he said, pointing to the pastry counter.

"Both are great, but I prefer the quiche Lorraine," said the shorter of the two men just before he licked the sugary spoon from his coffee and set it on his plate which held his preferred quiche option.

James put on his fake smile, the one he reserved for overly friendly strangers offering advice he had no intention of heeding. "The spinach quiche is fine."

The men wore suits and ties, a sure sign that they didn't belong here. Even after just a few days, James was already wearing jeans and a sweater. Anything to blend in and not draw attention to himself.

He inwardly chuckled. To these two men, he must look like a local.

The taller man removed a credit card from his wallet and paid for both meals. James couldn't help but notice it was a company card to a firm that sounded familiar to him. Vagrant Enterprises, he said repeatedly in his mind to try and remember the name.

And then it hit him. Vagrant Enterprises was a two-bit player in the property and acquisitions game. They bought up buildings and land when companies went under. They also bought any reusable or saleable stock or equipment. They were the vultures of the business world. Sad, but very much needed in these dark, economic times.

The company had sent proposition emails to him in the past, that is, until he ignored them or had his assistant Darin take care of them. He didn't make any appointments to meet with the company while in town. Were they here for something other than his plant?

His interest was piqued, so he quickly handed the woman his credit card to pay for his breakfast, and then leaned over to shake the shorter man's hand. "My name is James. Are you here on business?"

"My name is Martin," he said, accepting the offer. He then gestured toward the other man. "My partner's name is Barry."

Barry, who had a scowl on his face like he wasn't a morning person, gave a half–hearted smile and a head nod.

The three of them left the counter and had their choice of seats. Barry placed his tablet on the largest of the tables and the motion activated it, showing the screensaver page.

The Vagrant Enterprises company logo displayed. Deciding to snoop, James gestured to one of the seats and Martin invited him to join them.

"Mighty neighborly of you," James said, not sure why he chose to talk in a hick–southern accent when they were up in Idaho. "Cold enough for you?"

Martin rubbed his hands together before grabbing his warm coffee mug. "We're from back East so we're used to this type of weather."

The two weren't wearing any gloves, scarves, or hats. Maybe they thought Idaho would be warmer this time of year than the northeast. He vaguely remembered that Vagrant Enterprises was based out of New Jersey, like most companies due to the state's less vigorous corporate tax laws. But he recognized a New York accent when he heard one. "That's a long trek out to our neck of the woods." James inwardly chided himself once again for the stupid accent. "What type of business are you in?"

"We do a little bit of everything," Barry said. He stared blankly at James as he took a sip of his coffee.

An awkward silence filled the room until Martin asked, "What is it that you do, James?"

Martin, with his welcoming smile and morning personality, definitely seemed to be the more chatty of the two. James took note of that. "I run a business here in town."

With a gleam in his eye, Martin asked, "What kind of business?"

"Small. Family–run." It absolutely wasn't a lie, but he wasn't about to give them the upper hand. James leaned back in his chair and decided to play it cool. He took a sip of his coffee and eyed them both.

Martin gave Barry a sideways glance. The man was sipping his coffee and didn't look much like talking, yet he nodded back to his partner and gave a slight "go ahead" hand gesture toward James.

"Since you're a native of these parts, and a business owner, do you mind if we ask you some questions?" Martin asked, now that Barry seemed somewhat involved in the conversation.

James wondered just how far he'd allow this charade to continue. He had nowhere to be just yet, so he nodded yes.

"What kind of business do you run?"

He knew better than to reveal too much. "Retail." It was as short of an answer as James could make it.

"Store front and not an online store?" Barry asked.

Vagrant Enterprises didn't dabble in Internet businesses. He could guess what they wanted to hear, so he answered, "I have a shop in town. I own the building, the parking lot, and the land around it."

Barry's eyebrow rose and he shot a glance over to Martin.

"How many employees?" Martin asked, his voice rising an octave.

Staring them square in the eyes, James said, "It's over a hundred employees. We've lost some people recently, though."

It was hard to believe, and kind of eerie to see, but Barry smiled. It was a type of smirk that an evil villain would have when he found out his master plot would actually work. James would love to rope this guy into a game of poker with that transparent of a face.

Barry pointed at the table with his index finger. "Can you tell us what you feel is missing from this town?" he asked, accenting the last few words by tapping the table.

"Missing?"

Barry leaned in. "This is a quaint little town, but that's just it. It's little. Isn't there some sort of comfort that you'd love to have that only the bigger cities can routinely offer?"

"Reliable hot water," James immediately joked. He had been frustrated how long his home took to heat the water and how little hot water the home's water heater held. He figured most people were and it was a safe answer.

"We're serious," Barry said, even when Martin had laughed. Barry scanned the room and his expression soured. "We flew in a couple of days ago, even with all the damn snow. We represent some investors who are looking to put in a mall in the downtown area."

James took a bite of his quiche to allow him a moment to think of a response. He glanced down at the flaky crust and its savory taste and homemade quality impressed him. The quiche was probably one of the best egg breakfasts he had ever tasted. It impressed him so much that he almost forgot that Barry had asked him a question.

"I don't do much shopping," he finally said. He was never one to enjoy shopping at all, especially in malls. Besides, he had an assistant to be his personal shopper. "Do you really think the people in this town, with their small-time ways, would like a big mall downtown?"

"There really isn't a decent place to shop."

James was enjoying messing with them a bit too much, and said, "Amazon. They have drones now that will deliver your purchases." He motioned with his hand like a small airplane. "I hear the big cities use them. Is that what you fellas are talking about?"

He knew they weren't, but it was fun to watch Barry shake his head and give a slight sneer as if he didn't believe a local bumpkin could grasp the need for a large, local mall with a food court and franchised stores.

"We're talking about brick-and-mortar stores," Martin explained.

James took another bite of his breakfast, savored the wonderful taste, and then asked, "Do you think any store in a mall could make something this heavenly."

"They are really good," Martin said. "We had dinner here last night and they make a wonderful stew."

"Don't get us wrong." Barry waved dismissively

and returned the topic back to business. "We like your little town, but our investors think the people here might enjoy some different shopping options."

"Fair enough," James said with no fake accent. The men either didn't notice or didn't care that his diction had changed. "I don't like malls, but I know I'm only one person. I don't even make up the main demographic for shopping in this town."

Martin's eyebrow rose, which made James wonder if he should have used such marketing phrases during their conversation.

"The token representative person in this town is a woman. Mid–forties. Wife. Mother. Household income under sixty–thousand per year." Barry counted off on his fingers as he had listed them.

James was aware of the statistics. He was more interested in the working-class demographics, but he researched the place from many different angles before coming out to this town. "A mall would drive out businesses. Stores won't be able to compete and people will lose their jobs."

"They can work at the mall." Martin's smile was wide, pleased with his answer as if everything had come full circle. The response made James wonder if the man really understood the general public or not. "Not only can people work there, but a mall will bring in revenue to your town."

After having walked up and down the main area of town, and knowing its real estate fairly well now,

James had to ask, "Where were you thinking of putting up this mall?"

Martin sat straighter and his smile spread wider across his face. In between bites of his quiche, he said, "We're just here scoping out the place, and making offers for smaller retail sites—not the mall right now, per se."

"Rumor has it that the big paint plant will be closing down." Barry took a sip of his overly sugared coffee. "We're doing our best to negotiate with the factory owners on a selling price so our investors can move in."

Really? James's eyebrow rose and he was lucky not to have coughed up his last sip of coffee. Vagrant Enterprises was negotiating with the Nielson company? This was the first James had heard about it. Maybe they had approached the foreman Craig. James thought about it for a moment, but then dismissed the idea. Craig would have said something.

No. These two were bolstering their influence and position in the town—and for good reason. They thought he was a store owner with land—land that they were eager to gobble up. They wanted to be a big fish in this little pond, but their business ignorance and off–the–rack suits gave them away. And, honestly, if they had presented a bid for the negotiations to the Nielson company, James wouldn't have taken them seriously. They had acquisition lawyers on retainer for that type of service—not that Vagrant Enterprises probably was hoping that they didn't.

"The paint plant is shutting down?" James asked as nonchalantly as he could.

Martin looked around, as if checking that no one was eavesdropping, and leaned in. "Some of the factory workers have been talking about the head honcho showing up and inspecting the place." He made eye contact with Barry before staring back at James. "These workers are not happy. Rumor has it that the plant will close down soon after the holidays," he whispered. "You live here in town. Have you heard anything?"

James had to wonder if he had 'small town idiot' written on his forehead. These two had no clue how to keep a business plan confidential. It was a good thing he did. "I haven't heard anything," he said, shrugging.

Martin let out a deep sigh. "We met with the owners of a small diner, a shoe store, and a few other places. With the tough economy, they seem eager to sell." His eyebrow lifted, "We'd be interested in talking to you some more about your business and future in this town."

"Small diner?" James asked, his interest piqued and he ignored Martin's last comment. As far as he could tell, there was only one diner near the plant.

Had they approached his family about selling out the business?

Worse yet, had they convinced them to do so?

No more grandmotherly–handmade pastries. No more jobs for cousins to work. No more family business.

Maybe he wasn't in Newbury to save one family business, but two.

He now understood what errand his aunt had to take care of yesterday. She was meeting Tweedle Dee and Tweedle Dum to make arrangements to sell the place. Thinking back on his cousins, they all had smiles on their faces and carried on with their business. They didn't know what Aunt Sandra was planning to do.

Nodding, Martin said, "Not much parking available at the restaurant, but the place used to be a pretty good-sized mill. The lady who owns the restaurant owns all that land."

"Not that she's putting it to good use," Barry scoffed.

James's chest tightened and he had to take in a deep breath. These vultures had already begun circling and he wasn't sure if his aunt was business savvy enough to know of Vagrant's reputation. "You're talking about *Newbury Grill* on Fondern Street?"

"I figured you knew it." Martin grinned. "Just between us, that restaurant is outdated. That building alone is so old."

"Decrepit and old. I'm surprised it is still up to

standard building and food codes, but it is," Barry said. He took a sip of his coffee, making a slurping sound and finishing it, as he scanned the cafe. The expression on his face told James that he didn't find the place to be all that charming.

"Newbury Grill is a landmark. It is a renovated mill, like you said. Plus, the family has worked there for decades. The people in this town are used to eating there."

"Why would it matter if people like the place? A new and improved restaurant, with more variety will be there in the future. It's in a prime spot for a new diner, unless it's converted into a parking garage."

James's heart sank. Whether a new restaurant or a parking garage, the mill would be torn down. Dismissed as though it was nothing. His family's business—the second one—would be gone.

His thoughts immediately went to the family portrait which hung in the place. It had hung there proudly for generations. Those people were his family, his descendants, and his responsibility to look after.

He wasn't sure why he felt this way, but he did.

James didn't want to offer any business advice, at least, not any sound business advice that might give these two bunglers any more fuel to the flame, but he asked, "With the downturn in the economy, and with all the stores that are already closed, why do you think this town is in need of such large economic endeavors?"

The men stared at him and he wished he wouldn't have asked such a pointed question. He certainly didn't want to give away who he was. He revised his question by asking, "I mean, gosh, our town? Why would we need such things?"

"Logistics," Barry said. The man's eyes narrowed and a snarl appeared. "If you understood economic projections, then you'd know that the neighboring town of Wayford—just twenty miles away—has experienced a twenty-three percent growth in new business in the last two years."

"And," Martin chimed in, "a fifteen percent population growth in the last year alone."

Was that right? The main airport was on the north side of that town, and on the side closest to Newbury. He knew that because that was the airport he had flown into. And, it wasn't that long of a drive to his family's home. "And what does Wayford's growth mean for our little town?"

"If the plant closes, the stench will go away. Without the stench, this town is quite nice and a pleasant drive to all the new businesses in Wayford."

"Plus, AT&T Internet cabling is already coming to Newbury. They've already torn up the south side of the town installing cable."

Wayford wasn't mentioned in his company's projections, not that a growing, neighboring town would be a threat or an asset to the Nielson International Corporation. Most of this plant's business had been with the shipping of their paint to other states. "So, this little town is well positioned to explode in home value and retail properties... that is if the town can survive these hard times."

Barry glanced away and frowned. "You have to survive the hard times first."

"Get out now before franchised companies drive you out of business," Martin said reassuringly. "We're here to help the small business owners in this town."

James knew the exact opposite would be true. The land in this town, if what these idiots were saying were true, would only go up in value. Sure, the businesses might get squeezed out, but these store owners would make more money selling later.

He was sure that the Vagrant Enterprise's investors would undercut these people. They could spin any fact they want out of Wayford's growth, and they were putting a dramatic negative spin on it just to scare the business owners into selling for cheap.

He hated dealing with companies like Vagrant; hated their employees who bought into the mindset even more.

Barry shook his head and looked reassuringly at James. "You 'mom and pop places' won't be able to hold out forever to big corporations. We're here to make the transition easier on you." The tone of his voice was soft and reassuring. He may as well be a man sitting in a windowless white van telling children he had candy for them in the back.

James couldn't believe how fortunate he was to enter this little cafe at the right time and have these two jokers as breakfast partners. He had to do something, and fast.

21

There was nothing left to do at the plant unless a miracle presented itself. All day, James and the foreman, Craig, had reviewed financial records, with Craig doing his best to explain the issue and offer suggestions.

James was more determined than ever to keep the plant open, but all of Craig's suggestions wouldn't work.

He didn't want Vagrant Enterprises moving in, and he was right, Vagrant hadn't approached Craig —at least not yet. But there'd be other investors out there circling to pick the company's bones. He didn't want to imagine this building torn down and a mall in its place. Department stores, food court, and plenty of other franchised stores that made a town like this one feel plastic and fake, not comforting and real.

After spending hours grasping at straws, James left the plant deep in thought. He had made arrangements to meet with his Aunt Sandra, his mother's sister, to get some answers. His stomach twisted and he had to admit that he was a bit nervous to meet her. If anyone knew what had happened to cause the rift between the Petersons and the Nielsons, it would be her.

He drove around the neighborhood streets in a second rental car. The press already knew the make and model of the first one, so he'd thought it best to trade it in.

The streets' icy paths and dirty snow were clear now with the heat from the sun beating down all afternoon. Greeting him at the side of the road stood several snowmen, each grinning with pebble–formed smiles, old hats, and rocks for eyes. They were now a third their original height and melting, their original figures contorting to the strains of the sun.

Nothing could stay the same. The snow and ice were melting, but another blustery cold front would come in and new snowmen—snowpeople—would replace the old ones.

Heck, he may as well be the blistering sun coming to kill everything in his path. Kids, not unlike his daughter, lived here. They played here. They were the ones who made those snowpeople. Their parents probably worked at the plant, and the kids themselves likely figured they would one day, as well.

But that wasn't going to happen. James couldn't even think of a buyer for the big building unless Vagrant Enterprises could offer him a legitimate offer. The building would probably sit empty for years, a grim reminder of what it once was.

James's chest tightened in a way that he wouldn't have expected. This was supposed to be an open-and-shut case. Close a plant that wasn't performing anymore. No big deal.

Damn his father for having him come out here and meet with the local people, to stay in the family home, and to meet his mother's family.

Why had his father kept the family separate for so long? Originally, were his mother's kin after the Nielson family money? Was there some dark secret?

The townsfolk seemed too friendly and open to be gold-diggers. In fact, everyone seemed so nice. And this town? Picturesque and perfect for family life. Well, if you could ignore the paint stench.

He had to admit, the smell was wearing down on him. He was barely aware of it anymore.

James drove to the Starbucks, evidently the only one in town, and parked his car. He took a deep breath to center himself before walking into the place. Today, he planned to get some answers.

Once through the door, steam warmed his face

and fogged up his sunglasses. He took off his Ray–
Bans and gazed at the busy place.

A long counter filled with chrome espresso
machines, bean grinders, and coffee carafes with
aromatic brews lined the wall, with a line of people
standing in front of it.

Leave it to Starbucks to be the one busy place the
town had.

To that end, this town was no different than any
other town on the map. And if you've been inside of
one Starbucks, you know the layout of them all.

The smell of freshly brewed coffee mixed with
warm caramel and chocolate hit him. He welcomed
the scent.

People packed the noisy place, but James weaved
through the crowd and stood in the beverage line. He
read today's specials from the colorful chalkboard as he
listened to the soft music playing in the background.

They offered a latte and the usual holiday extras,
same as the Starbucks he frequented back home. He
didn't care for the sweet and fruity specials and
would order his usual dark house blend. At the very
least, some things were the same.

He snaked his way through the line, which
progressed rather quickly. Standing at the glass case
filled with muffins and other sugary desserts, he
ordered his plain coffee.

A tip jar lay near the register. James paid by cash,

and after the little ding of the cash register sounded and he was handed back his change, he placed it in the jar.

His order came immediately, possibly because he hadn't asked for extras—no blends, and no whipped cream. He turned and faced the crowd, wondering where to sit and if his companion had beaten him there.

He grabbed his coffee, and the mug warmed his hand. He gazed across the room of people, most of whom were either on their laptops, talking to a companion, or reading the daily news from newspapers.

That's when a small figure caught his attention. A gray-haired woman, sitting next to the window that offered a view of the street, waved to him.

Her familiar blue, twinkling eyes identified her. She was his aunt. Aunt Sandra, the mother of the waitress—his cousin—Patty.

The woman looked just as he figured his mother would look in her sixties. Still beautiful, still radiant, still... alive.

She had such a motherly look about her that his fear of meeting her subsided. He navigated through the dining room with its spaced-out tables and heavy iron chairs, dodging people's elbows and bags until he came up to the comfy leather couch where the woman sat.

"Are you Sandra?" he asked over the sound of people talking and coffee beans grinding.

Her face lit up, which caused her eyes to twinkle. "Mama was right. You do look a lot like your father." She raised her hand, delicate but firm, and shook his.

She was dressed in a lovely pant suit, in a color that complemented her complexion. Certainly her Sunday best, just to meet him. Perhaps she was a bit nervous as well, although it didn't show on her face.

"It's nice to meet you." He took a seat next to her and sank into the soft cushions. It was hot in the shop, uncomfortably stifling, so he set down his drink and removed his coat. Perhaps he was more nervous about meeting family than he wanted to admit.

"I met your mother, Lorraine, a couple of days ago." He picked up his coffee and took a sip, allowing its bitter warmth to cascade down his throat. "She mentioned that I look a lot like my father."

"Lorraine. Your grandmother." Sandra's smile, wide and ecstatic, conveyed her excitement about meeting him. She also hadn't taken her eyes off him, as though she were afraid he'd disappear if she blinked.

"Yes. My grandmother." Taking ownership of the relationship and titling it as such felt odd, but Lorraine *was* his grandmother. "She owns that diner?" He already knew the answer but didn't know what to ask or how to get the conversation going.

"It's been in the family for decades. Mama still comes in every day and bakes." She gave him a sly smile. "It keeps her active, although she usually naps during this time of day or she'd be here."

"I understand." Studies had proven how important it was to stay active in your later years. Something to do gave you a sense of purpose to keep your mind sharp. James's father planned to travel, to enjoy time with his new wife. It was a good plan, but one that would keep him away from his family—especially his new granddaughter.

Odd that the realization now bothered James.

"And you and your children work there?" he said, still knowing the answers to the questions he asked.

"Me and my daughters do. My sons work at the plant." Her face beamed with pride. She knew his family owned the factory and employed half the town. He was the heir to that fortune and her nephew.

A pang of guilt hit him. Everyone had a family member who worked at his company. But it wasn't just everyone. *His* family worked there, too. They were nameless, faceless people to him—at least at first—but they were blood nonetheless.

He noticed a book sitting next to her. "What's that?"

Sandra pulled out the photo album that lay next to her. "Let me show you some pictures."

The album had an heirloom feel with its black pictures and gold photo corners around each image. "This lovely lady," she said, pointing at a young teen-aged girl, "this is Natalie. Your mother."

He had never seen this picture before, but then again, there had been so few pictures of her at his father's home. "She's so beautiful."

"Oh," Sandra said smiling, "she caught the attention of all the boys." Sandra flipped through a few more pages. He saw images of his grandfather and great-grandparents—everything from formal portraits to candid snapshots during holidays and special events. Many pictures were black and white, with a few later ones in color. The more recent ones were square with white borders, the date stamped in blue ink on the bottom.

As she went through one image after another, explaining who each person was in relation to him, one question burned in his brain. "Do you know why my father never told me about you or that I still had so many relatives in this town?"

Her face paled. "He never told you?"

"No."

Her hands rested on the album, and she let out a sigh—a sound that sounded like she knew the truth. "The Nielsons and the Petersons were both founding members of this town. Both prestigious families. Both patriarchs were successful businessmen."

James nodded, listening intensely, even though the sound of the other patrons, the hum of the coffee makers, and the cashier calling out names was a din in the background.

"Avery Peterson and Mitchell Nielson were business partners." She flipped through the book and showed him a picture of the two men standing together in front of the first Nielson store. "They both started the plant, that is until your grandmother came between them."

"Lorraine came between them?"

"Your other grandmother, on the Nielson side." Sandra shook her head and gave a sigh as though the story were complicated. "Your paternal grandmother, Camilla, was a rare beauty. Educated. Strong. Both men fancied her, but she ended up marrying Mitchell." Sandra shook her head. "I doubt that's why your father never came back to the town, but Camilla was the start of a bitter rivalry between the families."

James had never even heard of Camilla before.

"Avery Peterson soon met the love of his life, my mother, Lorraine." Sandra pointed to a picture of a young Lorraine in a spring-time dress standing next to Avery.

Sandra's smile told him that Lorraine was in no way the runner-up. He had met her, witnessed her charm, and she had seen him for who he really was. It was likely nothing got past her.

"My parents met just before Camilla married your grandfather, Mitchell." Sandra flipped a few pages in the album and stopped at a newspaper clipping of a woman standing, all in white, next to a man in a suit. "Here is a picture of Camilla. Mama always said she was grateful to her for leaving my father alone. I think that is why she clipped this article, and kept it."

James stared at the image of his grandparents. It had been taken on their wedding day, and they were looking straight at the camera, stiff and still—like everyone did in the early days of photography. Even with the worn newsprint, James could tell that his grandmother was an attractive woman.

"Later, your father married your mother, Natalie, who was Avery's daughter—my sister." Sandra turned a few pages and showed their wedding picture. "Like the Hatfield's and McCoy's. Neither family got along, especially since the Nielson plant was originally the Nielson–Peterson plant. Your grandfather, although he did it legally, squeezed out the Peterson family from the paint business."

A dull pain flared deep in James's chest. His grandfather had had a partner. All those years ago, someone else—another family—had started the Nielson company and helped make it what it was today. James figured a romance wouldn't be enough to cause a family rift, it had to be tied to either money, fortune, or fame. He needed to clarify. "My paternal grandfather squeezed my maternal grandfather out of the business *legally*?"

"There had been some funds missing, and the guilty party was a member of the Peterson clan." Sandra shook her head and gave a wry smile. "My great–uncle stole the daily receipts and was caught."

James didn't know how much the daily receipts would have added up to back in the day, but legally severing the business ties to the plant would have cost the Peterson family a fortune over time.

His aunt's face pinched, and she looked deep in thought. "My uncle went to jail for... I want to say two years or so." She shook her head as if the time didn't matter. "But the trust was gone. Your grandfather bought the Petersons out of the business, and that was the end of it."

James did his best to follow the time-line. "Was that before or after my father married my mother?"

"Years before. The pain of having her uncle steal from the company and go to jail in shame was too much for Natalie. She and Gregory moved away. She wanted to return to the town once the initial gossip and rumors of their Romeo and Juliet romance died down, but your father had outgrown the place. He never wanted to come back." She shrugged. "At least, that's what she wrote to me in her letters."

James could believe that. He had been here less

than a week and, as charming as the town was, he was already going a bit stir crazy. "But surely my mother must have visited."

"She planned to, but she wasn't gone that long." Sandra let out a sigh, one that held deep sorrow. "She gave birth to you a year later, and planned to bring you home so we could meet you."

His mother had died in childbirth, and that trip had never happened.

Sandra wiped away a tear. "Your father never came back. I guess it's not surprising that you didn't know about all the family you have here. That man never even sent us a Christmas picture of you or even a school photo." She smiled and gazed at him. "You're such a handsome man."

His lips curled upward at the compliment, but he knew that his father would never send personal cards with family pictures. Maybe he would have had his secretary do it, but that still didn't sound like Gregory. Although, now, with his fourth marriage and being in his seventies, the man had seemingly softened. "My father is the one who suggested I come for a visit."

"Really? That surprises me. He always hated this place and claimed that Natalie was the only good thing to come out of the town." Sandra patted the album. "I have a mess of old photo albums at home if you'd like to see them."

"I'd love to."

22

*M*elanie and Arianna arrived early to Kinder Musik. Another diaper change was needed, some spit–up had to be dealt with, and a new outfit had to be put on.

Now that Arianna was taken care of, the baby lay on her Kinder Musik mat waiting for the other students and Abby to show up. She squirmed like a little angel, jiggling a set of bells in her hands and giggling at the sounds they made.

She seemed content and happy, so Melanie pulled out her phone to check her email. Her latest notice came from Vassar College with the subject, "Congratulations."

She had waited for so long for this email. The paperwork had already come, but so much more information was available online.

Her thumb hovered over the link. She had

dreamed of going to Vassar her entire life. She wouldn't quite be following in her mother's footsteps; she'd be taking the route her mother couldn't.

She clicked the link and dates appeared for freshman orientation. Dates as well as a fee to attend. Naturally. Nothing in life was free. She still had time to accept the offer to attend, could still make the orientation, she just couldn't pay to live for the next four years.

And, she needed money to live on. She was fond of eating, and didn't want to give it up.

Even though her tuition would be free, she'd still have to pay for a dorm room, meal plan, parking permit, books, and all the fees the college couldn't think of to tag onto the bill. Lab fees, library fees, gym fees, processing fees, and, of course, fees to cover the fees. She knew how that game worked.

A link to set up a student portal was listed in the email. She was teasing herself, but she clicked it. Arianna was still content on the mat and playing peacefully, so Melanie had a few minutes.

"There's no harm in at least setting up a portal and looking around." She gazed at Arianna and in baby speak said, "No, no harm at all. Portals are free."

She realized that Arianna would grow up in a world where portals were common. At least, until they'd be replaced by the next high-tech thing. Melanie had a different portal for each doctor she had and couldn't even schedule an appointment or check bloodwork without logging in. Heck, even her electric company now had a portal for her to sign into.

Arianna would take that as normal. She lived in a world where television was always paid for, where your phone was a computer, and when someone called, they called *you* and not your *house*, meaning you could never be 'out' and miss a call.

Arianna would never even know what a busy signal on a telephone was.

But technology was a blessing and it moved at the speed of light, even if it came later to such small tows as Newbury.

She set up the Vassar student portal and clicked a tab for "Student Resources." There she found links to student housing, meal plans, course selection, and scholarships. Being curious, she clicked on student housing just to see the costs and immediately regretted doing so.

How could people afford to live in New York? Even getting an apartment off campus would break her.

She was about to cancel the page and forget about Vassar when she decided to click on the scholarship tab. Dozens of opportunities appeared, which gave her hope.

"Some of these are just for freshman," she said to Arianna, who still played with a belled instrument on the mat. The girl seemed happy, so Melanie continued to study her phone.

Melanie scanned through the first page of the listing. "Some require an essay." She placed her hand on Arianna's tummy and patted it to make sure the child knew she was still there—although independent play was so important at this age for a child, and Arianna was enjoying herself.

"I have plenty of essays I've written." She tagged the ones she qualified for which needed an essay and kept scanning the list.

"Wow, some of these require a video. I don't know how to edit video and make something look professional, so... next."

She shook her head. "I'm not going to take pictures and put them on social media with certain hashtags either. I don't even have social media accounts." The fact that many of the scholarships required some sort of social media discouraged her.

"Some of these are very specific. I want to major in art not a science degree...Oh, here's one specifically for art." She clicked the link and became disappointed. "My parents aren't first responders so..." she exited that option and said, "next."

Once she filled out the very few scholarships she did qualify for, she bookmarked the page so she could come back quicker. She already had the tuition money with her free ride. Most of the scholarships were only to be used for tuition though.

Didn't people realize that it cost just as much to live during your college years as the tuition itself?

"I'll have to keep checking these listings. What I really need is a miracle." She clicked the app for 'Student Life'. Attending was only a pipe dream, but she could at least fantasize.

The first image she saw of Vasser was two rows of five-storied, red brick buildings. Between the rows lay a green courtyard. Surrounding everything were tall trees full of autumn colored leaves. "Look at this picture, sweetie." Melanie held the phone so Arianna could see the beautiful colors. "This is where I want to go. I want to study art and make a living from painting beautiful pictures."

Arianna had the toy in her mouth but she glanced up to the phone. An excitement overcame her at seeing the tiny screen. "Bwaa-aha."

Her hand reached for the device so Melanie pulled it away. "Not with those slobber hands." She reached into the diaper bag and pulled out a cloth to wipe the baby's mouth. She was definitely teething, but at least she wasn't in any pain and crying.

"The college is pretty, isn't it?" Melanie flipped through more pictures and showed them to Arianna, keeping the phone out of arms reach. Each image stirred an excitement within Melanie, a yearning. And, each image stirred disappointment.

"I hope you get to attend whatever college you want. I'm sure your father will set up some sort of trust fund or whatever rich people do for their children."

Tears welled in her eyes and she needed to put the phone away. She wanted Arianna to never worry about money, and she was lucky to have a rich father. She didn't want to begrudge the child for having been born into a rich family. It was nobody's fault that Melanie was from a small, humble town and had no parents. No college fund. No escape.

"I'm still young." Melanie wiped away a tear that had escaped. "Besides, if I ..." No, she wouldn't get rehired at the plant and save her money. She took in a deep breath. "I'll find another job, save my money, and maybe one day—one day soon I hope—I'll reapply to Vassar and then I'll be able to live the life I want."

Abby walked through the door and set down her bag with a thud. Gone was her relaxed mood and cheerful smile from the last class. Instead, Melanie could tell by the frown on Abby's face and the way she held her body—tight, her jaw clenched—that something was wrong.

"Are you okay, Abby?"

Abby spun around, and she seemed surprised to see Melanie on the floor. "Oh, you scared me."

"You look upset."

Abby raked her fingers through her hair and took a deep breath. Melanie could see that the woman wore no makeup today, and her clothes and hair were not quite as carefully picked out as previously. In particular, her hair band, shirt, and skirt didn't match.

"I'm fine." Abby walked to the counter and took out all the instruments the class would need, but she slumped her shoulders once she lay the boxes on the table. "My mother fell yesterday morning."

"Is she all right?" Since Arianna seemed content on the mat, Melanie stood and approached Abby.

Abby's hand circled the top of her head indicating where the wound was. "She got a deep cut when she hit the side of a table. We had to call an ambulance."

A head injury. A fall was bad enough if a hip or bone were broken, but a concussion or other head trauma, especially at that age, seemed more severe. The woman was also suffering from dementia. "Did she trip?"

"She's a fall risk—has been for a few months now. Sadly, this isn't the first fall she's had, just the worst one." Abby's gaze connected with Melanie's. "She's still at the hospital. She needed stitches over her left eye and her face," Abby gestured to the left side of her own head, "she has a bruise already forming that covers this entire side."

"Sounds like an awful fall."

"It was, but she's ready to be released now."

Melanie didn't know Abby's family, other than who they were and that they lived north of town, but she still wished the best for the woman. "That's good. That means she's stable enough to come home, right?"

"You don't understand. They will either release her to me, because..."—she let out a soft chuckle —"because *I* can take care of her. Or they'll release her to an elder–care facility." Abby's expression turned to one of sorrow. She opened the box of bells, the same ones that Melanie had found laying out that Arianna still played with.

She then opened a box of train whistles, and Melanie could tell she had tears in her eyes.

Melanie placed a hand on Abby's shoulder. "You did say your mother probably would need an elderly care center to take care of her."

Abby shook her head. "My husband works at the plant, so he'll probably be out of work soon. The little work I do, although part–time, does help. Of course, we now have a huge medical bill to pay off. My mother went by ambulance to the hospital, was seen by several doctors, and had an overnight hospital stay."

Yeesh. Melanie could understand the financial worry. The family would most likely be paying off the bill for years.

"It's not the money. I'm more concerned with my mother, of course. But..." Abby closed her eyes and let out a mournful sigh. "I'll have to quit my jobs and take care of her full–time. But if my husband loses *his* job, we'll need me to work. But," she said in a sarcastic tone, "I can always pay a facility four thousand dollars a month to take care of her."

Melanie's eyes widened, and the wind was knocked out of her. "Four thousand dollars a month?"

"It's memory care, not just retirement care, so it's much more expensive." Abby shook her head and Melanie could see the desperation in her eyes. "She'll also have to live in Canton, fifteen miles from here since we don't have a place that meets her needs in Newbury."

How on Earth could people afford such care? Melanie quickly did the math. "That's nearly fifty thousand dollars a year... and that comes out of your net earnings." Melanie stared in disbelief. "You'd have to make at least sixty thousand dollars a year just to take care of your mother, and that wouldn't even begin to cover your living costs—and you're a family of three."

"And I'll want to visit her," Abby continued. "A thirty-mile, round-trip visit several times a week will take up gas money and a lot of my time." She shook her hand and waived dismissively. "Not that my mother isn't worth me taking the time to visit with. I'm lucky to still have her..." She looked squarely at Melanie. The expression was a familiar one to her, one that Melanie saw often. "I'm sorry. I know you lost both of your parents. I shouldn't complain."

"No. It's fine." Melanie gently rubbed Abby's shoulder. Naturally, Melanie wished her parents were still alive. Even if she had financial difficulties in taking care of them, she'd gladly take money burdens on if she could have her parents back.

But it was nice, even if it were only a few minutes, that someone didn't tip-toe around the topic of parents with her. Being treated like a friend and not the lonely orphan was nice for a change.

Abby was a few years older than Melanie so her mother couldn't be more than in her sixties. "Your mother is still young. You'd be paying that kind of money for decades."

Nodding, Abby said, "She's turning seventy–two in a few months."

No spring chicken, but certainly not very old at all. "But, still."

Melanie had no idea that elder care could be that expensive. Melanie's parents were gone so she wouldn't need to worry about them, but eventually, her aunt and uncle may need help. And, more importantly, she wanted to be there for them if needed.

You do for family.

"That side of my family has longevity, too. Many family members lived to be in their nineties." Abby took in a deep breath. "Some became centennials and lived even over a hundred." She grabbed some train whistles out of the box and set them on the counter next to the bells she had gathered. The class would start soon and she needed to get ready. "I don't know what to do. I need a miracle of fast cash, and my husband to remain employed."

Abby's face pinched in pain. "You know it's sad when you hope you don't live so long to be a burden like this to your family."

"Oh, Abby." Melanie held her hand. "Don't think of it like that."

"Not that I see my mother as a burden. Don't get me wrong." A sniffle escaped. "It's just hard not to think of the money when you worry that you can't financially take care of your family."

"An answer will come. It always does." The words sounded hollow to Melanie. She had heard such things in the past and found them less than comforting, but still she said, "It will all work out in the end. You'll see."

"I'll need a miracle."

"Thank keep your eyes open for one. Miracles happen every day. There's no reason one can't happen for you and your family."

Melanie stared at the train whistles and the other musical instruments for the class. There wasn't a lot of money in teaching children's classes. A pang of guilt crept over her since she was probably the only local in town who knew about the plant's fate.

23

"She looks happy." Melanie sat across from James on the chair in the Nielson home's living room, folding some freshly washed baby clothes as he played with Arianna. The scent of the clean fabric mixed with the fragrance of James's cologne, and Melanie enjoyed the smell.

It was a Norman Rockwell type of smell, that is, if his paintings were scratch-and-sniff.

James gazed up at her. "Ten minutes of playing peek–a–boo. I think my brain is going to turn to mush if I keep this up."

Arianna let out a squeal as her father covered his eyes once more and then let out a "peek–a–boo" shout once he revealed his eyes once again.

"But, how can I stop if you love it so much?" He smiled down at his daughter, seemingly thrilled that they had found something to do together that didn't end with her crying. During the game, though, Arianna had become a slobbery mess, and her shirt, as well as the blanket he initially used to hide his eyes, was soaked.

"Does she look like she's sprung a leak?"

Melanie studied the amount of drool spilling from Arianna's mouth. "She's teething." She grabbed a teething ring from the table and tossed it to him. "Give her this, it's still a little cold."

He placed the ring near Arianna's mouth, and the girl gnawed on it. "She's getting teeth?" His face lit up as he helped his daughter to hold the ring in place. "I've missed so many firsts with her."

Yeah, he was a good dad. Inexperienced and nervous about spending time with her, but getting better by the hour. Melanie couldn't help but smile and take in the entire picture.

"She'll probably drool all over this, but it's okay." She handed him a cloth book with a bear on the front. "She's already in pajamas, has been fed, and now should slowly wind down so she'll go to bed."

"*Baby Bear's Big Day*," James said, taking the book from Melanie and reading the title. "I didn't even know they made books out of cloth." He gazed down at his daughter. "Looks like it's a super absorbent book for you."

Melanie finished folding the laundry as she watched James read the book. He pointed out the colors, talked about how the bear felt about his day, and how tired he felt at the end. The book even showed the bear being tucked into bed.

"Is it time for you to go to bed?" James read from the last page of the book and set the teething ring down. "Good night. We can play again tomorrow." He placed the book on the couch, and Arianna yawned and closed her eyes. "That was a good book, wasn't it, honey."

Melanie had noticed him calling his daughter *sweetheart* and some other terms of endearment, but *honey* seemed to fit. The word came out easily now when he talked to her, and he seemed to like the comfort of calling her that.

"I found that book at Wal–Mart today. I also bought a cool video monitor so I can watch her from any room in the house." Melanie stood and held out her hands. "I can put her to bed."

"I'd like to do it." Carefully, James stood and held his daughter tightly in his arms.

Wow. The baby steps were now big strides. Melanie placed a burp cloth on his shoulder. "You're doing a great job, James. She's happy and content to spend time with you and to be in your arms."

He took in a deep breath, and his beaming–with–pride face showed that he enjoyed the affirmation. "I'm really trying." He gazed down at his daughter, who lay half asleep in his arms. "She makes it easy."

She didn't want to intrude or suggest that he

couldn't do it on his own, but just to be sure she asked, "Do you need some help putting her to bed?"

James shook his head. "I read up on how to do it. No pillows, no blankets, no choking hazards in her bed..." He then shot Melanie a look as if he remembered the teddy bear incident earlier. "Maybe you should supervise."

A smile quickly came to Melanie's face, and she followed him up the stairs to her bedroom where James did a textbook–perfect job of putting his baby to bed.

"I NEED to wash the dishes and pick up the toys downstairs." As Melanie headed down the stairs with the new baby monitor, she was surprised that James followed her.

Surely, he had work to do. If the last several nights in the town had proven anything, the man liked to work in the evenings. From what she could tell, he worked into the wee hours of the morning. But then, he was probably calling people in Europe and taking care of his international business.

Melanie removed the diaper bag from the stroller, remembering that the baby bottles needed to be washed. "No work tonight?"

"I didn't work at all today. I met my aunt and had a nice talk with her."

It was odd to think of him not working, but she focused on what she knew of his family who remained in town. "Sandra at the diner?" she asked, heading to the kitchen.

His expression changed. For a moment, he almost looked hurt.

"I didn't even know I still had family in this town. Now I've met my grandmother, my aunt, and several cousins."

"You didn't know you still had family here?" Everyone knew the Nielsons had left long ago, but the Petersons—although not the wealthiest or most prestigious founding family—were still cornerstones in the town.

"I used to work at that diner."

His eyebrow rose. "Really? I didn't know you had worked there."

"It's where I got the recipe for the lasagna I made." She smiled and thought back to her first real job. "My parents had just died, and my brother and I moved in with my aunt and uncle. We sold my parents' home, and the money helped, but I still needed to find a job. Sandra allowed me to work after school and then full-time after that until my brother left for college."

Caleb was Melanie's pride and joy. Smart, handsome, and full of life. He looked so much like a mix of her parents that seeing him was a comfort to her. Making sure he had a good start in life with a college education was the one thing she'd felt she could do for her parents.

"Caleb's my younger brother. He now lives in Florida with his wife and baby boy." Her lips curled into a proud smile. "He's done well for himself, and working at that diner allowed me to get him to where he is today."

It wasn't concern or pity that she saw in his eyes, it was a comforting gaze—one that matched the slight smile on his face. "You did all that for your brother?"

"Of course. You're supposed to be there for family, no matter what."

"That's nice." His smile widened and he nodded his head slightly, evidently taking it all in. "What made you quit the job at the diner?"

There were so many reasons. After her parents' deaths, the whole town had rallied to help her and Caleb out. Free meals were delivered, free tutoring was offered by the school, and even free school supplies given by the local grocery store. The town had helped, but charity—especially when times are tough—can only last so long, and eventually, you need to overcome your adversities and move on.

"Sandra didn't need me as a waitress, which is why I quit. Her daughters work there, and even though they wanted to help me, her girls needed the work hours that I was taking."

She let out a sigh, thinking about how hard it

had been to find a job in town. Even having lived here her entire life, and being as well connected as she was, it was difficult. "It was time to move on. I worked at the daycare, Wal–Mart, the gas station...." She didn't want to go through the entire exhaustive list since it was quite lengthy, plus he had seen her resume when he had hired her. "I think everyone in town got to know me."

There was a pause in the conversation, like he wanted her to continue. Gazing into his eyes, Melanie found a man who not only listened but also showed compassion toward her. She never wallowed in her own pity and hated the emotion from others, but she felt the need to share.

"After a while, once you get to a certain age in this town, people expect you to get married and have kids." She bit her lower lip and thought back to Trevor and the life they would have had together, a life she'd chosen not to have—for several reasons. "I was engaged to that reporter, but I broke off the engagement."

She unpacked the diaper bag, James following her every step closely with his eyes.

"May I ask why you didn't marry him?"

The whole town knew one story, the one she had led them to believe: that she hated kids and wanted more than to be just a wife and a mother. But there remained an untold truth, one that had been eating away at her. She looked deep into James's eyes. He would be leaving soon, and it seemed harmless to share the real story with someone who would leave and never return.

"Trevor wanted kids and a wife who was always barefoot and pregnant." Melanie shook her head and took in a cleansing breath. It was James's soft eyes and concerned expression that gave her the strength to continue. "I probably can't have kids, so I told him I didn't want any. He decided to marry my best friend. Their baby is due this month."

As painful as it was to admit everything, a heaviness left her chest. Someone else now knew what her doctor had told her. She wasn't alone with the secret anymore.

One of his eyebrows rose. "You can't have kids?"

His voice didn't sound judgmental, not filled with pity either. His soft, blue eyes showed strong, caring emotions for her; his interest that made her feel safe.

"Long story. I had one ovary and fallopian tube removed for medical reasons, so my chances of conceiving are low." She thought back to how long it had taken for her to pay off the medical bills, but that was now behind her.

His hand came to rest on her shoulder. "I'm so sorry."

She fought back the urge to cry and glanced upward so the tears that were welling up wouldn't be shed. "Hormone therapy and fertility drugs will help when the time is right. The treatment requires money." She continued staring up at the ceiling, and a wry smile crossed her face. "It requires a man, too. I haven't had so much as a date since I broke up with Trevor."

Melanie felt her cheeks flush and she now looked over to James. She hadn't meant for that little part of her life to leak out. Why not just tell him that she was the least desirable woman in the county?

"You haven't dated since the breakup?" James's face still showed his concern, but now he was frowning. "That was, at least nine months ago. Are you still in love with him?"

She snorted, which surprised her. It was so unladylike, and snot nearly shot out of her nose. "Gosh, no. The bastard cheated on me with Stephanie. I've even heard recent rumors that he's been cheating on her while she's been pregnant."

James's face hardened. "My ex–wife was a cheater."

"I'm sorry." Melanie could have Goggled information about James but had chosen not to. She hated that everyone seemed to know everything about her, so why delve into someone else's privacy? It felt nice that he was opening up to her. It felt really nice.

And, overall, James having been married didn't surprise her. He was roughly a decade older than she was, rich, and, not to mention, incredibly handsome. "I didn't know you were once married."

"I was. She wasn't." He shrugged, but she could tell there probably was more to the story than that. "The marriage lasted only fourteen months. That was years ago."

In a town where people like her aunt and uncle remained married for life, fourteen months was a sliver of time. Melanie mustered up her courage and asked the one question that had been on her mind for days. "And you and Vivian Saunders? Are you two planning on eventually getting married?"

His lips went thin and his eyes cold. "There's nothing there but a future custody war for Arianna."

A bubble of excitement grew within her. She had suspected that nothing existed between James and the actress, and he had alluded to as much, but Arianna was so young, and sometimes relationships were complicated.

"She's a busy actress who abandoned our daughter. She's not going to win custody. I'll have my best lawyers working on it."

Melanie believed that he would fight for his daughter. For someone who had just found out that they were a father, she could tell James wanted to be a good parent and to have Arianna in his life.

"Children should be raised by caring people like you, James."

His face lit up and a tinkle showed in his eyes. "Thank you."

A flutter of excitement welled within her and she became very aware of how close he stood to her.

"You never did answer my question earlier," he said.

"What question?"

"Your ex–fiancé... Trevor, right?" When she nodded, he continued. "Why did Trevor say you were bad with babies? You're obviously good with them."

Her heart sank and she felt the air leave the room. She didn't want any lie between the two of them, especially since he had been so open with her about his love life and daughter. "Trevor actually said I *hate* babies not that I'm not good with them."

For someone she had just met, why was it that his eyes could see all the way into her soul? "I've let the whole town believe that I hate children, even though I'd love to be a mother one day. It's just easier to tell a lie than let everyone know the real truth. I'm already considered to be an old maid in this town. Once I don't have kids, they'll all suspect something anyway." She set the empty baby food jars on the counter to be rinsed and recycled, and the bottles next to the sterilizer to be washed and sanitized.

"So, you're living a lie."

It was more than just that, so much more. "No, I'm *surviving*." Tears welled up in her eyes once again and she turned toward the sink. "I think there is a bottle at the bottom of the stroller," she said, counting the bottles and realizing there was one missing. "Would you mind fetching it?"

JAMES WENT BACK to the living room, his thoughts consumed by what Melanie had told him.

Not just told him, but confided in him.

A woman who was a natural mother should definitely have children. The idea of her not having kids one day, it just didn't make sense. Why would someone like Vivian, who was in his mind heartless, be able to get pregnant so easily. And a good quality woman like Melanie couldn't? Fertility drugs were expensive, hard on the body, and didn't always result in a blessed visit from the stork.

Life wasn't fair.

Melanie was so beautiful. Her luxurious hair, emerald eyes, and high cheekbones should be passed down to a child. Same with her charms, gracious manner, and her wonderful ability to sing. In any town, even one as small as this one, there should be a ton of men wanting to take her out, put a ring on her finger, and claim her as theirs.

And she hadn't dated anyone in nearly a year?

That really made no sense.

Actually, Melanie never did say how long it was,

he had only assumed the man got his new bride pregnant and had to marry her. Maybe it had been years since the breakup, and her bed had been empty this entire time.

He took a deep breath and shook his head, not wanting to think about her empty bed and how easily he could fill it. She wasn't some cheap floozy that jumped into bed with a man just for sport. She was the 'take home to mother' type of woman, and he could respect that.

Melanie had shared more in these past five minutes than what he had learned about his ex–wife in the short few months he was married to her. It was more information than he had even gotten from Vivian, and they created another human being together.

Now, thinking about the quality of women that frequented his bed, none of them had ever shared their lives with him. All his past relationships had been about sex. He had seen a counselor after his divorce, and she had told him as much, but he didn't believe her—which is why he was only in therapy for a short while.

Gosh, he'd even dated his therapist after he stopped the sessions. That relationship was only one wild weekend in Vegas. He couldn't even remember her first name.

That slimy feeling of shame covered him. Was he as bad as Trevor? Trevor only wanted a mommy machine. All James had wanted were sex–toys. No commitment, no worries, absolutely no kids.

And now, he had Arianna.

His heart skipped a beat. What if someone, one day, treated Arianna like he had treated the women in his life? What if someone tossed her aside after... he didn't even want to think about that. Her heart would be broken.

No. He needed to focus on other things.

He needed to focus on moving forward. Moving forward as a better father and a better man.

Maybe now he needed to focus on stronger relationships with women. Ones that lasted longer than a few months or a weekend.

But women were usually only after his money.

"Did you find the bottle?" Melanie's voice rang out from the kitchen and reminded him of his task.

"I'll bring it right in," he said, walking to the stroller.

Melanie was different. She was like an open book, a volume that he wanted to read. There was no secret agenda, no undercover plot, and no games to be played. And, he never would have guessed the turmoil and hardship of her life. She had kept her family together after her parents died, was a hard–worker, and—as far as he could see—was grateful to this town and didn't gripe and complain about her lot in life.

Was it this town that turned out such honest and

caring people? He then thought about Trevor and... good Lord, how could the man have cheated on Melanie? Melanie was gorgeous, intelligent, caring... the whole package.

Maybe this town grew honest women. His mother, his aunt, his grandmother, Melanie, and her aunt, they were all wonderful.

James checked the stroller. The carriage portion was empty, so he checked in the compartment down below. There, he found the bottle as well as a letter from Vassar College. The torn envelope told him that Melanie had already read it.

Was she planning on attending the university? Or was she taking classes remotely?

Either way, it was an expensive school in New York. Vassar, which was only forty minutes from his home, was a college that most people couldn't afford.

He set the letter back in the stroller and returned to the kitchen with the bottle. Melanie now wore a blue–flowered apron tied around her thin waist. She wiped her hands on the cloth and took the bottle from him.

There were no sequins, silk, or chiffon. No expensive shoes, handbags, or jewelry. She stood at the sink, her back now to him, in jeans, a T–shirt, and an apron. Her hair was pulled up in a messy but sexy bun that showed the nape of her soft and kiss-able neck.

"Do you need some help?" He had never washed

a dish in his life, but he was willing to scour every pan in the place just to be near her.

"It won't take long, but thanks."

He glimpsed Arianna in the video of the baby monitor. She was still asleep, and it was still early.

"I need just a few minutes to make a call." He went to the pantry and pulled out a bottle of red wine. "Thank you for keeping Arianna safe today."

"Of course." Melanie filled the sink with water. "I'll have to wash everything in cold water I guess..."—she paused a second as the pipes squealed to life—"oh, wait, the hot water just turned on."

Every night as he went upstairs to work, she had cleaned the kitchen, put away the toys, and kept a close ear on the baby monitor when she wasn't physically taking care of Arianna.

He didn't know how often Arianna woke up in the middle of the night, nor did he know how many diapers she went through during the day. Melanie made everything look so easy.

Melanie was also, probably, going to school. She was intelligent, caring, and... his eyes studied her bottom as she washed the dishes. Sexy. So incredibly sexy.

"You're a lovely person, Melanie."

She turned and stared at him. Her expression was soft as if she enjoyed hearing the compliment. He thought that made her look even sexier.

"Thanks, James." She gave him a slight smile, and her cheeks blushed; he liked the innocent schoolgirl look.

But he needed to take care of something before he forgot. "I'll be off my call shortly. Would my partner in dodging the press be interested in a glass of wine when I come back down?"

24

A glass of wine?

A glass of wine with the most handsome and eligible bachelor in town?

Heck, yes.

Melanie quickly rinsed the suds off the bottles and placed them in the sterilizer. She set the timer and realized that her shirt held the stench of sour formula from an unfortunate spit–up accident earlier in the day.

And her hair was a mess.

When was the last time she'd brushed her teeth?

She took a deep breath to calm her nerves. Just because James had asked if she wanted a glass of wine didn't mean that he saw her as anything but an employee. After all, it was the holiday. Christmas was just a couple of days away.

But when did a boss enjoy a glass of wine with the domestic help?

Okay. Melanie needed some clues. Signs to indicate what he actually meant by her having a drink with him.

She paced as she took off the apron. She could decipher this.

Placing the garment on the counter, she held up her hand and counted on her fingers.

James had opened up to her about his fears. Check.

He had touched her shoulder when she told him something personal. Check.

She stared at the two fingers that she held up in the air. Was there a third check? A third would be the telltale sign.

The compliment! He had said she was lovely. There may have also been a *caring* thrown in from yesterday.

Her face pinched. Caring sounded like he was pleased with his nanny selection. Lovely is what you said to an old aunt who knitted you a sweater.

She took a deep breath and was reminded of the sour smell wafting from her shirt. No matter what the wine invitation represented, no matter what might happen, she couldn't spend the evening with Arianna's spit–up on her blouse. Thank goodness she'd gotten more clothes from her apartment.

Melanie crept up the creaking stairs and heard

James's muffled voice coming from behind his closed bedroom door. She slowly entered her room, but could barely see since she couldn't turn the light on with Arianna sleeping.

Using touch alone, she found a clean T–shirt and her hairbrush. She got a glimpse of the crib with Arianna still sound asleep. The floor heater had made the room toasty... at least warm enough so that Melanie didn't have to go to bed at seven thirty in the evening to keep Arianna warm.

If Arianna followed her usual pattern, she'd be asleep for a few hours, want something to eat, and then would go back to sleep with some cuddling in the big bed.

So, there were at least two or three hours of adult time that could happen. Wine, conversation... yeah, adult stuff.

Melanie felt her skin flush, and an ache began in her core. She had actually told James that she hadn't been on a date in nearly a year. It had been even longer since she'd had a man in her bed.

Glancing at Arianna, Melanie knew the latter wouldn't happen. But, having a man hold her, having that close connection, maybe even a kiss... her life had been so empty, so lonely. Melanie's heart fluttered at the thought of James touching her.

She crept out of the room and made her way to the bathroom, noticing that James's door remained closed. She'd planned to give herself only five minutes of prep time before she went back downstairs.

She closed the narrow bathroom door and stared at her reflection in the mirror. Messy bun... gone. No hair blowout, but a good brushing made her hairdo somewhat passable.

Brushing her teeth and then drinking wine? That sounded awful, so she brushed without tooth-paste and rinsed thoroughly.

James's razor and kit sat on the side of the sink next to a stack of newly bought towels that still had price tags on them. The case was black leather. No fuss, just manly. The tiny bag smelled of his cologne and aftershave, which held a powerful and robust scent.

Melanie took in a deep whiff and enjoyed the smell. She had noticed the scents every time he was near her, and especially tonight when he sat so close to her.

She had been lonely for too long.

Five minutes were up. Melanie studied her reflection. Not the best, but it was a far cry from being the hot mess she'd been earlier.

She heard James's door slide open, so she dashed out of the bathroom and turned off the light.

"Is Arianna all right?" he asked, his gaze moving to the bedroom door.

"She's fine." Melanie led him back down the stairs, wondering where the night was headed.

Two wine glasses, a bottle of Merlot, and some soft Christmas music played in the background.

James had finally realized the beauty of this house, but it had more to do with Melanie, who now sat next to him on the couch, than anything else.

He wanted to comment on how beautiful she looked, or offer her another compliment, but instead, he said, "It's too bad we can't start a fire in the fireplace." James glanced at the stonework and the mantel, pretending to be interested in the fine craftsmanship. "We'd have to have the flue cleaned, I'm sure."

Melanie pulled the blanket off the back of the couch. "If you're cold, we do have blankets." She draped the soft weave between them.

His hand gently touched the fabric. "This is a nice blanket. I wonder if my grandmother made it."

Why was he talking about the blanket and his grandmother? He'd never had a problem talking to women before, at least not to the ones he usually attracted. Within the last year, he had been with three wealthy heiresses and a... he guessed a beauty pageant contestant. She had certainly bored him enough talking about her trophies.

James set the blanket aside and took the opportunity to slide closer to Melanie. "I'm fine."

Melanie took a sip from her glass. "This wine is nice."

He had picked up the cheap bottle at a small grocery store near the plant. Overall, the wine wasn't bad for costing under twenty dollars.

An awkward silence hung between them until Melanie said, "Tomorrow is the town's fair."

"A fair?"

"I go every year. Actually, most people do. You can get pies, and side dishes... pretty much anything you may need for a Christmas dinner except the turkey. There are also last-minute gifts you can buy."

It was as if a sledgehammer had hit him squarely in the chest. He hadn't even thought about buying Melanie a gift, or even some for Arianna. Arianna would be enjoying her first Christmas, and he didn't have a single present for her.

He was worse than Scrooge.

"We should definitely go." He glanced around the house and noticed how undecorated it looked for the holiday. "I know Arianna is only a baby, but maybe we should get a tree. This place doesn't look very Christmassy."

Her smile reassured him. "I think that's a great idea. The fair will have plenty of decorations to buy."

He stared at her lips for a moment and decided not to kiss her—at least, not yet. "So, tell me," he said, pausing for a moment to gather his words, "what type of gift does a busy college student need?"

Her eyebrow furrowed and he saw a hint of disappointment in them. "I'm not going to college."

He pointed to the stroller. "I found a letter."

"Oh, that. No. I... They accepted me for the spring semester, but I'm thinking of maybe attending Vassar *next* year."

It made sense that she would go to college now. She had worked after high school to help raise and support her younger brother. Naturally, now that she had more time, she could go back to school. "You said your job was on hold..." He paused and corrected himself. "It's ending. Why wait a year? Vassar is a fantastic university."

She looked away, took a deep breath, and then finally admitted, "I can't afford to go right now. Maybe after I save up for a year... or two... I'll go."

James moved his arm around the couch and leaned in. "I often find that there's no time like the present for what you really want."

"Is that so?" Her soft voice held a promise of what was to come, especially since her gaze drifted to his lips.

Capturing her lips with his, he applied soft pressure, only deepening the embrace once she kissed him back.

25

*L*ast night had been a two–hour make–out session on the couch, like Melanie had done back in high school and there was nowhere to have sex. There was definitely his bed upstairs, and that's probably where James wanted the evening to end, but the relationship wasn't ready for that type of step—at least, not yet. The anticipation of still having a first night together felt exciting. Kissing, touching... the enjoyment she had felt last night made her body flush in the present. In truth, Melanie had wanted the evening to continue beyond second base, but Arianna had cried.

She sat in a chair at the kitchen table feeding Arianna pureed string beans and peas. The girl wasn't interested, and Melanie couldn't blame her. She hated the taste of peas and saw them as the 'fillers' in life's menu.

"I'm not going to give you bananas." She eyed the child skeptically. "You're not going to teach me to give you dessert first, young lady."

When Arianna spit up the last bite that Melanie was able to place in her mouth, Melanie set the spoon down, placed a burp cloth on her shoulder and proceeded to work out any bubbles the child might have in her tummy.

Melanie stood and rocked Arianna in her arms as she burped her. She stared at the ceiling. "Your father is making a late day of it. It's almost ten in the morning and we haven't seen him yet, have we? No, we haven't."

With a few more pats, the child burped.

Was James spending more time in his room because he was hiding? Maybe he regretted the makeout session last night and didn't want to face her?

Placing Arianna back in the highchair, she wondered if she had done anything that would have upset him.

Thunderously loud footsteps sounded down the stairs and interrupted a spoonful of peas from reaching their destination as Arianna turned her head and looked out the kitchen door.

James entered the room and marched straight to the coffeemaker, barely giving them a glance.

"Are you all right?" Melanie asked.

James took a mug from the cabinet. "Good morning." He nearly slammed the cabinet door shut and then he let out a sigh.

Melanie wasn't sure if she should ask him about last night. The kissing and holding were fantastic, and she couldn't complain. But he was a man and had probably assumed the heat would turn up and the two would have spent the night together.

Not that a night together was far from her thoughts either. She stared at his back as he made himself a cup of coffee. She couldn't see his face, but she could feel him being distracted and upset. Before she had a chance to ask him about last night, James turned and faced her.

"My lawyer called this morning. Thanks to your local news station, Arianna's mother found out where we are and is planning to come to Newbury today."

Found out? Melanie didn't like the sound of that. "You weren't exactly hiding out here."

His serious expression shifted to one of dismissal. "Of course not. I just haven't prepared myself to deal with her... at least not yet."

"And Vivian is coming here," she said, nervously. It wasn't as if the woman was super famous, but definitely the biggest star that this town had ever seen.

"Her flight lands at one o'clock. My lawyers tried to stop her, but they had no legal right to do so."

Melanie glanced at the clock on the wall, even

though she was well aware of the time. "We're a good hour from the airport."

He nodded. "She isn't here for me, she isn't staying, and she isn't welcome. But, she's Arianna's mother, and we haven't finalized any agreements yet when it comes to our child."

"Agreements." Melanie's mind raced with the information. Naturally, since the child had just been so callously dropped off at the office, James didn't have the time to set down visitation rights with the woman. No child deserved to be abandoned like Arianna was.

Melanie glanced down at the young girl who was spitting out green mush. It wasn't as if she could lay claim to the baby, but she wanted to at least protect her from any more harm. "What does Vivian want?"

James studied Arianna and then made eye contact with Melanie. She had never seen such a determined and hurt expression from him before.

"I'm sure she wants money. I'm also sure the visit won't be long. Please make sure Arianna is here at two o'clock on the dot so she can see her mother."

They had no classes today and were only planning on doing some grocery shopping. There'd be no problem in making sure Arianna was ready. "Is there anything you want me to do while she's here?"

He shook his head, his face still hardened. "I don't trust the woman, so I'll be here as well."

"I thought you were going to the plant."

His eyes remained on his daughter. "This is more important." He stared at the green mush on his daughter's face, hands, and highchair tray. "What is this stuff?"

"It's yummy sweet peas," Melanie said, her voice an octave higher and gazing into Arianna's eyes. "It's yummy yummy for your tummy tummy."

JAMES SMILED at Melanie and his heart skipped a beat. "How can you so easily do that?"

"Do what?" Melanie said, wiping off the baby's face.

"Yummy yummy tummy stuff."

She gazed his way as she wiped Arianna's hands. "Baby talk?"

"I hear you talking to her in the mornings when I walk past your room. You talk to her when I get home when you're feeding her and even later when you're bathing her." He made eye contact with her and wished he could be as comfortable around his daughter as she was. "You're a natural."

"I'm not a natural, believe me." Melanie let out a slight chuckle. "I used to babysit a lot when I was younger, then I worked in a daycare center. I had to practice at the baby talk so I could survive those jobs."

Truth or not, she looked like a natural mother

taking care of her young. And, oddly enough, this was the second time she mentioned something about surviving—first the town and now her jobs. Perhaps she wasn't all that happy here in Newbury and needed a change.

"If you had seen me a few years ago with children, you wouldn't think I'm such a natural. Practice, terrible jobs, and more practice."

He didn't believe that for a minute. "I'm sure there's more to it than career planning and making the most of it."

Arianna let out a squeal and put her clean hand in her mouth.

Melanie gently touched the girl's nose and gave her a big smile. "Nice and clean. Yes, you are," she said in a sing-song voice.

She didn't even skip a beat. She could turn it on and off so easily moving between adult and baby conversations. "I guess practice does make perfect." He'd only feel like a fool talking such nonsense. Actually, he wouldn't even know how to begin.

Melanie shook her head and lay down the soiled napkin. "Baby's are a great audience. They have no idea what you're saying as long as you say it in a pleasing way." Her eyes shifted and she looked deep in thought. "I read her a story yesterday about three lost kittens, and she loved it. I could have read to her the..." She looked over to the refrigerator, "I could have read the service agreement to the refrigerator or the dishwasher and it would have been the same. It's the tone of your voice and the eye contact that is important."

James touched Arianna's cheek. "I guess you're right."

"I mean, simple words are best. Talking about colors and objects around her will help her pick up language skills faster... but you can talk to her about your super secret wheelings and dealings when you're alone with her doing company stuff." A grin spread across her face. "It's not like she'll be a corporate spy and ruin your business."

"At least not yet. No, no you won't," James said in baby speak, feeling silly. He leaned closer to Arianna and spoke in a higher voice that he thought made him sound like Kermit the Frog.

"That's the right idea." Melanie went to the cabinet and picked up a small jar. "Here are some peaches. Why don't you feed her while I make you some breakfast?"

He reached for the baby food. "You don't need to make me breakfast." Melanie was a great cook, and he was hungry, but she didn't need to serve him food. After the makeout session last night, he wasn't really sure where the line was now between employer and employee.

Just thinking about the evening last night made his body excited.

"Just feed your daughter and enjoy the moment."

She gave him a devilish grin. "She's going to love peaches."

Melanie took the eggs out of the refrigerator and grabbed a bowl from the cabinet.

He watched as she moved effortlessly through the kitchen. He had always dated women whose only domestic quality was that they lived in a house. He never thought he'd be attracted to a woman who was so... so homey.

Before she had a chance to begin cooking, he lay the jar of baby food down on the table and crossed the room.

"Melanie," he said, his voice soft.

She turned around and for a moment she looked surprised to see him standing so close behind her, but then she smiled.

"Thank you." He wrapped his arms around her tiny frame and pulled her into his embrace. She felt warm and wonderful in his arms.

"You're very welcome, James."

26

*V*ivian was late, which didn't surprise James with how much snow had fallen, just irritated him.

He had thought about catching the next plane out of Newbury to avoid seeing Vivian again, but he didn't want to play games. His lawyers had advised him to allow her to see the child, but he worried that she might take Arianna from him.

He sucked in a deep breath and a heaviness settled in his chest. It had only been a few days, so how was it that he already couldn't live without Arianna? Her smile was already etched on his heart, her gentle coos forever echoing in his head, and her tiny hand gripping around his finger—that was a daddy-forever type of moment that he needed more of.

"I thought her flight landed at 1 pm. Was it

delayed?" Melanie paced the living room with Arianna in her arms. She swayed side–to–side rocking the child as she stared at the wall clock.

"Only by a few minutes. According to my lawyers, she said she'd hire a car and come right out."

"If she doesn't get her soon, Arianna will be asleep." She glanced down at the silk dress the child wore, a dress that was bought an hour ago at the local department store. "She already has a stain on her outfit."

"Don't worry about it." The dress, with matching bow, was her new Christmas outfit. He could have it laundered in time for when it really mattered. For now, Vivian was just lucky that he had told Melanie to get the child dressed in a nice outfit.

"Everything will be all right," Melanie said, a concerned expression marring her face.

He wasn't reassured. Tapping his vest pocket, he said, "My lawyer drafted up a 'waving of rights' agreement. I'm going to see what she wants and then ask her to sign it." He gazed at Melanie. "It will require a witness's signature."

"Of course," Melanie said, nodding. "Whatever you need."

He knew Melanie would be on his side and help out with whatever she could. There was no question about that. She was a trooper.

The doorbell rang, which momentarily woke

Arianna. Melanie shifted her to the other hip and took a step toward the door, but James said, "I'll get it."

Whatever his ex–fling wanted, it had to be important for her to leave New York and come to a little town in Idaho. The woman was reputed as never liking to travel south of 15th street, let alone leave Manhattan unless on location and filming.

He took a deep breath to steady himself. He knew he had the best lawyers and could counter any new demands she may have; he just didn't need her drama. Arianna didn't need the drama either, and she'd be the one who would suffer the most.

Opening the door, he found two men with camera equipment. They stared at him for a moment until a look of recognition hit both of their faces.

"You're James Nielson." The shorter one said.

Wha…? James glanced around outside and didn't see Vivian. When his eyebrow lifted in surprise, the taller man asked, "Is this Vivian Saunders' residence?"

He took in a deep breath, his chest tightening with the cold, outside air filling his lungs. They weren't with Vivian. They weren't here to talk about the plant, either. No, they were here to discuss his personal life. And that was much worse.

"We're not interested in any press release," he said while trying to shut the door.

The reporter moved closer to the door and was just one move shy of sticking his foot into the door jamb. "We're here for the Vivian Saunders interview. We set this up yesterday with her people."

His heart raced. This was about Vivian. And now it made sense. This visit wasn't about him, the plant, or even about Arianna and Christmas. Vivian was being interviewed for something. He was certain the topic was frivolous and something he wouldn't care for, but most likely something he could not dismiss.

He thought about sending them away since he hated the scandalous side of the press, but thought otherwise. He didn't need to upset Vivian when he needed the papers signed. Plus, she was going to handle her own PR so it might as well be somewhere that he could—on some level—control it.

"Come in." He opened the door wider and the wintery air invaded the house, bringing a crisp chill in the room.

The men entered and looked around the foyer. Their expressions were more of surprise than anything else. James wasn't sure if they reacted to him or the decor of the home. He hoped their reaction was to his house since the place looked old–fashioned, but he didn't think the furnishings were that far removed from what people thought Holly-wood–Chic would be. No, the men were eyeing him as though they'd have a chance to interview him as well.

He didn't do interviews.

"It's a private residence," James said, trying to redirect their interest. "It's been in the family for generations," his voice dismissive.

The reporter held out his hand. "I'm Seth. My camera man is Justin." Seth gazed around the home. "This house is kind of a legend. It looks so different since it's not boarded up anymore."

James should have realized that the crew would be local. And, of course, they knew all the town stories, knew about this house, knew more than they needed to. "What news stations will be picking up the interview?" he asked, hoping their feed wasn't national.

"'Good News Daily', but it's available on Reuters within forty–eight hours after initial broadcasting," Seth said.

Damn. They had a national feed. Not exactly what James was hoping for, but it was what it was. Any news affiliation could pick up the segment and air it within a few days.

Justin scanned the room and then focused on Melanie and Arianna.

"Hello," Melanie said.

"Please take her to the kitchen until Vivian arrives," James said in a controlled yet commanding tone—the one he reserved for hired help. Melanie's eyes widened and he regretted his harsh words.

She gave him a quick nod, as though knowing

that his irritation was not directed toward her. She turned and walked to the kitchen.

Arianna would get no extra camera time. She'd have limited exposure. He smiled, knowing that Melanie would do what was needed to keep his daughter safe.

"Since your family owns the Nielson paint factory, would you mind if we ask you a few questions about the chances of more layoffs or even a plant closure?"

Crap. Of course, the plant would come up. He didn't want, nor did he need, any bad publicity right now. In fact, his father had urged him to find some good PR to throw at this situation so it would have a positive spin. He had an idea of what to do, but nothing that was set in concrete as of yet.

But there was an even bigger issue going on than the plant closure. Right now, he needed to keep Arianna safe and handle Vivian. He couldn't think of business at a time like this. "No comments will be made about my business holdings."

Seth glared at him like he had wasted the trip out here. "We're just doing the one interview," Seth said to the cameraman.

Justin held up a light meter and seemed pleased by the light coming from the window. "I'll set up in here."

No request. Just come in and tear everything apart type of manner. James hated people who disrupted his order of things, but he supposed they were just doing their job. A job told to them by Vivian and her 'people'.

He needed to play nice. At least for now.

"What exactly is this interview about?" James asked, hoping it was a personal expose on how Vivian tossed her daughter out like garbage, but knowing better. He could only guess that Vivian—or her agent—called the newspaper and made the arrangements for such a blatant publicity stunt. James's stomach tightened and he felt ill. This interview was going to shine a positive light onto the situation, with Vivian being touted as a wonderful person.

Other than two wild weeks with the woman, all James really knew about her is what he read recently online about her. Expensive trips, wealthy men, and even a trip to rehab a few years ago. It all boiled down to one thing. All the woman cared about was herself.

"We're doing a piece on..."

A knock sounded on the door.

Crap.

He didn't want to see Vivian, let alone play up to her pretend perfect status. His heart raced, and not in a good way. He walked to the door as the two men prepared for the interview.

Taking a deep breath, he opened the door and put a smile on his face. Vivian wore a hat and sunglasses, which contrasted sharply to the fur coat she was wearing and oversized Gucci bag. She plastered a smile on her face, one that looked fake to James. It was a smile most women he knew wore on their faces when they wanted something from him. Something he wouldn't want to give them.

"James, darling." She leaned in and kissed the air two inches from his cheek. "I'm so happy to see you."

The last time he saw her—when their two weeks in Maui had ended—she was naked on the bed and telling him that she agreed there'd be no strings attached to their affair. There were no promises of a relationship, no cutesy nicknames, no false pretenses. Just two fun weeks, with one very adorable string being attached—and she was hiding out in the kitchen.

Closing the door, he noticed a van parked outside with the television station's name on the side. Vivian knew the press had arrived before her. Now, having her call him 'darling' made sense. Her act was already in place, and she was performing her role beautifully.

He also noticed that her driver was waiting in his car. That was a good sign that she didn't intend to stay long.

"Hello, Vivian." He shot her back his own plastic smile and let her in.

She instantly went into her fake Hollywood persona, which he now believed may be her real personality. She greeted the two men and mentioned how beautiful the town was.

She threw her bag and expensive mink on a nearby chair. Her hat and sunglasses followed. "Darling? Where can I freshen up?"

At least the nick-name wasn't pookie or some other crap. "Upstairs, first door on the right." He hated the idea of her traipsing through his home, but there was only one working bathroom.

"I'll be back in a minute," she said to the news crew.

Justin held some equipment in his hand but managed to look her way and say, "We'll be ready by the time you get back."

Vivian left without another word. She didn't ask about Arianna. She didn't ask about how James was managing as a single father this past week. She didn't care.

The tabloids were right. It was always about her.

"Miss Saunders sure is something." Seth said to no one in particular, his gaze still staring toward the staircase where Vivian had disappeared. He was practically drooling.

James wondered if he had been so taken by Vivian when he first met her. She had always been beautiful, and her body a perfect ten. Most men were attracted to her right away, and she had caught his attention on the fashion runway. One thing led to another, and off they went for a vacation on his yacht, away from the press and the world in general. He had never taken the time to know her.

Overall, he didn't think he missed out on much.

Melanie emerged from the kitchen, a very excited, and now awake, Arianna in her arms. She glanced around. "I thought I heard..."

"She's in the restroom freshening up."

Seth walked over to her, ignoring the fact that Justin was set up and ready to do some test shots with the camera. "And who exactly are you," he asked with a sensationalist edge in his voice as though hoping for an even juicier story.

Melanie shifted Arianna from one hip to the other. "I'm just the nanny."

"If you don't mind, Ms. Frank." James nodded back toward the kitchen. "These men need some time to set up, and I'd like to talk to Vivian for a few minutes before they get started."

Melanie quickly returned to the kitchen and he heard Justin mutter that they needed only a few more minutes to set up. Regardless, they would have to wait until he talked with the mother of his child.

27

"*V*ivian, a word." James knocked on the upstairs bathroom door.

The door opened and the smell of hairspray immediately hit him. "It's been so long James." Her voice was soft, feminine, and alluring. She hugged him and tried to kiss him, hitting his chin instead as he turned away.

"So, it's going to be like that. That's a pity." A scowl appeared on her face, but then one eyebrow lifted and her gaze traveled the length of him. "We did have an amazing two weeks together," she said in a softened tone. "I wouldn't object to another vacation with you."

"I don't *vacation* with women who keep secrets from me." His voice was flat and he held back any anger he felt toward her.

She returned to the mirror in the tiny bathroom

and applied lipstick. "The lighting in here is terrible."

There was barely enough room for two people, but he squeezed in and closed the door behind him for privacy. "I'd ask you how you've been, but I already know. Pregnant."

She set down the lipstick and her face pinched. "I knew you'd feel this way."

His jaw tightened. He had gone over what to say to her hundreds of times in his head. He wanted to scream, but he kept his voice down. "You don't even know me. You have no idea how I feel," he said, his tone sharp and enunciating each syllable.

"Really," she said, applying mascara. "I have no idea?" She stopped fixing her face and then waved dismissively at him. "You would have told me to abort the child."

Guilt hit him square on. It was the first thought he had upon hearing the news. But not now. Arianna was a blessing, and he never wanted to think about not having her in his life. Narrowing his eyes at her, he wanted to lash out. "No," he said, through gritted teeth.

"Oh, please." She tossed all the makeup from the counter into her bag. "You don't want this kid anymore than I do."

He let out the breath he didn't know he was holding. She didn't want Arianna? She had left the child at his office, but he suspected she had been in a momentary panic and would come to her senses and demand her daughter back.

He had to play it safe, but had to ask, "Then why didn't you..."

"Have an abortion?" She took a deep breath and put her purse over her shoulder. "A mystery baby is good press." Shifting from one foot to the other, she said in a nonchalant voice, "I got a lot of mileage out of the pregnancy and the single–mom birth."

Bile bubbled up. She had used their daughter for Hollywood glitz and gain. He had hoped she had more morals than that, but he didn't really know her either. "And now?"

Her eyes narrowed. "And now I have a fabulous television show and a career–making second movie to star in." Her face glowed in a way that was only depicted on villains in the movies. "I'm going places."

Vivian made a move toward the door and James stepped aside to allow her to do so. He then followed the most cold–hearted bitch he had ever known back down the staircase to the downstairs floor.

"I'm ready," Vivian announced as she reentered the room and made a grand appearance. "Where's my baby girl?" she asked, in a drippy–sweet voice.

"Ms. Frank," James said loudly in the direction of the kitchen.

The kitchen door opened and Melanie entered the living room with Arianna in her arms. Melanie looked motherly and warm as she smiled at James and straightened Arianna's dress.

Vivian approached Melanie, without questioning who she was and why she was holding her child. "Hello, sweetheart," she said to Arianna. Arianna didn't react to seeing her, so Vivian said, "It's Mommy." Her tone was light and uplifted, as if that alone would excite the child.

Arianna's hand had taken hold onto some of Melanie's hair and she lay with her head nestled to Melanie's neck. She looked a bit tired, but was perking up with the lights and the visitors in the home.

"Mmbb... gaw," Arianna said, pointing at the camera. She kicked her legs in excitement, still not looking at her mother.

"She's tired." Vivian said about the wide–eyed baby, as if being sleepy were an all–access pass for a child not excited that her mother was nearby. She took Arianna from Melanie's arms, pulling Melanie's hair in the process, and held Arianna like a sack of groceries. She then walked to the couch with Arianna crying. "Are we doing the interview here?"

Arianna let out a sharp squeal when Vivian sat down, one that would hurt your eardrums if you were too close. Vivian's quick head turn seemed to indicate that Arianna had hit a nerve.

"Yes, ma'am." Seth took a seat next to her and gestured to the camera man to start filming.

Arianna kept crying, and Seth said, "cut." He smiled at the baby, but irritation showed in his face. "We can wait until you're settled down with her."

Vivian shifted Arianna from one hand to the other, but Arianna still cried. James knew she had just eaten and had on a clean diaper. Something else was wrong.

"Why aren't you happy." Vivian's voice held a certain level of anxiety mixed with anger that James picked up on.

"Her leg is caught in the sofa." Melanie dashed over and fixed the baby's leg so she'd be more comfortable. "Here you go, sweetheart." She showed the baby a pacifier and Arianna opened her mouth to take it.

Now with Arianna quiet, Vivian plastered a smile on her face. "We're ready."

Seth held up the mic and told Justin to start filming again. "We're here with an exclusive interview of Miss Vivian Saunders for GND and its affiliate stations. Vivian has quite a following with the younger crowd and has been aloof about doing any interviews this past year due to her mysterious pregnancy. Today, we get to meet that baby as Vivian opens up and tells all."

Seth eyed James and gave him a sly smile. "The father is none other than Billionaire CEO James Nielson, heir to the Neilson International Corporation." He nodded toward James in an unasked invite to have him join them on the couch. "She kept the secret of the two of you very tight lipped. How long have you been dating?"

James took in a deep breath, knowing he was able to keep the conversation off of him. He had no intention of going on air, least of all talking about anything private in his life. "Keep the questions just for Vivian."

Seth's face showed his disapproval. With his hand doing a 'cut' gesture across his neck, he said in an irritated manner, "take two." He adjusted his tie and then raked his fingers through his hair before putting on his fake smile and redoing the intro—this time without trying to bring James in. "In this segment, Hollywood career mothers who juggle having it all."

28

*I*f there had been any more ridiculous crap being said in the living room, Melanie would need a shovel.

She stood in the back of the room and listened to the interview, sick over how much time Vivian said she spent with Arianna, that she had suggested their daughter spend some time in the country, and blushing whenever Seth gave her a compliment.

How could she juggle being a working Hollywood mother? The answer was easy. She didn't. She wanted the world to believe otherwise, but the non-responsive look from Arianna told the truth. She wasn't excited to see her mother again. The woman had abandoned her in an office building. What was worse, James hadn't even been there to collect his daughter from her.

To make the situation even more tragic still,

there were no follow–up phone calls or any communication from her to see if the child was all right.

The reporter Seth was also getting on her nerves. She didn't know the man, but the wedding ring on his finger said he was off limits. He shamelessly flirted with Vivian and she ate up his compliments like it was diet cheesecake with a calorie free brownie crust.

It made Melanie sick to her stomach. She knew women like Vivian. It was all about the show, and nothing about substance. Their lives were too busy to be burdened by anything that didn't bow down to them. Vivian's perfectly manicured fingers and hair were a perfect example of someone who never rolled up their sleeves and got messy.

"So, what is next for you, Miss Saunders?"

A smile so charming you could see the fakeness crossed her face. "My show *Visions* has been picked up for another season," she began. She droned on for a few minutes about all the plans she had in Hollywood for the next year, including some filming she planned to do in Europe over the summer with a movie, but she didn't mention Arianna.

"And you must have an excellent relationship with your baby daddy, the wealthy James Nielson of Nielson International Corporation." Seth gestured for James to join them on the couch but he shook his head.

James, who had been standing in the background, didn't budge. "This interview isn't about me or the Nielson company. It's all about Vivian and our daughter."

Melanie heard the fake sincerity in his voice and wondered if anyone else picked up on it. The interview continued with a quick "we'll edit his reply out in production", so she figured they didn't.

Melanie touched James's hand and then nodded toward the kitchen. Once out of earshot, but within sight of Arianna, Melanie whispered, "What a piece of work. She's holding Arianna like she's a greased-up pig, shifting her from one side and then the other. She's going to make that child seasick."

Staring back at his daughter, James said, "Arianna vomiting would mess up Vivian's perfect interview." A slight snicker followed, but Melanie didn't see anything funny about the situation.

James had chosen to be with the type of woman that Melanie had always thought of as the 'Princess' type. Melanie classified all women into three categories: the Princess, who couldn't do anything and needed pampering; the Show Off, who talked a good game, but never accomplished anything; and then the Doers, who proved that Wonder Woman wasn't just a person but a title.

Oddly enough, the title of 'bitch' was in all three categories.

"So, what's your plan," she whispered.

"To get her out of this house?"

Melanie shook her head. There was a bigger picture here to consider. "To get her out of your life."

"I'm going to ask her to sign the papers. Hopefully she'll do so and leave," he whispered back. He then added, "The note she left with Arianna suggested she had lawyers. I'd rather her just sign what my people drafted and be gone."

She doubted it would be that easy. "Do you think her lawyers will try to take advantage of you or Arianna?"

He gave her an 'are you kidding' glance. "That's what you pay lawyers to do."

She knew that was true. Her personal experience trying to settle her parents' estate had worn her out years ago, and had soured her opinions of the entire legal profession. "Do your papers screw Vivian out of anything?"

Shaking his head, and keeping an eye on his daughter, he replied, "No. Just a standard release of her parental rights. Really straight forward."

Men were so clueless when it came to women. Vivian wasn't the type to do the right thing, she was the self-serving type that had to believe that what she did was in her best interest. "That type of woman needs to have things done her way. If you're going to get her to sign anything without her lawyers jumping in, you'll have to make her believe it was her idea."

James leaned in, his cologne scent filling the gap

between them and smelling divine. "I'm game. What do you have in mind?"

The plan was only just forming in her head, but she figured she'd be able to play the woman. "Just follow my lead." Melanie stepped back into the living room with James following her.

"Thank you for the interview," Seth said as he concluded the visit. Justin was turning off lights and packing up his camera. "Can we get your autograph?"

Melanie rolled her eyes. Were these men really fan-girling this fake, cold-hearted woman? She stared at the woman's features and tight body. The packaging was beautiful, she'd give Vivian credit for that. Her perfectly exercised and tone body was obvious, even under the bulky wintry clothing. She also had an hourglass figure with perfect and perky boobs. She had the body any man would drool over.

Glancing over to James, a hint of jealousy caught her and squeezed her tight. James had slept with this woman. They had spent time together in some romantic hideaway, removed from the prying eyes of reporters, for what he had said was a two-week fling.

Two weeks. He had touched and caressed her. Kissing probably every inch of her body.

Vivian had also touched, caressed, and had kissed every inch of James's body. Catching a glimpse of him through the corner of her eye, Melanie thought about his strong jaw and neckline.

She mentally trailed kisses down onto his shoulders down to his chest. She sighed remembering his sexy chest hair.

Hmmm. It was very nice. She imagined for a moment what he would look like with his shirt off, the sun gleaming down on his tight body, with the wind in their hair as they sailed aboard one of the man's boats she assumed he owned.

Melanie sucked in a deep breath. The ruggedly handsome picture she was painting in her head was mere fantasy. The reality was that there was no boat ride for a barren country girl that was stuck in a backwater town with no job. A romantic holiday fling? Maybe. But not something substantial. Not something permanent.

A lump settled in her throat. She did want something permanent with the right man. A man who would love her no matter what.

But it wouldn't be James. Vivian, with her Hollywood star status had garnered the attention of a sweet man like him. Rich billionaires didn't come to small towns and fall in love. No. Men like him were only seen in the ritziest of places with the elites.

Elites like Vivian.

Someone who didn't deserve him.

Anger welled up within her. How could Vivian be pregnant and not tell James he was to be a father? How could she give birth and still keep her secrets?

How could she abandon her child for such selfish reasons as the making of a movie overseas?

There was no need to judge James for being with someone like Vivian. Most men would have fallen for her female charms. It wasn't up to her to measure his love life with her own moral ruler.

No reason at all.

She would help him get custody of his daughter, she would see that the plant got closed, and she would say goodbye to James and Arianna and get back to her life.

Vivian's eyes lit up and she beamed with delight at the request for an autograph. She pulled out some 8x10 glossy images of herself from her bag and signed them. Melanie thought it boded well for them that Vivian understood the idea of having something super handy to sign.

James was already at the door. It took less to tear down the equipment than it did to set it up, and they were ready to leave in minutes. "Thank you gentlemen for coming."

Vivian slumped back on the couch once the men were gone. "I don't appreciate hunting you down in freezing Antarctica."

"We're in Idaho." James walked back to the couch.

"Same difference." Vivian tried to stand, but Arianna's sleeping body was too heavy. She lay the girl on the couch in much the same way someone would lay a sack of potatoes. "She smells." Gazing at Melanie, she added, "She needs a new diaper."

"She has a name. It's Arianna." Melanie pulled a diaper from the diaper bag that lay on a side table.

Vivian shot her a side–ways glance. "A nanny with an attitude. Your mother must be so proud of your accomplishments."

"Don't talk to my household staff in such a manner." His eyes shot daggers at Vivian. "Ms. Frank is the only nanny I could hire in this town, and she's the best I've ever seen."

Melanie took that as a compliment, a very distant and formal one, but still. At the very least, it got Vivian to shut up.

After a moment, Vivian walked to the window and glanced outside. "They're gone, so I'm off."

Melanie picked up Arianna who was now in a clean diaper and quickly headed Vivian off before she made it to the door. Holding the smelly diaper in her hand, she used it as a magical wand—one that hopefully would make Vivian disappear.

"One moment Ms. Saunders," Melanie said, pointing the diaper at her. "We need to discuss the logistics of my job."

Vivian closed her eyes and averted her nose. "I don't know what you're talking about."

"I'm sorry. I just assumed that I'd continue with my nanny responsibilities now that you're here to take your daughter back." She juggled Arianna in her arms and made a fake attempt to hand the child —and smelly diaper—over.

Taking a step back, Vivian now turned and addressed James. "I was hoping that you could watch over her. I do have a movie I'm filming overseas."

James's gaze darted past Vivian over to Melanie, who was shaking her head. Obviously, he must have picked up on the non–verbal signals because he said, "I'm flying to Europe myself on business." He waited for Vivian's reaction, which Melanie couldn't see but guessed the woman's face turned to one of panic.

"Ms. Frank can have Arianna's belongings packed in short order and you can take her with you," he added.

"No. No." Vivian paced the floor. "I appreciate you not saying anything to the press about how I asked you to watch over her..."

"How you abandoned her," Melanie said.

"Does the help really have to be here and listen to our private discussion?" Vivian said in a dismissive tone.

James's face hardened. "The *help* is the only one in this room who knows how to take care of our child, so yes." He shook his head and gave her what Melanie could describe as being his best 'what can we do' face.

Vivian's expression looked determined. "If you could watch over her until..."

"Until when?" he asked.

"I don't know," Vivian said, her voice filled with frustration. "I'll be on site with the film for at least six months, maybe longer. I'll also be flying back and forth for my television show."

"A movie? Your ongoing successful television show?" He pointed at Arianna. "You need to take her. Now."

"I'm available to work overseas," Melanie chimed in. "I have a passport. Plus, babies aren't all that bad on planes—especially long flights that are overnight."

The audible grunt from Vivian spoke volumes.

"Arianna will need to go to school eventually. She'll need some sort of structure in her life." James wiped the back of his neck with his hand and gave her another 'what will we do' expression.

"She'll need to go to a proper school," Melanie said. "Maybe an arrangement where you have her exclusively for six months of the year and where Mr. Nielson has her six months..."

Vivian groaned and panic displayed in her eyes. That's when Melanie noticed the cross she wore. Now it made sense why the woman continued with the pregnancy even though she didn't have a maternal bone in her body.

Shaking her head, Melanie walked closer to Vivian, the diaper still in hand. "You know, that schedule might not work. One of you should have her full time."

"Full time?" Vivian's breath was nearly a gasp of fright.

"You'll want her doctor to be familiar with her when she gets sick. Trust me, you will want someone who knows her very well when she's crying at three o'clock in the morning with a high fever."

Vivian rolled her eyes. "Oh, I know. We've already done that. If it wasn't for my own hired help I never would have managed. And, even then... the sleepless nights. I can't be on camera after I've been up all night." Her hand touched her face. "It just isn't fair."

"Plus, she'll need to be socialized with other children," Melanie said, ignoring Vivian's complaints. "Have some play dates at your home. Naturally, the house will have to be child protected." With fake enthusiasm, she added, "I can help you childproof the hotel rooms we stay at."

Vivian took a seat on the couch and her hand wiped across her brow. "Ok, what are we going to do? I'm on location all the time, my schedule starts at five in the morning, and I can't have this woman," she said, pointing at Melanie, "following me with a screaming baby all day."

"It looks like Mr. Nielson's schedule is more flexible. Maybe if he had full custody of the baby, then a regular pediatrician can be used, a good school picked out..."

"Wait," James said, his eyes widening with what looked like pretend fear. "So, *I* should take her?" James asked Melanie.

"Would you?" Vivian asked, her eyes hopeful.

"Ugh." James did a little nervous pace in the living room and winked at Melanie when he knew Vivian couldn't see his face. He then stood straight and tall, his face pinching deep in thought as he locked eyes with Vivian. "Well, if you think it's for the best." His hand went to the papers in his breast pocket. "I'll need you to fill out some paperwork."

Once the paperwork was signed, James quickly marched her to the door. Taking a peak outside, he said, "Your car is still waiting for you."

Without kissing Arianna goodbye, without even grunting toward James, she grabbed her bag, put on her fur coat, and left.

James closed the door and watched from the window as her car pulled away.

Melanie walked to the window and joined him. "She may have been different when you knew her, but your ex–lover is a bitch."

"Tell me something I don't know." He turned from the window and gave Melanie a big hug, sandwiching Arianna in between.

29

"*L*ooks like Arianna isn't the worse for wear after her mother's visit." Melanie said, straightening the child's outfit and brushing her hand through her curls.

James took her from Melanie's arms and kissed the child on her chubby cheeks. He held her close and took in a deep breath smelling her delicate baby skin. "I thought I'd need to have lawyers involved and fight to get full custody of you." He gave Melanie a sideways glance and then said in baby speak, "Yes. Yes, I did. But you're a daddy's girl."

Melanie took in the sight. Father and daughter. Arianna certainly did love him.

James sat on the couch and placed his daughter in his lap so the child could face him. It was their usual stance for a round of peek-a-boo or for some light ruff-housing.

"Bb–mmb," Arianna let out excitedly.

"Did you hear that?" he asked, a wide grin on his face as he looked up at Melanie. "She said 'da–da'." His voice was light and she could tell he was joking.

It was beautiful to see him becoming more comfortable with Arianna. She was such a good baby and the two of them were such a nice family. Melanie sat next to James, her thigh touching his. "She's trying to put weight on her legs."

He studied the child's legs as her feet plastered themselves onto his lap, her polished black baby shoes—which matched the outfit—giving her more sure footing. "Yep. A bit too early since she can't sit up by herself yet."

For someone who didn't know much about babies, he knew some big milestones. It was impressive and very endearing. Melanie knew she had started caring for this little family, which only would make it that much harder when they left.

"I've done some research." James's voice held a certain level of fatherly pride. Melanie figured it wouldn't be long before he'd be telling the stereotypical 'dad jokes'.

"Thank goodness for the Internet," James added. "I don't know how parents managed without it." He paused and then corrected himself, "How my father managed without it." He let out a deep breath and steadied his daughter on his lap, getting her to sit down. "I would be so totally lost if I couldn't Google for things." He smiled at Melanie and the twinkle in his eye shown. "Well, I'd be lost without the Internet and you."

He was an honest man, too. She liked that. Most men bragged about their abilities or professed to have no issues and that they understood everything, even if it were obvious they didn't. "You're doing a great job with Arianna." She looked into his deep soft eyes. "You really are a wonderful daddy."

His beaming smile told her that he was thrilled with the title of 'daddy'. Last week, before he knew about Arianna, he was an unknowing Baby Daddy. When Melanie first met him, he was a man who had fathered a child. Today, he was a daddy. He also had full custody of Arianna, not because it was forced upon, but because he fought to get it.

The two made a nice family.

The two of them.

They hadn't talked about their kissing session last night, and she wasn't sure how to bring it up. Was he just looking for a fling? Or was he wanting something more substantial than that? He was becoming a family man, but was that just due to the charm of this small town? Once back in his big city life, would James change?

James reached for a toy on the coffee table and showed the plush toy, that had a teether rubber part, to his daughter. She was able to hold onto it, and it immediately went into her mouth.

"She should get some teeth any day now," Melanie said, trying to focus on something else.

"Melanie," he said, "When I first arrived in town I didn't think I'd enjoy my stay." He placed his free hand on her leg. "You have made the holidays very enjoyable."

Noticing that his eyes gazed down at her lips, she moved closer. Sitting next to him, with a child in his lap, didn't make it easy, but she found his soft lips and kissed him.

He may be a ruthless businessman, but he had a softer side. A side she enjoyed being with. But how long would a city mouse be interested in a country mouse?

JAMES DEEPENED THE KISS, keeping his right hand safely around his daughter. The kiss, which started out soft and sweet, could have turned into something more passionate—which is what he wanted, but he knew he was treading on some rough waters.

He pulled away and adjusted Arianna on his lap. She dropped the toy and he tried to hand it back to her, but her hands went to her eyes and she let out a yawn.

"It's past her nap." Melanie glanced briefly at his lips, but then shifted her gaze to Arianna. "I can put her down."

She picked Arianna up and held her closely, snuggling with her in a motherly way. "There's a pacifier upstairs," she said, patting the baby's back. Arianna eyes closed and her body molded into Melanie's shoulder, her head cradling next to Melanie's neck.

James watched as the two left the room. He needed to talk to Melanie about last night's kiss. Well, kiss and more kisses. Plus, the kiss they just shared.

Crap.

He was falling for her. Falling for her hard, and he couldn't do this.

Taking a deep breath, he leaned back into the couch and felt the cushions give under his weight. Melanie was his employee. Even just a temporary one, he can't start a relationship with someone under his employ.

That was business basics 101.

And she wasn't just any employee. She was his daughter's nanny. It was a bad romance novel coming to life. Sexy nanny. Rich billionaire.

He placed his head in his hands in deep thought. She was doubly his employee because she technically still worked at the plant. She relied up him for a paycheck. What he was doing—and what he was feeling—could be seen as pressuring her for physical intimacy with the threat of losing her way of supporting herself financially if she didn't return the favors.

At least, that's what a lawyer would say if this were to become a sexual harassment suit against him.

He had never dated anyone from work before—always steering clear of the young new hires, never checking out the secretarial pool, never hiring the sexiest woman to be his assistant.

Heck, Darin was his assistant. Nothing sexy or tempting about him.

James rubbed his temple and let out a long sigh. Why did he have to have feelings for Melanie?

He heard a soft sound coming from upstairs so he craned his neck and listened intently. He could barely make out Melanie's words, but knew she was singing. He had a Mary Poppins perfect nanny, singing to his child, and all he wanted to do was strip her down on this couch and make... have sex with her.

No, it was making love.

A wave of panic nearly overcame him. He had never made love to a woman before. His sexual encounters were hot, passionate, and very temporary. Hollow encounters that involved body parts other than the heart.

Making love seemed even more passionate. The idea of stripping Melanie down, caressing her smooth silky skin, hearing her pants of desire and feeling her nails dig into his back as they...

A lone groan escaped his throat, and he stood and began pacing. He needed to keep his hands to himself. He just didn't want to.

The creaking boards from upstairs sounded on the ceiling and he knew she was pacing the floor while she sang. Melanie was a good person. Someone wholesome and kind. Was he taking advantage of her?

In a few moments his daughter would be sound asleep and he and Melanie would be alone again. His heart pounded just thinking of having her in his arms.

He needed a diversion, something to keep him from thinking of her in any way other than a woman.

Work. Work was always a good distraction.

His computer lay nearby so he returned to the couch and picked his Mac up. The light shown as the device came to life. But, once again, no Internet.

"You've got to be kidding me," he said to no one in the room. He tossed the computer aside and pulled his phone out. There were no messages, but then again, people were already taking off for the holiday. Craig at the plant also knew that James had some personal business to attend to, and he didn't seem like the type to contact him unless there was an emergency.

Not that an emergency would happen at a plant that was barely running.

Shoot. He still didn't have an answer as to how he could keep the factory open.

A bubbling filled his gut and he knew closing the plant, which seemed like such an easy decision not too long ago, would be difficult to do now. He'd have to wait until after the holidays to tell people. He didn't want to ruin everyone's Christmas.

His calendar app had a tick mark on it, so he opened the day's appointments.

'Dinner with Aunt Sandra and Grandma Lorraine.'

He had totally forgotten. They wanted to meet Arianna and find out more about him and how his life turned out. Normally, he would have shied away from opening up to a stranger about his life, but he could make an exception for his family. The women were open and caring. It was hard not to like the and be yourself around them.

Some squeaky floorboards announced Melanie's presence back downstairs. "Arianna is down for her nap."

He glanced at his watch; it was later than he thought.

"I met my aunt and grandmother the other day," he said.

"Sandra and Lorraine. You told me that already."

That's right, Melanie used to work there. She

knew his family probably better than he did. "I was thinking I'd take them and Arianna out to dinner..." His gaze drifted to the staircase behind Melanie. "But she's taking a nap and I told them that I'd meet them in an hour."

"You can eat here."

There wasn't much in this town, at least not many places he had seen when he had explored the surrounding area, so he had to ask, "What restaurants deliver?"

"No." She walked over to him and touched his arm, rubbing it gently and causing a warm feeling to surround him. "I'll make something."

"You'll cook for me?" She had made dinners for them in the past, but this was family coming over, a small dinner party of sorts. It felt very domestic.

No, that wasn't the right word.

It felt personal and loving.

She gave him an angelic smile. "If you don't like my cooking, you just have to say so."

He couldn't remember any woman, other than nannies and personal chefs, ever cooking for him. He knew women did that for the men they were dating—not that he was dating Melanie—but he had never personally experienced a home cooked meal lovingly made. It made her extra special.

His arm reached out and curved around her waist before he could think better of it. "I like your cooking." He leaned in, closing the gap between them and moving into her personal space. The smell of her perfume enticing, her body warmth comforting, and her smile welcoming.

"I like everything about you." He didn't know where this relationship was heading, he just hoped it would last and that it wasn't a lawsuit later for sexual harassment. He leaned in and claimed her lips with his.

Her mouth opened and invited him in, and for a moment, he was lost in her charms.

At first the kiss was light and gentle, but it quickly turned into a burning passion. He tasted the sweetness of her lips, felt the passion of her body, and before he knew it, he was kissing her neck and shoulder. His hands slid down her thin waist, gripped her bottom firmly, and pressed her firm body into his. The two of them bumped into the wall and he held her tightly against it. Feeling her heart beating next to him, he wanted the moment to last forever.

"We... we should start on that dinner," she said in a breathy, labored voice. She swallowed hard and he could hear her catching her breath. "Or, we could go out. It's not snowing that hard."

"We'll wake Arianna and head out," he said, still kissing her.

Melanie, whose hands had gripped him firmly, her body on fire only a second ago, now giggled. "We're not going to take her out in this weather. I better get started in that kitchen." She licked her lips and stared at him, her lipstick now gone, her hair tussled, and her sexy bedroom eyes looking back at him with a promise of what could be in store for later. "We wouldn't want to eat our food raw."

"I don't know. It depends on what we're having."

His hands pressed against the wall and allowed his body to encircle hers even more. Her lips were still swollen from passion and he dove in to kiss them once more.

She turned her head, depriving him of the joy. "I have ingredients for enchiladas. Chicken enchiladas."

He didn't care. His body was on fire for her.

"Your aunt and grandmother will be here soon. Or have you forgotten?"

Dammit. It was too late to call off dinner, and they would be here shortly. He pulled away, giving her his best pouty look. "Enchiladas are better cooked, anyway." He took a deep breath. "I'll help you."

30

"*T*he salad is mixed."

Why was a man in an apron so sexy?

Melanie wasn't about to correct him and say that salads are tossed, not mixed. He had helped to shred the chicken and had grated the cheese. He had proved himself useful in the kitchen, and she had always thought it was incredibly fetching when a man knew how to cook.

He had no idea where anything was in the kitchen, but was eager to help.

She watched him from behind as he 'mixed' the salad with one more final stroke. He looked adorable in the apron. And those tight jeans he wore? Well. She shouldn't be thinking of them with his aunt on her way over, so she gave herself exactly ten more seconds of staring before looking away.

The doorbell rang and she quickly glanced at the baby monitor. Arianna stirred, but was still sound asleep. For a second nap, it was a bit on the longer side. Which meant she'd be up for quite a while tonight.

And there'd be little to no time for her and James to be alone.

She suspected something more than just a fling existed between them, but she didn't have the time right now to explore her feelings. Feelings that had been growing for days and she could no longer ignore.

"Come in." She heard James say as he opened the door in the living room. The enchiladas were ready to come out of the oven so she removed them and carried them into the dining room. The table was already set, and she noticed James had set out four plates and the highchair. He didn't see her as just the help.

She mentally surveyed the table and counted the empty trivets James had placed in the center. The rice, beans, and the salad needed to come out. Taking a deep breath, she realized how nervous she was. She didn't think cooking for her old boss would cause her such pause—especially since she had known Sandra for years. And then it hit her. Was her nervousness due to the fact that she was eating and socializing with James's family?

"That's too bad that she's sleeping," Sandra said,

walking into the dining room. A smile quickly came to her and she walked over to Melanie. "It's so nice to see you again."

"Hello, Sandra. Hello, Lorraine." Melanie gave a nod to the table and the wine bottle. "James, if you'll open the wine, I can get the rest of the dinner."

"Everything smells so good. You know, James, I..."

Melanie walked back into the kitchen, her heart pounding. This felt way more like a married couple dinner than she had originally thought. Baby upstairs sleeping. Husband opening some wine. She wasn't scared by the situation, she just wanted to embrace it and own the moment. But it was too soon. Way too soon.

With the food on the table, and the wine poured, the four of them began the meal. The baby monitor sat proudly in the middle of the table with everyone keeping an eye on it.

"I wanted to ask you about the diner," James said. "How are you managing?"

Sandra's eyebrow lifted. "What do you mean?"

James put down his fork and Melanie saw a shift in his persona. It was slight, but definitely there—like he was in his element and going to weave his own magic.

"I'm not blind, Sandra."

Sandra glanced at her plate and then set her own fork down, followed by a huge sigh.

"Most of the stores in this town are closed or

closing. Is the restaurant soon to follow?" James said in a very business-like manner.

With some slight head nods, Lorraine said, "We're keeping afloat. For now."

James placed his hand over his grandmother's frail one. "Vagrant Enterprises seems interested in buying you out."

Sandra's gaze darted over to James, her mouth momentarily opened, but then she shook her head. "Just talk for now."

Melanie wasn't sure what Vagrant Enterprises was, but James—in his jeans and sweater— looked formidable. She didn't think he'd be any sexier if he were in a three–piece suit and tie.

Taking another look at him, she felt the fluttering of excitement deep within her. A suit wouldn't hurt. She bit her lip. No clothes wouldn't hurt either.

"Ladies, I know we just met," James said, "but I'd like to offer you some business advice."

Sandra's eyes told Melanie the true story. She had known the woman for years. She was proud and determined. If there were a way to keep the restaurant running, she would find it. If she was looking for selling out, then it meant one thing. Sandra was at the end of her rope and couldn't hang on anymore.

Lorraine looked to be near tears.

Melanie studied Sandra. She was a "Doer" type

of gal. But, even a "Wonder Woman" needed a break every once in a while.

"I met with two representatives of Vagrant Enterprises the other day," Sandra said, her voice soft and sad. "They told me about your plans to sell the plant." Sandra's gaze drifted to Melanie. "So many of us want the plant to stay open." Swallowing the lump in her throat, she continued, "Melanie needs her job back, my husband and sons need to keep theirs. And, of course, the restaurant." A tear escaped, and she wiped it away. "Without the plant the restaurant hasn't had much business lately. A mall would..."

"A mall?" Melanie asked, staring from Sandra to James.

"No," Lorraine said. "I don't want a mall to..."

Sandra put her hand on her mother's shoulder. "Mama, we've talked about this."

"A mall isn't going to happen. At least not right away," James said. He then added, "Never, if I can help it."

"What do you mean?" Sandra asked, her voice sounding hopeful. "Our restaurant can't compete with the fast food of a mall."

James shifted so he faced more directly toward Sandra. "Vagrant Enterprises has not reached out to the Nielson International Corporation. They're not buying the plant. Heck, I wouldn't sell it to them."

"But the plant is closing." Melanie didn't think it was giving too much away since Sandra seemed to already know the details.

"I'd like to keep the plant open, and I'm still thinking of ways on how to save it." He gave them a compassionate gaze. "Vagrant Enterprises wants to scare you into selling your land for cheap, threatening you with how everyone else is selling and how you'll lose more money in the end."

"That's what they said." Sandra's watery eyes pleaded with James. "We've already lost so much money in the past two years, I just don't know how much longer we can hold out." She bit her lip and Melanie could tell she didn't want to cry in front of her mother. "I don't want our family's legacy to end." Sandra's eyes pleaded with James. "We really need the plant to remain open, and back to producing again."

Lorraine let out a frustrating sigh, one filled with heartache. "The restaurant was fine until all the construction tore up the roads." She stared at James. "I guess you can't speed up the road work, huh?"

"I don't know who got the highway contracting bid, but I could look into..."

"No," Sandra said, "We're just grasping at straws. It's just that..."

Her face appeared so sad. Melanie wished there was something she could do since Sandra had stepped up and helped her when she needed it the most.

"Our family doesn't know how bad it is," Sandra said in a soft, sad whisper. "Mama and I have kept this a secret."

The story sounded so familiar to Melanie. She had kept the family money problems a secret from her brother during his high school years. Her only goal was to get him off to college and for him not to worry about her or how she was working two jobs at the time.

"If the plant were to miraculously stay open and in full production mode, then the restaurant will be fine," James said. "If the factory closes, and investors do come in to buy, the land the restaurant is on will be worth so much more."

"What about the mall?" Sandra asked.

He rolled his eyes. "I've made no deals on selling the building or the land. Regardless," he said, "hold out and don't sell."

"We don't have the money to stay afloat anymore." Desperation sounded in Sandra's voice.

"There's always hope," Melanie said. She had heard that line so many times in her past. Being on the receiving end of it sucked. Saying it to someone who you know was hurting was even worse.

"There is hope," James said. "I'd like to personally invest in the restaurant. After all, it is my family business too, and Arianna's legacy."

"IT'S BEEN A LOVELY EVENING," Aunt Sandra said, holding onto Arianna, who finally woke from her nap. "This little one is so darling. You two are certainly blessed."

James's ears perked up.

Sandra's face reddened. "I'm sorry." She looked from James to Melanie and then back again. "I know Melanie isn't the baby's mother. I just forgot for a moment that she's the nanny." She gave James a wry smile as she handed Arianna to Melanie.

"You two do make a nice couple." Lorraine studied the two of them. "Yep. You look really nice together."

Was his family playing matchmaker? Or could they read his thoughts and knew what was in his heart?

"Well, we better be going. Tomorrow is the fair and we'll be selling pies." Sandra nearly started to cry, and then she hugged James. "I know the paperwork isn't done yet, but thank you so much." She pulled away and a tear was on her cheek. "Make sure to come by *our* table and get a free pie, *partner*."

"We will." He opened the door and frosty air blew in.

"No need to walk us out. Good night."

Still wanting to make sure they were all right, he

went to the window and pulled the curtain back to watch them enter their car. He figured the town was safe, but if they tripped on the ice or had problems starting the car, he wanted to know.

31

*J*ames walked back into the living room. "They're gone."

At least someone's Christmas wish had been answered tonight. Melanie may not be all that close with the Peterson family, but a warm feeling of relief washed over her knowing that the restaurant was saved. "That was very sweet of you to invest in the place."

"I couldn't see it torn down for a parking garage."

She thought about the times she had spent there, not just working, but also with her family in happier times. "Having it bulldozed down would be terrible." Arianna was wide awake in her arms and playing with her hair. "We should clean up the kitchen."

"I think Arianna has gotten bigger just since I've known her." James picked her up from Melanie's embrace. "Do you think she's grown?"

Melanie led them back to the dining room where she picked up some dirty dishes. "You've just known her a week."

"And she ate and slept a lot today." He held Arianna firmly in one hand and then picked up the portable playpen and carried it to the kitchen.

Stacking the plates, she ran the water in the kitchen sink while Arianna played in the secure pen. The pipes roared to life after a few minutes, and she began rinsing the dishes and handing them to James.

"This place needs a dishwasher," he said, drying the plates.

"I grew up without one, so I'm used to it." At the time, she hated washing the dishes after a big holiday meal with her family. Now it was a fond memory. She and her mother had many heart–to–heart talks over a sudsy sink.

"Uh, oh." James looked down at his daughter and how her face had reddened. "Oh."

The smell of a dirty diaper filled the room. Melanie dried her hands and then reached for the girl.

"I'll do it," James said.

"Really?"

"I think I'll need you to walk me through it, but I'd like to try."

Melanie wasn't going to argue with that. It wasn't as if Arianna was a major poopy diaper maker, but

Melanie was glad for the break. Having a messy diaper right before bed was also a good sign, and she hoped the child would sleep through the night.

They quickly finished the last of the dishes and then laid Arianna on a blanket on the floor, the diaper bag and plenty of wipes handy.

"I'm ready." He undid one tie and then the other, slowly peeling the diaper down. The smell hit her nose as he did so.

"Oh, geez." He turned his neck and sat taller, doing his best to avoid the smell.

"Wipe," Melanie said, handing him a clean cloth.

"Why is it so green?" He made a passing wipe but missed most of the mess.

"Peas." Melanie handed him a second wipe.

Wiping a bit better, Arianna started to cry.

"Am I doing it wrong?"

"No, she has diaper rash." Melanie reached in the bag and took out some ointment.

He wiped a few more times and then slid the diaper out. Melanie folded it and got rid of the pungent odor.

Smearing ointment on her tender bottom, he asked, "What about butt powder? There is such a thing, right?"

Melanie broke into a wide smile at the phrase 'butt powder' and nearly laughed. The words seemed so funny coming from James who moments ago was talking about the financial value of real estate and other business stuff. "Yes, there is 'butt powder' but you don't use powder on little girls."

He looked like he was about to ask why, but then said, "That actually makes sense."

Once the diaper was taken care of, he picked Arianna up and the new diaper sagged against her hips.

"You can make the tabs a little tighter," Melanie said. "You don't want the next mess to fall out."

His eyes widened. "No, we certainly wouldn't want that."

She threw the old diaper out and the two of them took turns washing up.

Outside they heard a boom and some laughter.

"What do you think that was?" he asked.

Melanie carried Arianna to the living room window and glanced outside. The back end of a truck was screeching out of sight. Hanging from the tree in the front yard was a strand of tissue paper. Bending down, she took a good look at the tree through the window. Swaying in the empty branches were streams of toilet paper.

She gazed back at James. "We have a problem."

"It seems that not everyone is happy to have me in town." James could have guessed this response to his visit, but it had been days since he had arrived. He was hoping everyone in this town, with their friendly ways, was not seeing him as the 'boss man' who could affect all of their financial lives.

"Arianna hasn't been up long, but she may go down if I bathe her and put her pajamas on. Why don't I do that while you start cleaning up. I'll join you as soon as I can."

"Can't we call someone?"

"The police?"

That sounded good for a start. His house had been vandalized and he found it odd how personal he took the attack. "Sure."

"We don't know who did this. I doubt you'll get fingerprints off of toilet paper."

She was right, but it still hurt that thugs would do such a thing. He glanced out the window and took in the messy sight. "Couldn't we call someone to clean this mess up?"

She let out a deep sigh. "Maybe, but we have to hurry and get that paper off the tree."

He bent down low to see how high up the toilet paper went. There were streams of it, even as high as the tallest branches. "Why is that?"

"Dry paper is easy to clean. Wet paper is messy. Like, really messy. See if there is a something in the garage that will help you get to the higher branches and I'll hurry and put her down."

Melanie went upstairs as James put on his coat and opened the front door. Plastered on the door were two broken eggs. It was cold outside, so he walked past them and made his way to the garage.

The large, metal garage door was manual. He pulled the handle and lifted it up, the gears squeaking and complaining the entire way.

He entered the garage and found a light switch. The place was respectively clean, with not even oil stains or gas fumes. He figured there hadn't been a car in here in decades. Several boxes stood in the corner and he read the markings on them. 'Christmas decorations.'

There were two boxes for Christmas and another two for Easter and Halloween. The boxes were dusty, but they didn't look like spiders or rodents had crawled in. He made a mental note to bring them into the house in the morning.

Behind the boxes were a stack of gardening tools. Sticking out was a rake.

The sun had already set and he used the outside garage lights to guide the rake along the branches. Snow fell and hit him in the face and all he could think about was the waste of the all the 'Snow Falls' that he could have had with Arianna the next day.

"She's asleep." Melanie carried the baby monitor with her and walked up to the tree. "You did a good job. Looks like you got it all out."

He glanced back to the house. "I just have to clean up the door."

"Good thing you have all this toilet paper, huh?"

A cry came from the baby monitor. "I have to..."

"I'll finish up here and check on you in a few minutes."

Scraping half–frozen egg off the front door didn't take long, and he threw everything into a garbage bag and left it in the garage. Taking another look at the boxes of Christmas ornaments, he grabbed them and went into the house.

He placed the boxes in the living room, removed his coat, and then walked upstairs. The warmth of the home enveloped him with each step. His feet were numb and so were his fingers, which he rubbed together.

At the top of the stairs, he heard Melanie singing to Arianna. He wasn't sure, but he thought it was another lullaby. She must have known several of them. He paused and listened for a moment. A smile quickly came to his face. She had a beautiful voice.

He washed his hands in the bathroom and then returned and knocked on the open door to her room. The smell of lavender had filled the room thanks to the diffuser, and a light coming from the floor heater in the corner gave the room a warm and cozy feel. He inhaled deeply, enjoying the scent. Lavender was calming and restful. Hopefully it would help Arianna get some well needed sleep.

"How is she?" he asked, poking his head into the room.

"Wide awake. You must be half frozen." Melanie

patted the bed and invited him in. "Come and lay down with us."

It was picture perfect and a nice family moment. He removed his bulky sweater, knowing it'd be too hot soon after he got in bed with them and that a t–shirt would be more comfortable. "Someone isn't sleepy?" he asked in baby talk.

"Bbbl." Arianna turned her body and slunk down on her father's chest once he lay down. She giggled and put her fingers into her mouth.

"Too many peaches." He tapped her tiny nose and she looked up at him. "You, my little sweetheart, have a sugar high."

Melanie moved her body so the two of them made a barrier on either side of Arianna. It also had her lay much closer to him. "Lay down, baby. It's night night time," she said.

James couldn't remember the last time he lay in a bed with a woman and didn't have sex with her. If he had to guess, he was an awkward teenager probably, if ever.

But lying here with his daughter and nanny did bring back a fond memory. It was a memory of one of his nannies. She was an older woman who had watched him when he was about eight years old. All his friends were into horror movies and he pretended to be brave and watched them as well, even though he hated such films. He remembered the nanny laying with him and singing to him as he fell asleep. It made him feel safe and special.

He hoped Arianna felt protected and loved.

That is what was important.

He could make out Melanie's outline in the dark, with Arianna's silhouette sitting up in between them. "Good night," he said to both of the women in his life.

"I think she needs a story to fall asleep."

James didn't know any childhood stories off the top of his head, but he said, "Long time ago, in a magical place called Newbury a company was started." He told the story of his family as Sandra had told it to him, except he told it in baby talk. Melanie had asked a few questions, but the story seemed to work its magic and make Arianna tired.

"The man came to the town ready to close down the factory," he continued. He knew Arianna had already fallen asleep in his arms, but Melanie still lay awake. "The man came to the town and met a fairy princess named Melanie."

He moved his arm so Melanie could place her head on it. He took a deep breath, his heart pounding in the little room. His mouth felt dry, so he licked his lips and continued. "This princess was the answer to what the man needed in his life, and he was so happy to have found her."

32

*M*elanie weaved her way through the crowd, avoiding stray elbows and people bumping into her as she led James into the Newbury Dance Hall for the Christmas Eve fair. The place smelled of freshly baked pies and doughnuts mixed with corn dogs and pretzels.

"My family comes to this fair every year." All of it represented fine holiday fare to Melanie. There would be jelly, hot sauce, and bread to taste, as well. A little something for everyone.

The usual vendors were there, including some new ones. She noticed a bouncy castle outside and a portable jungle gym. She figured all the kids running around, especially those with their faces painted, were enjoying themselves. They probably didn't even notice how cold it was outside.

They passed a portable heater and she paused a

moment to get warm. The place had several of them all roped off and in strategic places. Her numb fingers tingled with a bit of pain as they came back to life.

"I didn't expect it to be so big." James pushed Arianna in her stroller and tightly held onto Melanie's hand. His skin felt warm, and she enjoyed the closeness. His physical nearness wasn't all that made her happy; it was also being able to share a Christmas tradition that she looked forward to each year.

James was turning into someone she cared about. Someone she wanted more time with. He may be gone in a few days, but he was here now. She didn't want to think of him leaving, not when they had just started what seemed like the sparks of a relationship. She took a deep breath and smiled to him.

"Merry Christmas, Mel," a woman said, followed by two men who also wished her warm holiday wishes. Others nodded acknowledgment to her as she walked past them, while still more stared. She figured they wondered who accompanied her, especially since they had a baby with them.

"Seems like a festive group." James dodged other partygoers and walked closely beside her.

"Like I said, the entire town turns out for this event." Melanie pointed down to a crowd of people to where a '4H Events and Demonstration' sign hung.

"We can get a *Charlie Brown* pathetic, last–minute tree down there." She waved her hand in front of her where some balloons were. "Delicious food is in front of us." Waving to the right, she added, "Gifts and auction house down there."

"Sounds like we have a lot to see and do."

"Hello Melanie." A vendor wearing an apron said and got her attention. "Merry Christmas."

"Ms. Nancy. Hi." Melanie gave the woman a half hug and asked how she was doing. "Ms. Nancy, this is James." She didn't use his last name since she agreed with him that there was no need to call attention to themselves, especially with the press lately.

"Ms. Nancy was my third-grade teacher," she told James. "She now makes the most heavenly jams and jellies."

"Only the best." Ms. Nancy smiled at James and held out her hand. "It's good to meet you, sir."

He shook his head and a slight smile formed. "There's no need to call me sir. Just James will do."

She nodded slightly and studied him. "You're James Nielson. My husband works at your plant."

James's expression soured and Melanie knew Ms. Nancy as one of the sweetest women around, but she didn't want her ex–school teacher to cause a scene. James had worn comfortable clothes, jacket, and a hat just to blend in and go unnoticed.

"People have been talking all over town about

your visit." Her eyes narrowed in on him. "Are you planning on closing down the plant?"

Melanie glanced all around to make sure no one was listening. A pain hit her in the chest. They had barely gotten through the door and this was the welcome James got?

And, how was it that Ms. Nancy could always put you on the spot and call you out? Memories of having to go to the whiteboard and show her work on math problems flooded Melanie's mind. James didn't deserve this.

"I don't know," James said with a genuine pain-stricken tone. "I sure hope to save it."

Ms. Nancy eyed him, but after a moment her scowl disappeared. "Want to try some preserves? I've got to make a living somehow."

"That's not fair," Melanie protested.

"It's fine." James scanned the samplings on the table. Peach, pear, strawberry, they were all standard jelly varieties. "They all look so good."

Regardless of Ms. Nancy's rudeness, Melanie pointed to the jar with the light purple sticker on it. "She makes the best vanilla lavender jelly around."

"Vanilla lavender?" he asked.

"They're $12 apiece, or three jars for $30," Ms. Nancy said, bringing out a paper bag.

"A bit pricy," Melanie said, "but well worth it."

It was adorable that Melanie would think that he knew the price of a jar of jelly. The latest Mac computer? Or even the cost of a Tesla? Sure. But not jelly. He supposed they usually went for the $10 a jar range in any normal grocery store, but he wasn't sure.

He glanced around the hall and at all the vendors. "We have a lot of tables to visit, so I'll just take a jar of the peach." He noticed a sign that indicated she took the Square so he handed her his credit card.

As Ms. Nancy turned away and grabbed a container of peach jelly from the bin behind her, James said to Melanie, "At least I know Arianna can have peaches. She needs to be older for the strawberry, and maybe some other flavors."

Melanie couldn't help but smile. She placed her hand on his shoulder and gently rubbed. "You've really been studying those parenting websites."

His eyes twinkled with pride. In a whisper so only Melanie could hear, he added, "And, at least I know the jelly is sealed. I don't need to worry about it containing any spit."

"Here you go," Ms. Nancy said as Melanie let out a slight chuckle.

"Thank you," he said quickly as Ms. Nancy handed him the bag and a tablet so he could sign for the purchase.

He placed the jelly in the stroller down below. "Where to next?"

Melanie wanted to get Arianna a gift and maybe

something for James, plus, she told her aunt and uncle she'd meet them here. She took the stroller from him. "How about we split up and meet at the Christmas trees in an hour?"

At first, he looked hurt, but then smiled. "Sounds good." He grabbed a few grocery bags from under the stroller. "I'll see you soon."

———

JAMES WATCHED as the two women in his life walked down the make-shift aisle toward the row of what looked like home-made soups and dips.

"Ms. Nancy," he said, getting her attention from another customer that walked up. "I'll take another jar. This one vanilla lavender." It wasn't much of a Christmas present for Melanie, but a decent stocking stuffer.

He glanced around. They should probably buy some Christmas stockings while they were here.

After he made the jelly purchase, he walked in the opposite direction of the jams, towards the crafts. Homemade candles, children's clothes, and even toys. There was so much and he didn't know where to begin.

A musical toy caught his attention and he bought that and a few other gifts for Arianna that seemed like they would be fun. Overall, his daughter was easy to shop for. All he had to do was look for toys and clothes that were suitable for a six-month-old child.

Getting something for Melanie, besides a jar of jam, was much harder.

He passed a vendor that had quilts on display, and he had to stop. The table was filled with brightly covered blankets and she had some hung over racks so they could be more on display. They were practically works of art.

"This one is a 'wedding ring' quilt. This orange one is called a 'starburst'," the vendor explained as James lifted one quilt up, looked at another, and then searched through even more.

The craftmanship was amazing. "These are lovely."

"Thank you."

He saw a sign that indicated king–sized quilts were $200. He studied the quilt in front of him and inspected the intricate design and colors. The quilts were light and airy, but warm and inviting. The stitching went through the blanket and even made a nice design on the underside—making the quilt practically reversable. "That price can't be right."

She turned and eyed the sign. She then looked back at him with a concerned expression. She stood taller, squaring off her shoulders, and her lips thinned. "Please feel free to make me an offer."

He had already seen at least four quilts he wanted. He had his father to shop for, Arianna's crib wouldn't need one, but he still wanted to get her one, and he wanted one for himself. They were just too exquisitely crafted not to have.

"Two hundred dollars just seems..."

"I can go down a bit on the price, but don't forget," she interrupted, "twenty–five percent goes to charity."

"What?"

She looked almost apologetic. "Each vendor can select what percentage to give, with the minimum being twenty–five percent." She looked nearly embarrassed for selecting the lowest amount of her earnings to give away.

"So, you don't even make two–hundred dollars off of these quilts?" When she shrugged, he asked, "how long does it take you to make one of them?"

Her hand patted several of the quilts and a smile of pride crossed her face. "I made all of these in the last five years," she said, modestly. "I'm selling them since my husband lost his job at the plant..."

Guilt coated James. She didn't recognize him. She had no idea who he was and what power he held over the plant. He swallowed the lump in his throat. "I'll take these three."

He then thought about gifts for his grandmother, aunt, and of course, Melanie. "As well as those three quilts hanging up."

Her face lit up and she quickly went to work pulling down the quilts and folding them.

"If I pay extra, can you have three of them shipped to New York? Like an extra fifty dollars?"

She shrugged. "I don't see why not. They won't make it in time for Christmas though."

"That's fine."

He handed her his credit card and she rang up the charges. When she handed the tablet to him, she said, "That'll be $1200. Please make sure the order is fine and then sign."

He adjusted the order to include a hefty tip, signed it, and handed the tablet back. "They're easily worth $500 apiece, and that's what I'm paying for them."

Her expression was priceless.

"The extra $300 per blanket is for you, for all your hard work." After making arrangements for the shipping of three of them and the delivery of the other three, he left to find his family's table of pies. But, first, he noticed a sign with the name of a church on it and something about a food bank. He'd go there next and make a donation to their worthy causes.

33

Melanie's enjoyed her favorite Christmas carol, Silent Night, which played on the overhead speaker. The holiday music played softly, and she found herself singing it quietly in her head.

"This little one is so precious." Aunt Eva cooed and looked at the sleeping baby in the stroller.

The song switched to Rudolf and Melanie wondered what Arianna's favorite song would be. "This little girl is the perfect kid." She was surprised at how easy Arianna was to take care of. She went down for two naps a day, like clockwork, rarely cried, never screamed. This wasn't your typical kid.

But then, she felt closer to Arianna than all the other kids she had taken care of in the past. Working in a day care center, or even babysitting, just wasn't the same. Arianna cuddled with her at night, smiled at her when she woke from her naps, and loved to hear her sing.

It was probably as close as she would ever come to having a baby of her own.

"Your uncle is in the art corner handling your paintings," Aunt Eva said, pointing to the sign with "Art" across it. Scanning the amount of people over there she added, "Doesn't look too crowded. At least, not yet."

"I'm so glad he agreed to sell them." She couldn't bear haggling over the cost of one of her artworks, or, even worse, hearing critics sneer as they walked past them. It was best that they sell and the deed be done as quickly as possible.

But she wasn't hopeful that her paintings would sell. All the artwork, including the pottery, was marked at the $40–$150 range. She had listed her work as a 50–50 split with the auction house, which would allow perspective customers to actually bid on her paintings as well. She'd hate for to be auctioned away for less, but not selling at all? That would be worse.

"Your paintings will sell—and at your suggested pricing," her aunt said, obviously noticing the look of uneasiness on her face. "Maybe someone will even offer to pay more."

"Doubtful." She let out a slight chuckle. "But thanks."

"It's a good turnout this year." Aunt Eva stopped

and looked at some homemade salsas. "I should probably pick up some sides for Christmas dinner. We got those delicious rolls here last year, and that sweet potato pie."

"And the Dutch apple cake." Melanie couldn't forget that cake. She knew she probably should buy a pie from James's family, but he said he would pick some up—and she loved the apple cake.

Noticing her aunt checking out some aprons and cookware, Melanie asked, "You picking up some Christmas gifts?"

"Me? No. You know I've already sent your brother his presents and I already have a little something for everyone."

Money was tighter this year than the year before. The family had agreed to only buy gifts for the children this year, but she knew her aunt would break that vow and get her something. Of course, she had already picked up a little gift for each of them as well.

"How is it working for Mr. Handsome?"

"James?"

"Now who else would I be talking about? I haven't seen you and that baby since we were at your apartment." She slowly let out a sigh. "He sure is dreamy looking."

Melanie felt her face flush. "Things are going well."

"Personally well?"

The place was too crowded to really have a good conversation. Melanie led her aunt to a bakery table and got them each a sweet bun. They then sat a table in a corner of the dance hall away from people.

Aunt Eva took a seat. "Okay, spill."

There was so much to share. "Ok, first... I can't tell you what he's told me about the plant."

"I wouldn't ask." Aunt Eva quickly shook her head and had a stern look on her face, one that told Melanie she was serious. "That could jeopardize your job... and anything else that might be going on." Her face turned into a sweet smile with a twinkle in her eyes.

Melanie figured she wouldn't ask about the business. Of course, what was going on personally in her life? Yeah, that was fair game. "I really like James."

A pleasant smile spread on Aunt Eva's face. "And?"

"And... I really should buy him a gift for Christmas," she said, deflecting the question. She took a bit of the sweet bread and enjoyed the chewy texture. She thought about the real problem with getting James a gift, and said, "I'm working on something for him, but I don't know if it will work out."

"What is it?"

She shook her head. "I don't want to jinx it. But if I can't pull it off, I don't want to be empty handed. I just don't know what to get a rich man who has everything."

Aunt Eva's eyes narrowed. "Just because a man's got money doesn't mean he has everything." Her hand lay on Melanie's arm. "Just give it some thought and ask yourself 'what does he really want' and you'll have an answer."

Being surrounded by handmade doilies and crafts wasn't going to help. Any food they bought would be eaten before he left for New York.

New York.

"And?" Aunt Eva said, prying.

A heavy feeling sank in her chest. She hadn't wanted to even think of him leaving, let alone talk about her feelings about how she had grown to care, not just for James, but for both him and Arianna. "He lives in New York," she finally said.

A dismissive look crossed her face. "You could always move." She took a sip of her coffee as if her last statement was as easily said as done.

Moving away was what Melanie had always wanted. Leave Newbury and live in a big city with all the glitz and glamour. Have the time and the luxury to be an artist one day, to have art gala openings, and to sell her work. To be known as an artist... but then reality settled in, as it always tends to do. She'd be a starving artist. "I have no job there."

"Well, certainly jobs are hard to come by, but couldn't you remain as his nanny? Or has he hired one in New York?"

She hadn't thought about that, but in any case, she didn't want to just be a nanny.

"Go."

"What?"

Aunt Eva glared at her as if Melanie had lost her mind. "Go and be with that man." Her head swiveled and she searched the crowd for him. "You need to decide what to do, but that man is only here for a few more days and you're wasting your time talking with me."

"I'm not wasting my time."

"You know what? Invite him and little Arianna for Christmas," Aunt Eva said, the tone of her voice light and cheery. "It'll be fun having a little one around on the big day."

Melanie shook her head. "I think he already has plans to be with his family."

"Oh, that's right. He does have a lot of family here." She let out a sigh. "I sure would miss seeing you on Christmas Day, but why don't you see about spending the holiday with his family."

God, this woman loved her.

"I'm going to spend it with you." She leaned in and kissed her aunt on the cheek.

"Well, I don't want to be greedy, but I would prefer that." She again glanced back into the crowd. "You should spend as much time with him as you can while he's still here." She stood from the table.

Like your mother always used to say, "seize the opportunity."

MELANIE HAD REJOINED James and they walked down what he thought was the most exciting part about the fair. The art that was for sale.

Arianna was wide awake and sitting in a baby sling around his shoulders, which allowed her to face outward to the crowd. Melanie had bought it from one of the vendors, and it certainly looked sturdy to him. He felt like a kangaroo with a chest-pouch, but had to admit, it was much easier than carrying her.

He picked up a piece of art. "The statues are from a mold," he said, inspecting a bird statue with some hearts. "The clay pots are nicer. They were made from an actual pottery wheel." He wasn't that fond of figurines, but wanted to give each exhibitor some time. Spending a few minutes at each table took some time, but he couldn't remember if he'd ever been to a fair like this before. He loved it.

The paintings were next, and he was much more excited to see them.

The art was hung on partitioned dividers with the artists' names on signs beneath them. They walked past some paintings depicting outdoor images and some that were still life. Arianna stared at the paintings and cooed at the bright colored ones. They were nice, but not his style.

When they turned down the next aisle, his eyes widened. His gaze darted from one painting to the next from this artist. Exquisite colors, bold strokes, and his favorite style—cubism. Not many modern-day painters did this form of painting, which he thought was a shame.

His hand went to his mouth and he let out a sigh of awe. "Beautiful," he said. "Amazingly beautiful."

As if also showing her approval, Arianna squealed with delight.

Gazing at one painting and then the other he said, "Different sizes, too. The whole collection works so well together."

Melanie's eyes lit up and she watched him intently as he studied the paintings. "Do you really like them?"

He nodded. "Absolutely." He looked at the small placard and read the artist's name. "These are *your* paintings?" James stared at the bold, primary colors and the cubist–style portrayal of the animals. A bubble of excitement stirred within him, and he stood mesmerized by the beauty of Melanie's artwork.

"I've always loved to paint," she said modestly, her cheeks flushing.

"Mma–blb." Arianna kicked her legs and stared at the bright colors.

He stepped closer to the image featuring three cats, careful not to let Arianna touch the work of art. The stark simplicity and raw emotion he detected from the brush strokes spoke to the artist in him.

He turned to face her, his smile beaming with joy. "Your work rivals Franz Marc," he said in an excited, school–boy tone of voice. "It's like you've studied under him for years and have captured his style."

"I don't know Franz Marc." She shifted her gaze to her paintings and them back to him. "He wasn't one of my teachers."

He let out a slight chuckle. "I would hope not, seeing how he died before World War I. He was a founding member of Der Blaue Reiter, a collection of famous artists." Naturally, getting a degree in business had been important since James had his family business to run, but minoring in art history had been his passion.

He knew so much about the art world and had no one in his life to share his love of art with. At least, not until now.

Melanie studied her painting and shrugged, apparently not realizing how significant he found her work.

"Franz Marc is my favorite artist. Nazis censored his work in World War II." Gosh, he could go on and on about the man, his struggles, and his work.

"Really? I heard the Nazis stole a lot of artwork."

"Paintings, mostly, but also statues and other art." James could give a history lesson on the stolen works, but instead, he glanced at the price tag on the bottom of Melanie's painting. "Only eighty dollars?" His gaze darted toward the biggest one of the pieces. "One hundred dollars for that one?"

The prices seemed ridiculous. Even more ridiculous than the quilts he just bought. He stood back and studied the paintings, focusing on the entire collection as a whole. "These are worth much more than that."

She blushed in a way that told him that she didn't believe him. "I'd be happy if any of them sold. I split the money with the charity house." Her eyes then lit up. "Or, I could give you one as a Christmas gift!"

Pointing at her paintings, she said, "I'd love to gift one to you. Pick out whichever one you want."

That was very sweet of her, but he suspected she was selling these masterpieces because she needed the money. "I don't want to break up the collection."

A worried look crossed her face, but then she smiled. "I can give them all to you as a Christmas present."

"Absolutely not. You're an artist and deserve your commission on your paintings." He then remembered what the people at the charity booth had told him when he made his donation. The price share was up to seventy–five percent. He hoped Melanie wasn't donating that much, but he knew her generosity. "Let me guess, you're giving seventy-five percent to the charity running this fair."

She shook her head. "Fifty."

"Fifty percent?" That seemed ridiculous. Naturally, the charity needed donations, but the canvas, the paint, her time... it was worth at least twice what the price indicated. The masterpieces she created? That was worth so much more in his mind.

He felt giddy inside. "I must buy them all."

"Really? You don't have to feel like you—"

"I *must* have them." His voice sounded commanding. "They're outstanding. Marc is my favorite cubist, and your paintings are rawer than his, but they show the same passion and spirit." He studied them once more, a huge smile spreading across his face. "Actually, I think you're my favorite artist now. Who do I see about buying them? I'll want them shipped to my home so I can display them."

She smiled a beam of pride, her face flushing red. "My uncle, Craig, volunteered to handle my table." She glanced around. "Let me know if you see him."

"Do I know him?"

"He's the foreman down at the plant. I imagine he's the one you've been talking to."

James was speechless. He had spent days with

the man and he never said a word. "Craig is the uncle who raised you?"

She nodded. "Don't worry. He didn't say anything confidential to me about the plant. And, you know I would never say anything."

"Craig?"

"Yes. Craig."

This town really was small. James could not see a family resemblance and assumed the man was related through marriage. In any case, the man was thoughtful and very pleasant during his entire visit. James could tell where Melanie got her sweet disposition from.

"All right. We'll find him and buy these paintings. But," he stressed, "you're going to earn the true amount on these beautiful works of art."

She really looked confused to him and pointed at the price tags. "They're priced..."

"Incorrectly," he interrupted. "Let's find your uncle so I can buy these beautiful paintings before anyone else does. Then we need to buy a tree."

She walked down the painting aisle and searched for her uncle, pausing to look around, she stood underneath an archway that read, "Santa's Village."

"Melanie," he called out to her.

She turned and made eye contact with him. "I'm sure my uncle is somewhere nearby."

Closing the gap between them, he could feel the

heat of how she studied his eyes and waited for his next word. The smell of her perfume mixed with the pine scent of the nearby Christmas trees, and her smile simply stole his heart.

She slightly tilted her head. "What is it?"

"Don't move." His arm wrapped around her waist and he pulled her closer to one side. "Would it be a big scandal in this little town if I kissed you in the middle of this fine fair?"

Her gaze darted to his lips. "In this little town, it just might."

He nodded to the mistletoe, which hung above them. "Then I guess we could just break with tradition."

She smiled when she saw the plant dangling from red garland on the archway. "You know, it might just cause an even bigger scandal if we *did* break tradition. So, I think a kiss in is order."

Leaning in, he found her soft, eager lips and gently kissed her. She applied more pressure and he matched her desire. For a moment he closed his eyes, and they were the only two people in the hall. Nothing mattered in that instant. Nothing that is, except how to make this beautiful moment last forever.

34

"*I*s everything all right?" James asked, now that they were home—all purchases taken care off—and decorating the house.

Melanie set her cell phone on the coffee table. "I just got a call from Arianna's Kinder Musik teacher." Her face beamed with a smile. "She wishes all of us a Merry Christmas."

"That's very nice of her. I guess she's calling all of her students."

Melanie shrugged. "I don't know. She is an old babysitter of mine and we've revived an old friendship through the class."

James strung the colored lights on the small three-foot fir that now stood in the living room of his family home. "I'm so glad they could deliver the tree." His height overpowered the tiny fur. Taking a strong whiff of the pine scent, he added, "It's not as grand as what I'm used to, but I do like it."

"It's a sad, little thing, but I think it's perfect." Melanie shifted Arianna to her other hip as they checked out the tree.

"You ready for some pretty colors?" James asked his daughter. Plugging in the lights, he watched as Arianna's eyes lit up and she let out a squeal of delight.

Melanie's face also lit up.

"I think your daddy knows how to make you happy. Doesn't he?" She placed the child in a playpen near the tree. "You can watch the lights from in here, little one. Where it's safe."

Melanie crossed the room and picked up a small box marked 'ornaments' from the table. "I can't believe these boxes sat in the garage for so long."

"What's in the little one?" He eyed it carefully. "Be careful. It's cold outside, so I doubt there'd be bugs in it..."

"Here," she said, handing the box to him. "I don't want a spider jumping out at me."

He took the box. He wasn't a fan of bugs himself, but it always amazed him how a strong woman, who could move emotional mountains and do great feats of courage, could run away from a tiny speck of a bug. "Scared of spiders?"

"Scared of anything with multiple legs that wants to bite me."

He took the box with one hand and then leaned into her. He gave her a soft kiss on the neck and then began nibbling on her ear. "*I* have multiple legs."

"Mmmm." She placed her arm around him and allowed him to trail kisses down her neck, but just for a moment. "Multiple legs as in six, or eight. *You* have a *pair* of legs. There could still be a spider in that box."

"I'll handle it." He opened the tiny box, wondering whose handwriting it was on the side. Maybe it was his great–grandparent who stored all the holiday stuff before leaving here. Whoever it was, he knew the items in these containers were quite likely family heirlooms.

He opened the box and a towel covered an ornament. Carefully unwrapping it, he discovered a beautiful glass tree topper. "Wow. It's a beautiful star."

"That's really nice. And old." She took the towel from his hand and he held the star up to the light, taking in the delicate design. She noticed that there was writing on the towel, and she recognized the style. "This is an old tea–towel."

She unwrapped it and the creases were stiff and age had covered it with brown spots. Her face lit up. "It's a calendar towel. They used to be very popular." Her mother had some dating back to the 1970s, but they had been lost between... well, her mother's death, the selling of the house, you name it.

Melanie read the date on the top of the towel. "1912."

His face quickly turned from the ornament to Melanie. "That towel is over a hundred years old?"

She inspected the fabric. Stains covered it but it was salvageable. "I think I can clean it."

His gaze went to the other box, the much larger one. "Let's see what that one has in it."

He opened the box, and more ornaments were protected by towels, but the 1912 was the only tea-towel that was a calendar. "I guess there wasn't such a thing as bubble wrap back in the day."

"These are incredible." Melanie held up some glass ornaments. "They don't make any like this anymore."

"And these are spun–satin ornaments," he said, holding up some red and white balls. "I've never seen real spun–satin balls before."

They placed each ornament onto the tree, selecting the sturdiest branches. The tree's bald spot —well, the *worst* bald spot—was turned toward the window.

"I think we did a good job." James took a step back and enjoyed their handiwork.

"And now for the star on top." Melanie handed him the tree topper.

The top branch was sturdy and he placed the tiny treasure in its place of honor. "This may be the prettiest tree I've ever seen."

"Bllllbbb."

"You agree with me, sweetheart?" He smiled at Arianna. "I guess it needed to be the best since it's your first one." He took a good look at her. "Is it just me, or is she a drooly mess?"

Arianna's watery mouth dripped drool.

"I hope she cuts these teeth soon." Melanie walked over and wiped the baby's face. "That's why she's wearing a bib right now."

"Poor baby. Do you think she might be hungry?"

"We bought some banana bread and some iced sugar cookies at the fair." Melanie picked up Arianna and sat on the couch with her. "We also picked up some vanilla custard baby food for you."

The girl reached for the sugar cookies. "Maybe next year," Melanie said, moving the plate farther away from her.

Next year, James thought. Glancing at the fireplace he saw the matching stockings they had bought. Each one was embroidered with their names, and looking much like a family set.

He was beginning a relationship with Melanie and would very much like to be with her next year as well. But she lived in this small town and he had a business to get back to.

There were so many possible ways this relationship could work out. Excitement fluttered in his stomach and he wondered if she'd agree to an idea he wanted to suggest. He just didn't know how to approach the subject.

"Here you go." Melanie opened a jar and gave her a spoon of baby food. She then gazed up at James, who helped himself to some banana bread. "You're going to spend Christmas day with your aunt?"

"Sandra invited me a few days ago." Only a part of him wanted to visit with his family. Mostly, he wanted to spend the day with Melanie, but he figured she also had plans.

"You're spending the day with your aunt and uncle, right?" he asked.

"Yes. This is my brother's off year, and he'll be with his wife's family." Since Arianna wasn't hungry and content to lay by herself on the couch, Melanie stood and walked to the side table. "Here is Arianna's gift." She went to the tree and placed the package on the embroidered tree skirt they had bought. "She can open her gift tomorrow morning."

A squeal came from the child. She had managed to take off her sock and was now waving it in the air.

Melanie shot him a devilish smile. "Or, she can open her present now. The toy will be more fun than playing with a sock"

"The gifts I bought her were delivered to my aunt's house, so let's allow her an early present tonight."

He sat on the couch and put Arianna in his lap.

Arianna fussed because she wanted a cookie from the plate on the table, but quieted down when he placed the present in front of her.

"I'll help you open it." James opened the gift and revealed a colorful play set. He pushed a button, and the toy sprang to life and played some music.

Arianna's face lit up, and she whacked the toy with her hand, causing another piece of music to play.

"I think she likes it." James had seen this toy at the fair and had bought the same one for Arianna. He figured he'd give the one he had purchased to charity.

"I also have a gift for you." Melanie sat on the couch, her eyes wide and her grin spreading from ear–to–ear.

Her wide smile held a secret, one that he hoped involved another make–out session that might end with them in his bedroom tonight. Of course, taking things slow might be the way to go with a woman of quality like Melanie. At any rate, any special 'adult type' of a gift like that would have to be later once his daughter was snugly asleep.

"I have a way you can keep the plant open," she said, her voice overflowing with excitement.

He hadn't wanted to talk about the plant in days, but a ray of hope spun its magic, and he felt as though if a miracle could happen, it would be at Christmas. "How so?"

"The Robin Reading Railroad has been dead in this town since a sinkhole destroyed some tracks on the north side of town."

"I know. After you told me about the train tracks the other day, I looked into it. The tracks are still under water." Her information wasn't news to him.

"But,"—her eyes lit up—"what if you could move the tracks?"

"Move them?" The tracks were destroyed, and the land they lay on could not be used to reroute the tracks.

"Just alter the track to go around the water."

He shook his head. He had already looked into that. "The land in that area is bad. Much of it is also under water."

"The state–owned land, sure. But not all the farmland. There are neighboring plots around the sinkhole that were not affected by the underground water."

He had researched the possibility of circumventing the bad patches of land, but had run into a roadblock. "Farmland circles the town. We'd have to convince a farmer to sell," he said, his voice trailing off. "It's been my experience that farmers do not sell their land to large corporations. In the past, I've had my lawyers working on acquiring land for this plant as well as for future plants in other towns, and each time—"

"What if a farmer *wants* to sell the land?" Her

eyes lit up again, as though another secret lay behind them.

James didn't want to get his hopes up. "It'd be nice, but we tried a few years ago and nobody wanted to sell."

Melanie's gaze fell on her cell phone. "The Kinder Musik teacher's name is Abby. She owns a huge plot of land just north of the town. She just called to tell me that she is willing to sell you what you need to redirect the train back into the town."

Melanie's voice sounded giddy with excitement. He didn't know why Abby wanted to sell, but it would solve his problem of getting the raw materials to the plant.

"She's willing to sell?" James sat straighter on the couch, his mind racing with legal matters. "I'd have to talk with the city and state regulators, get my surveyors out to the land, do an assessment of the plot and its potential to also have sinkholes, get a contract with the railroad... but if she's really serious, it may work."

"She's very serious."

"But no one wanted to sell a few years ago."

Melanie shrugged. "Life happens. She's ready now to talk. Besides," she added, "like my mother always said, 'recognize the opportunity and take advantage of the situation'."

An ache that he had carried in his heart lifted, and he found it easier to breathe. He could possibly save this plant, honor his grandfather, and... he glanced at Melanie, who now fed Arianna some banana bread.

He wanted to take her away from this town, to show her the world, to keep her in his life. But, in doing so, wouldn't he be doing exactly what his father had done when he left this town with his mother? Did his mother regret her decision to leave?

Or would Melanie stay, forcing him to go back to his old life. He didn't want to say his next sentence, but did so anyway. "You could get your job back if the plant stays open."

MELANIE'S HEART SANK, and the bubble she had made of love and family just burst.

She hadn't thought about her job in days. Naturally, she'd have to return to it if they called and told her to come back. It was a good job, one that she needed.

"My life can continue as normal once you leave and things go back to what they were," she said, her voice drifting off as she glanced away. "It'll be good to have things back to normal."

The stare he gave her wasn't reassuring. He would move back to New York with Arianna. He would reclaim his old life and probably wouldn't think twice about this town or her.

"I have a gift for you, too. But I didn't wrap it, and I'm not sure you'll want it."

She took a deep breath. James was here now. Arianna was here, too. Melanie didn't need to start missing them until they were actually gone.

She mentally told herself not to cry. "You have a gift for me?"

A beautiful smile beamed on his face. "A scholarship to Vassar."

She wasn't sure she heard that right and her mind raced. "What do you mean?"

"Nielson International Corporation has had a lot of bad press because of the recent layoffs. To offset the bad stuff, you always want good press."

Melanie could understand that, but how would that mean a scholarship?

"Setting up a scholarship is one way we can give back to the community."

Giving back to a community sounded like charity. It came across as pity. It was not what Melanie wanted. Her chest tightened. "I don't need charity."

"It's not charity."

Money must be a wonderful thing to have. James had only yesterday found out about her not being able to afford to go to school, and now, as if by magic, a scholarship opened up? "And now you instantly have a scholarship that's perfect for me?"

"I set everything up last night with my lawyers. It's why I went upstairs to make that phone call. I only got the idea for a scholarship once I saw your letter. It wasn't until this morning when I saw your art that I realized how perfect you are to receive the funds."

Not just a scholarship, but one in her field of study? "And it's conveniently an art scholarship?"

"My family's business began in paint. I have a minor in art history. It isn't that far of a leap." He pulled away from her on the couch and handed Arianna a hard teething cookie. "My company needs the tax break, my father asked me to do something to shed some good light on the company after the recent layoffs, and I just got this great idea after seeing your letter and your work."

The muscles in her jaw unclenched, and she could breathe again. "So, the scholarship is real."

"And based on your, let's call it a portfolio that I've seen and bought for $1000, you are the most qualified. You need to go to art school and achieve your full potential."

Her jaw dropped. "You paid $1000 for my paintings?" she asked, her voice squeaking out the cost.

"I paid $1000 for *each* of your paintings. I paid $2000 for the largest one."

Her heart rate increased, and she could feel the pounding in her chest. James had spent seven thousand dollars, just like that. No planning ahead of time. No saving for months to make sure he had the money. He just whipped out a checkbook.

Good Lord. That meant she had earned half of what he paid, since 50% went to the charities.

Did James think so much of her art that he'd so easily spend a small fortune on it? Or did he want to give her money and this was the only way he thought she'd accept it?

He laid his hand on her knee. "You are very talented, Melanie. You need to pursue your gift."

Things were going so fast. "Is this charity?"

"I made a separate donation to the charities at the fair. I bought your paintings because you are an amazing and gifted artist."

Amazing. Gifted. She took a deep breath.

"Believe me, that wasn't a pity–payment. You deserve every cent I paid for them." He gave her what she considered to be a pained expression. "This scholarship will save my butt with the press. You'll be doing me a favor by accepting it. The idea that someone who got laid off from the plant—"

"Furloughed."

"Right, someone who got furloughed from the plant and probably would be laid off being the recipient of the scholarship will be a big win for my company."

Maybe she just needed the hope, but his story made sense. However, Melanie just couldn't accept his money. "James, the offer is nice, but—"

"Be smart," he said, interrupting her and smiling a boyish grin. "A wise person once told me to 'Recognize the opportunity and take advantage of the situation.'"

She heard her words thrown back at her. Taking a deep breath, and letting all the worries leave her body when she exhaled, she knew what her heart wanted to do.

Melanie couldn't believe it. She was going to college.

EPILOGUE

Melanie lay in bed, staring at her phone's time display. Five o'clock in the morning. She still had hours until the big event, but she felt too nervous to sleep.

"It's too early." James turned and smiled at her, the dim light radiating from the cell phone casting a slight glow across his face and the rest of the room. "We don't have to be up for a few more hours," he said, his tired voice coaxing her to lie back down.

She took a deep breath to help her focus. "Your Aunt Sandra, grandmother, and my brother are already in town. My aunt and uncle should be landing at nine. They said they'd take a cab from the airport."

"I'm glad your uncle could get some time off. The plant has been keeping him extra busy these days..."

James's sleepy voice trailed off. He then yawned and opened his eyes halfway to look at her again.

"The gala will be over at six." She powered off her cell phone and set it on the nightstand. "The reception shouldn't last more than a couple of hours." She mentally worked through her schedule. "I'll drive Arianna to kindergarten and then check in with the museum."

She was nervous. The day was too important. How many artists made their public debut at the Whitney Museum of American Art? Of course, perks always came to those with a degree in art from Vassar College. Plus, her last name now being Nielson had opened many doors that were not generally open to others.

"I told Arianna she could skip kindergarten today. Besides," James added after a yawn, "she wants to spend time with her grandparents before they leave on their next cruise. The three of them will be at the museum on time."

What a relief. This was another "Wonder Woman" moment and she needed a break. Having her in-laws help out was a relief. It solved so many problems with trying to get Arianna to and from the art museum when it opened to the public at noon. "That's a good idea. I hope she won't be too bored."

James opened both eyes and stared at her. "I'm taking the day off, so she can, too. You know the rule:

family first." He glanced at the clock on the night-stand. "You need to come back to bed and rest for a few more hours."

Melanie had planned to take their daughter to school, but now she could spend the day with her. She lay back down and cuddled into James's arms, her body sinking into his muscular one.

"The paintings are already on display, and the museum has taken care of everything. We don't even have to be there until eleven this morning." James then added for good measure, "Everything will be perfect." He kissed her cheek and allowed his hand to caress down her body as he spooned her. "Just relax, and don't let the day stress you."

His hand now cupped her rounded belly. "Plus, stay off your feet as much as you can. The baby is due in a few weeks, and you don't want to wear yourself out."

He was right. This was one of the special days Melanie had dreamed about her entire life. She could lie in her husband's arms for a little while longer and enjoy the anticipation.

THE END

Please do the author a favor of leaving a review.

You can find links to all retailers at:
http://www.reginamorris.com/christmas-in-
newbury-info

ABOUT THE AUTHOR

Dear Readers,

I hope you enjoyed reading my novel, Christmas in Newbury: A Billionaire Dad & Nanny Romance. Please leave a review on the retailer site where you purchased the book.

You can find a link to all retailers at: reginamorris. com/christmas-in-newbury.

Please visit my website (http://www. reginamorris.com) for more information about my other novels and short stories. A list of my books and descriptions are below.

Please feel free to contact me through my website, through my many social media sites (see my website for the a list) or by email at mailto:regina@reginamorris.- com?subject=Email from fan.

I like to play games and have fun in my monthly electronic newsletters. Please sign up at newsletter.regi- namorris.com

By day, I work in a small cubicle as a computer programmer, but at night I write about vampires, billion- aires, and other romance combinations. I capture my creativity on the pages of my passionate stories. I write about second chance romances, mature romances (where the characters are 40+ years of age), and about vampires.

My contemporary romances are mostly sweet romances (please check descriptions to confirm). The romances build a connection between two people with happily-ever-afters. No cliff-hangers, but complete stories.

The books in my series are all stand-alone novels that can be read in any order.

My COLONY series is about vampires who can alter their aged appearances by the amount of blood they consume. The series is about a covert team of sexy vampires who protect the President of the United States. This series' success prompted me to launch another series ("COLONY World") that involves the same world, but about civilian vampires who live among unsuspecting humans.

The heat level differs from mild to hot in my books. My stories involving the Historical Preservation Agency and time travel are mild. My COLONY series, COLONY World series, and some of my contemporary romances are hot. These hot stories have an age warning of 18+ on them. My contemporary short stories are mild. My contemporary novels vary.

I live in Austin, Texas with my husband and two children. I graduated high school in Germany and I attended the University of Texas at Austin, where I received a degree in Computer Science with a minor in math. After enjoying a career in software engineering, I discovered that writing is in my blood, and had to put pen to paper!

The opinions I express in my novels are my own. My stories are my own intellectual property. Copyright (c) 2012-2021, Regina Morris

Sincerely,

Regina Morris

ACKNOWLEDGMENTS

Special thanks to my husband and our children for their love and support; to my sister for believing in me and encouraging me to follow my dreams; to my critique partners, Jean and Pennie, for being with me every step of the way; to my editor Chelle (Literally Addicted to Detail); and my proof reader team. I also want to thank my beta readers, and street team. This book would not be possible without the support I have had from all of you.

Contemporary Sweet Romance Short Stories

Taking Chances

978–0–9966192–9–5 (ebook)

Available as an audio book

Broken engagement, a disappointed father, an emotional mother, what else could a wounded soldier ask for? Tommy has no idea that his sweet nurse remembers him prior to his injuries. Always professional, Abby treats Tommy no differently because of their awkward past. Once the truth is out, what will become of their friendship and budding romance?

Christmas Joy

978–1–948997–18–8 (MOBI)

978–1–948997–19–5 (ePub)

978–1–948997–20–1 (Paperback)

Jake needs to clear out his father's old cabin and sell it. He's prepared to deal with the freezing cold weather and the remote location, but not with the sexy woman, who was once his late father's nurse, still living in the place.

More Than Puppy Love

978–1–948997–01–0 (MOBI)

978–1–948997–02–7 (ePub)

978–1–948997–03–4 (Paperback)

Ex-wallflower, now veterinarian, Kacie Preston is eager to go to her ten-year high school reunion where she can meet up with the boy she crushed on for years. But then his dog, her patient, shows up at the event mistreated. How well does Kacie really know her old heart throb?

FANASY / TIME TRAVEL BOOKS

Just in Time (Short Story - Prequel to Time Historian)

ISBN: 978–0–9966192–5–7 (ebook)

ISBN: 978–0–9966192–6–4 (paperback)

Managing teams to send recorders back in history is stressful enough, but when the government makes a play for proprietary technology from the Historical Preservation Agency, Caleb must rely upon a well-connected, and sexy, developer at a government agency for help. Can the two of them keep time travel in the hands of historians?

Time Historian

ISBN: 978–0–9966192–8–8 (Print)

ISBN: 978–0–9966192–7–1 (ebook)

Also available as an audio book

Hank McConnell's is having a bad day at the office. First, he just destroyed history. He finds himself living in the Confederate States of America, Lincoln was convicted as a war criminal, and slavery existed for another fifty years. Secondly, his blunder erased his family from existence and his alternate self works as a lonely tenured professor instead of at the Historical Preservation Agency.

He doesn't have much time. He travels back to Lincoln's presidency to right what went wrong. Unfortunately, correcting time is like herding cats and one fix leads to more and more changes.

Is he willing to do the unthinkable to make the world whole again?

PARANORMAL (VAMPIRE) ROMANCES

COLONY Series Books

Vampires exist among us. They can be our neighbor, our best friend, our child's teacher...

They alter their aged appearance based upon the amount

of blood they consume. They move to a new area, drink a lot of blood, and appear young. Slowly they limit their intake of blood and age, right in front of our unsuspecting eyes. After decades, they fake their death, move, and do it over and over again.

Most live quiet lives in an effort to blend in.

Some, however, want power and control.

The COLONY is an elite group of vampires sworn to protect the President of the United States from these rogue vampires. Few humans are privileged to this knowledge.

Eternal Service (Book #1)

Top 100 Bestseller

978–0–9888222–0–7 (ebook)

978–0–9888222–1–4 (paperback)

Available as an audio book

Vampire Raymond Metcalf has too many balls to juggle and life is getting more complicated by the minute. As if working with a covert team of sexy vampires to protect the President isn't enough, he has to deal with his rebellious half-breed son, save the President from a crazed vampire, and break in a new director for his team since the last one, his best friend and the only human he trusts, has decided to retire. Why does his friend's replacement have to be the most beautiful human woman Raymond has ever seen?

Career military woman, Alex Brennan, is being offered the promotion of a lifetime, and with it a romance that she has desperately been seeking. Does she dare accept the position as Director of the COLONY, an elite group of deadly creatures of the night and risk a dangerous romance with a man who isn't even human? Together, can they save the President?

United Service (Book #2)

Top 100 Bestseller

978–0–9888222–6–9 (ebook)

978–0–9888222–7–6 (paperback)

Available as an audio book

Sterling Metcalf is a modern–day vampire who clashes with his father's antiquated ideals. Being the half–breed of the COLONY group, Sterling hates being the team's weakest link. He jumps at an opportunity to do some fieldwork rescuing kidnapped vampire children and is accompanied by Kate Spencer, the nanny of one of the children.

Kate is a purebred vampire with a secret of her own. Can Sterling put aside his bad–boy ways and woo the lovely Kate? Will Kate accept the advances of a half–breed? Together, can they save the children from a religious cult who wants to kill them?

Enduring Service (Book #3)

Top 100 Bestseller

978–0–9914034–0–0 (ebook)

978–0–9914034–1–7 (paperback)

Available as an audio book

Colony Agent Sulie Metcalf, the President's private physician, has been in love with the same human man for nearly thirty years. She refuses to allow herself the joy of true love because her feelings are unrequited by her human boss, Jonathan Dixon. As Dixon's retirement looms near, and his memories of Sulie and the last thirty years of his life are about to be erased, does she confront her fear of intimacy and take a leap of faith before it's too late?

Dixon has decided to retire and enjoy what time he has left. When his best friend Sulie, a vampire team member, is kidnapped during a medical emergency, Dixon realizes that retirement means giving up everything, and everyone, he's known for the last three decades. Will he risk his life, and his heart, to save her?

Equality of Service (Book #4)

978–1–948997–07–2 (MOBI)

978–1–948997–08–9 (ePub)

978–1–948997–09–6 (paperback)

Available as an audio book

Fifteen years ago, COLONY Agent William Wardell met his future wife Jackie Pearlman. She's sexy, opinionated, and finds him to be a mockery of the American dream of equality for all.

Can a past Freedom Rider and racial activist from the 1960s, now turned vampire, prove to the love of his life that he's not a political puppet?

Reliant Service (Book #5)

978–0–9914034–2–4 (ebook)

978–0–9914034–3–1 (paperback)

Available as an audio book

After faking his death from an assassination attempt on the President, and retiring his first and only alias with the COLONY, Daniel Brighton discovers the mandatory sabbatical to be less than exciting. He chooses to do a favor and act as a security guard for a fading pop–singer, Lori Austin, whose career is winding down. He travels across Europe with her and discovers her past to be one of deception and intrigue with a history leading directly back to the COLONY itself.

Lori Austin is struggling to keep her career alive, and is willing to do what is necessary to save it. From bad press and scandalous stories, she travels across Europe on a relief tour to revitalize her career, but doesn't realize she is traveling with a vampire. Discovering a hidden family secret, she realizes that the one man who can save her is the handsome security guard she fought so hard not to hire.

Echo of Service (Book #6)

ISBN: 978-1-948997-31-7 (EPub Ebook)

ISBN: 978-1-948997-32-4 (MOBI Ebook)

ISBN: 978-1-948997-33-1 (Paperback)

Also available as an audio book

After the President of the United States is poisoned, Vampire COLONY agent Mason Warner steps in as the man's double. He manages the President's hectic schedule just fine until the political party sends in a public relations expert to clean up the President's image. She is the one woman from Mason's past whom he has never forgotten—the woman who is the measuring stick he compares all other women too—but he compelled her decades ago to forget their one night together.

Nicole Banner is assigned by the party to do a makeover on the one man from her past she despises the most. Years ago, her short-lived secret fling with the Senator of Massachusetts, now President of the United States, left her with a son to raise on her own.

Mason can't risk her remembering their tryst from decades ago since she believes him to be the President. Nicole has always hidden her affair from prying eyes, until now.

He still desires her. All she wants is revenge.

COLONY World Series Books

These vampire romances feature vampires from the COLONY world, but these vampires do not work for the government.

Winter Wishes (Book #1)

ISBN: 978–0–9981866–0–3 (ebook)

ISBN: 978–0–9981866–1–0 (paperback)

Available as an audio book

Sammy needs a holiday miracle. The Vampire Council is after him, he's falling in love with his best friend's mother–in–law, and there's artwork hanging on the wall that was stolen by the Nazis. Life is spiraling out of control for this Jewish vampire as he spends the Christmas holiday baking cookies and wrapping gifts for the needy.

Louise is busy with her charities and hosting her annual Christmas party. Putting a smile on her face proves difficult when her soon to be ex–husband arrives with a bimbo on her arm, her proposed divorce settlement is far from fair, and the sexy stranger she's starting to fall for believes she's a Nazi.

Destined Desire (Book #2)

ISBN: 978–1–948997–16–4 (EPub ebook)

ISBN: 978–1–948997–15–7 (MOBI ebook)

ISBN: 978–1–948997–17–1 (paperback)

Available as an audio book

After a car accident nearly kills his immortal father, Alexander rushes to his father's side only to discover that his parents want him to marry and stay closer to home. He's already been down this path once before with a less than desirable outcome, so he refuses. He's steadfast in his decision until his parents threaten to financially cut him off and he's forced to approach the Vampire Council for a new marriage contract.

Dionora is enjoying her new job at the Vampire Council Marriage Office. The holidays take an exciting turn for her when she discovers the next match she does is for her ex–fiancé.

Revenge is sweet with this sensual romantic comedy.